About the author

Rebecca Muddiman is from Redcar, in the north east of England. She spent many years working in the NHS before becoming a full-time writer. Her first book, *Stolen*, won a Northern Writers Award and the Northern Crime Competition in 2012. She spends far too much time living in the fictional worlds inside her head. The rest of her time is spent watching Game of Thrones and dealing with her two unruly dogs.

Also by:

Stolen

Gone

Tell Me Lies

Murder in Slow Motion

Rebecca Muddiman

Chapter 1

DS Nicola Freeman looked down at the shattered glass, coloured with blood. The picture frame was destroyed, crushed beneath someone's foot, glass scattered across the floor. She thought about turning it over, taking a look at the photo, but decided to leave it in-situ until the crime scene team had been through. She imagined the picture was nothing more than a snapshot of the unhappy couple, presumably in happier times.

There wasn't a huge amount of blood on the frame. Some had pooled on the floor around it, and there was a trail towards the sink. Someone had tried to clean it up but hadn't done a very good job. If they were trying to get rid of evidence, they were idiots.

As she turned away, she glanced at Andrew Blake, the man who'd called it in. He was standing by the back door, half inside the house, half in the garden. He met her eye, moving forward again, opening his mouth to speak but she held up her hand and he froze. She'd already told him to stay put but he wasn't getting it and kept trying to move towards her, asking the same question on repeat: 'What do you think happened?' She knew that Andrew had already been inside the house, had wandered through the kitchen, probably disturbing things as he went. But he swore he

1

hadn't been anywhere else in the house and she wanted to keep it that way.

'Martyn?' Freeman said, and one of the uniforms who'd been first on the scene turned to her. She glanced at Andrew and Martyn nodded back, stepping towards Andrew, keeping him where she wanted him.

Freeman left the kitchen and walked through the house. There was only one other room downstairs, a long living room-dining room with the kind of modern decor that Freeman hated. Magnolia walls, brown leather sofas with cream cushions, and laminate floors. She stood in the middle of the room and looked around. Nothing seemed out of place. The room was tidy, no clutter, no mugs left festering. It was as far from her own flat as it was possible to get.

Her eyes skimmed across the walls and she noticed there were no more photos of the occupants, just a signed Boro shirt in a frame and one of those shop-bought sepia triptychs of some city or other.

As she left the room, Freeman looked back through to the kitchen and saw Martyn trying to placate Andrew Blake. As she caught Andrew's eye, he called out to her but she ignored him and went upstairs. She could see why he'd be upset but if he let her get on with her job in peace she'd have answers for him sooner.

At the top of the stairs was a small bathroom. She pulled on the light. It obviously hadn't been decorated by the current occupants, only a few knick-knacks seemed in line with the downstairs decor. The rest was 1970s style, original not retro. The bath looked like it had seen better days and Freeman assumed that tearing it out would be high on the occupants' list of jobs when the money was there.

Freeman was still waiting to find out who the house belonged to. From what Andrew had said it was a man and woman, a couple, but he didn't know anything else useful such as their names. She wondered who was in charge of decorating. Mostly it screamed 'bachelor pad' and she wondered how long the man's other half had been there. If she was looking at the house without any information at all she would've assumed the relationship was new, that the woman hadn't had time to start making herself at home, to start leaving her mark on the place. But from what Andrew had told her, his neighbour's relationship wasn't a stable one. Arguments were frequent. Freeman wondered if this was the reason there was little trace of the woman in the house – because he was the boss.

As she turned to walk out of the bathroom, Freeman noticed something in the sink. She squinted and bent down for a better look. On the side of the avocado-green sink there were blood stains. She stood up and sighed. Might be nothing. Could be from a shaving incident that morning. But she'd check just in case.

Leaving the light on, Freeman moved to the next room: what appeared to be a spare room. Things weren't as tidy in there and she could tell from the layer of dust on the shelves and dresser that it was a room rarely used.

She walked to the front bedroom, and noticed the unmade bed and the stale smell in the air. As she walked inside she saw the mess on the floor – clothes, books, more broken glass – although she couldn't tell where it had come from. It wasn't just an untidy room; it looked like there'd been a fight in there. Was this the aftermath of the argument Andrew and his girlfriend had overheard?

Freeman turned back to the door and something caught her eye. The white laminate bedside cabinet was stained red down the front. A bloodstain no one had tried to clean up. Freeman crouched down in front of it and noticed more blood on the carpet: a long, thin smudge.

She sighed. Maybe Andrew Blake was right. Something *had* happened in this house. But to whom had it happened?

She left the room as she heard a car door slam outside. Hopefully the crime scene team had arrived. She left the room as she found it, and walked to the top of the stairs. As she descended, another bloodstain caught her eye on the landing, this one leading towards the stairs but petering-out before it got anywhere. Had he attacked her in the bedroom and then she walked out, trying to get across the hall to the bathroom to clean herself up? But what about downstairs? Was that a separate event?

And how was Andrew's girlfriend involved?

Freeman went downstairs, back into the kitchen where Andrew's eyes lit up as she entered. She spoke to the crime scene manager, letting her know what she'd found, where they should start.

'Did you find anything?' Andrew asked, his cheeks flushed.

'Let's go outside,' she said, and led him out of the way. 'I want you to tell me again. From the beginning.'

4

Chapter 2

For the previous six months Andrew and his girlfriend, Katy, had been listening to their neighbours. Noisy wasn't the word. They argued all the time. The man's voice in particular echoed through the walls. It clearly wasn't a happy relationship; it was one dying a slow and painful death.

For Andrew it was more of an annoyance. As far as he was concerned it was nothing serious, just two people who shouldn't be together, unable to see it for themselves. But Katy would get upset. She worried that this woman next door was in danger. She suggested calling the police, but Andrew said no – that it wasn't serious enough to call the police. And, besides, it wasn't any of their business; how would she have liked it if people interfered with their relationship? People like her mother, for instance. The answer was that she wouldn't.

But two nights earlier, they'd been in bed, almost asleep, when it had started. Voices had raised, and Andrew had sighed and reached for his earplugs. The best thing he'd ever bought. He'd tried to go back to sleep but the noise from next door had gotten louder and louder, and he'd seen Katy lying awake, worry written all over her face.

Suddenly something was thrown, hitting the adjoining wall, shattering. Katy had sat up in bed and turned on the light. Andrew had felt himself beginning to get pissed off; what was wrong with these people?

And then more screaming. This time he'd heard the woman's voice. She'd sounded afraid and for the first time Andrew had wondered if Katy had been right and they should call the police. But then it stopped. The quiet had been overwhelming. Andrew and Katy had sat there in bed, neither saying a word, listening for movement, for a sign that it was over, that things were okay.

They'd heard a door slam. They'd heard a squeal, maybe from the dog. More raised voices. And then nothing.

Andrew had lay down again, prepared to go to sleep. But Katy stayed sitting up. She'd kept asking, 'Should we call the police?' In the end Andrew had talked her out of it. It was over, he'd told her. Go to sleep.

Andrew had slept fine that night but in the morning he'd seen that Katy had been restless. The bags under her eyes were heavy and she'd spilt the milk all over the table when she'd made breakfast. She'd brought it up again while they'd eaten, and Andrew had told her to leave it alone. If someone wanted help, they asked for it; this wasn't their concern.

That night when Andrew had come home from work, Katy had brought it up again as soon as he'd walked through the door. To be honest he'd been a little tired of hearing about it. If something had happened, they would've heard by now. He'd told her to drop it and she hadn't mentioned it again all evening.

6

That night there had been no arguments next door; everything was quiet and Andrew had thought it was the end of it. He'd left for work the next morning and Katy had seemed fine. She'd made his lunch and said she might spend the day putting the books into alphabetical order. He'd left her to it and gone to work.

Later that day he'd got a message from her. He'd been in a meeting so hadn't answered the phone when she'd called. He'd listened to her message telling him she was worried and was going next door to see if she could talk to the woman, see she was all right.

Andrew had checked the time she'd left the message, noticing it was an hour earlier. He'd tried to call her back to see if she was satisfied, if she'd spoken to their neighbour. But there'd been no answer. He'd tried a few more times but had given up when he'd had to go back to work, knowing she'd tell him all about it when he got home.

After work he'd gone straight home but Katy hadn't been there when he arrived. That was unusual. He'd tried her phone again but still got no answer. At this point he'd been a little worried. He'd wondered if Katy could still be next door … if she'd got talking to their neighbour and like old fish wives had been chatting all afternoon, oblivious to the time.

He knocked at the neighbour's front door. There had been no answer and when he'd looked through the window he hadn't been able to see anyone in there. He'd gone home and waited a short while, getting more and more concerned; it wasn't like Katy to just vanish like that, without telling him where she was going. Eventually he'd decided to try the neighbour's again, this time trying the back; if they were sat in the kitchen gossiping, maybe they hadn't heard him knock.

He'd gone round and found the back door open – not wide, just not shut tight. He'd nudged it open and shouted Katy's name. He'd stepped inside and found the kitchen in a bit of a mess: there was a photo frame on the floor, smashed, blood all over it; the cupboard under the sink was left ajar, a trail of blood weaving its way down the wood to the floor. Then he'd seen Katy's phone on the worktop.

He'd shouted again, a bad feeling coming over him. Why hadn't he come home sooner? Why hadn't he told her once and for all not to get involved?

Andrew had left the kitchen and gone into the garden where he'd finally dialled 999. Maybe if he'd done that sooner, Katy wouldn't be gone.

Chapter 3

Freeman thought about Andrew's story as he looked at her expectantly. He had a puppy-dog type face, round and open, with red cheeks like a young boy. She thought he might start crying any minute. But she didn't want to make any assumptions. Something had happened in that house but it was too early to say what that something was. Yes, there were signs of a disturbance and more than a trace of blood but that didn't mean anything had happened to his girlfriend.

The most obvious explanation, so far, was that these neighbours had had a fight, one that had gotten out of hand and led to one or both drawing blood. The fact that neither Andrew nor Katy had seen their neighbours since the big fight meant little. Andrew claimed that they didn't know these people, didn't know their names, barely saw them at all, just heard them. So wasn't it likely that they'd had a fight and then gone about their lives as normal? It was likely that they'd both come home from work shortly and wonder what the hell was going on.

So really what they had was a grown woman who just wasn't there. Andrew said Katy had called him late morning to say she was going next door. She might not have been in touch since but so what? It was only a few hours. Maybe she was just doing something else, shopping, having a drink with friends.

But then … clearly Katy *had* gone next door that morning because her phone was there. So if she'd found the smashed photo frame and the blood, wouldn't she have called the police? Andrew said she'd been worrying for days. If she'd walked in and found the place like that, wouldn't she have done something?

Freeman looked at the back door. It wasn't broken. The glass wasn't smashed. So how did Katy get in? Had one or both of her neighbours been there? And if so, what had happened when she'd seen them? Had they assured her things were fine and she'd left knowing she'd done what she could, for some reason forgetting her phone? Or had this man, the neighbour, been there when she'd come poking her nose in? Had he lost his temper with her too?

Freeman sighed. She couldn't assume anything until the place had been checked for prints, the blood had been analysed, and they'd spoken to these neighbours. Until then, nothing was certain.

'Can I hear the message Katy left for you?' Freeman asked, turning back to Andrew.

He nodded and pulled his phone from his pocket. Freeman waited while he tapped the screen, searching for his voicemail. He put the phone to his ear for a second before passing it over.

She listened as the robot told her the message was left at 10.45 a.m. that morning before Katy's voice came on. She sounded younger than she was, which was twenty-nine according to Andrew. By voice alone she could've passed for a teenager.

'Hi Andrew, it's me.' There was a pause and Freeman could hear Katy breathing. 'Look, I know you said I should keep my nose out of it but I'm really worried. I think something might've happened to ... that woman. I can't stop thinking about her. So ...' There was another pause and Katy took a few breaths. 'Don't be mad but I'm going to go over. I'll just knock on the door and see she's all right. I won't be long. I promise.' Another pause. 'See you later. I love you.'

Freeman hung up and Andrew took his phone back. 'See?' he said. 'Something's happened to her.'

'DS Freeman?' one of the crime scene techs said, and she nodded to him that she'd be there in a second.

'Look,' Freeman said to Andrew, 'we don't know whether any of this has anything to do with Katy yet.'

'But what about her phone?'

'Doesn't mean anything's happened to her. She could've just left it behind.'

'But what if he's done something to her?'

'Who?'

'The man who lives here. What if he's hurt her?'

'What makes you think he would?'

'I've heard him. Heard what he's like. There's blood,' Andrew said, as if that explained everything.

'But you said you didn't know him, don't know anything about him.'

'No, but—' His face dropped and then he stared at Freeman with even more panic in his face. 'What if it was that other man?'

Freeman racked her brain trying to work out which other man Andrew was talking about, whether she'd missed something, wasn't paying attention. 'Which other man?' she asked, when she couldn't think of anything.

'I've seen it on the news. That man who breaks into girl's houses,' he said.

Freeman nodded in realisation. She was aware of the case but not all the ins and outs of it. And she doubted that was what they were looking at here. Besides, Andrew had been sure his neighbour was responsible two minutes ago. He was grasping at straws, panicking.

'Have you seen anyone hanging around recently?' she asked though, just in case.

'Not really,' he said.

'Well then. Let's not jump to any conclusions, okay?' She patted Andrew on the shoulder and went inside to see what was happening.

'We've collected blood samples from the four locations – kitchen, bathroom, bedroom and upstairs hallway. Fingerprints could take a while,' the tech said.

Freeman thanked him and wandered back to the hall away from the noise, trying to think what to do next. She needed to get hold of the homeowner. She was about to walk back to the kitchen, to retrieve Andrew and take him home where she could question him some more and take a look around his house – and then she stopped. She hadn't noticed earlier, but the post from that day was still on the mat by the front door. She bent over and collected the mail.

A couple of flyers and a bank statement addressed to Lee Johnston – that was a start. She put them on the sideboard by the door. And then she looked at the last envelope, a letter from the Dogs Trust. Freeman looked at the woman's name on the address label.

'Shit,' she muttered to herself. She put the letter down with the others and took out her phone. Gardner was going to want to know about this.

Chapter 4

Freeman followed Andrew through his home, noticing that the layout of the house was the mirror image of next door. The only difference was the decor and the fact that this house felt warmer, cosier. Maybe that was psychological. Maybe the fact that the house next door was a crime scene made it seem colder, less welcoming. Or maybe it was the decor itself.

Freeman's eyes scanned the walls of the long living room-dining room. It was covered in photographs in frames of varying sizes. Each one showed Andrew with his arm around Katy at some tourist attraction or other. She noticed that they looked happier in some than others, wondered if the cheery ones were from the start of the relationship when everything was new and exciting.

'How long have you and Katy been together?' Freeman asked and Andrew turned to her, seemingly puzzled by the question.

'Two years,' he said after a moment. 'Why?'

'Just curious.' She wandered away from him, towards the kitchen, finding the room immaculate. No dishes left in the sink, no crumbs on the worktop. Looked like Katy kept a clean house.

'You said Katy didn't work?' Freeman said, trying to recall what Andrew had told her earlier as he'd shot down every suggestion of where Katy could be.

'No,' he said. 'She was made redundant earlier this year.'

'Must've been hard.'

Andrew shrugged. 'Well, she never liked the place anyway. And we manage on my salary.'

Freeman wondered how she'd feel about being home all day. To be fair, some days she wished she didn't have to go to work, but on the whole she thought it would drive her mad if she had nothing to do all day. She'd have to find some hobbies.

'You've tried Katy's friends, family?'

He shook his head. 'She would've mentioned if she was going somewhere. Her friends would have been at work.'

'What about family?'

'There's just her mum but she lives in Cumbria.'

'So you haven't spoken to her?'

'No.'

'Okay,' Freeman said and left the kitchen with Andrew following close behind her. She started up the stairs and asked Andrew to show her their bedroom. He went in first and she noticed the cleanliness again. The bed looked like a hotel maid had been in there, all tight corners and pillows at angles. There was nothing out of place, no junk left in the corner, no laundry tossed on the floor. It would be immediately obvious if something was out of place.

Freeman opened the wardrobe and she noticed that the clothes were hung in order of colour. Everything looked ironed. These people had serious issues.

'Does it look like anything's missing?' she asked, moving aside for Andrew to take a look. He stood for a moment, staring at Freeman.

'Why would anything be missing?' he asked, and then realisation spread across his face. 'You don't think—'

'We have to make sure we cover all bases, Mr Blake. So could you just take a look, see if it looks like anything's missing. Any clothes or a bag?'

Andrew ran his fingers across the hanging clothes before opening the door to the second cupboard. There was a suitcase at the top and Andrew reached up, pulling it down. He unzipped the case on the bed and found two smaller cases nestled inside like Russian dolls.

'They're all here,' he said.

'She doesn't have any other bags?'

'Just her handbag. It's downstairs.'

'Okay,' Freeman said. 'What about on here?' She pointed at the dressing table. She looked it over beside Andrew and noticed that everything was lined up in straight lines, not a speck of dust anywhere.

'It's all there as far as I can tell,' he said.

Freeman nodded and looked at the pictures surrounding the mirror. It was the only bit of the room with any life to it. There were a few more photos of Andrew and Katy together, and in a couple of strips of photo booth pictures, from back when they were fun, a much younger Katy pulled faces next to an older woman.

'That's her mum,' Andrew said, nodding at the pictures.

It looked like they were close but Freeman hadn't noticed any more pictures of the mother in the rest of the house; in fact there hadn't been any pictures of anyone else at all. She wondered if that was weird. But then, she didn't have *any* photos up, so who was she to talk? She shifted her focus to the other pictures stuck around the edges of the mirror. A couple of postcards that were tatty around the edges, both with greetings from Scarborough. She pulled them down and read the backs. One was addressed to Katy from her mum and dad, hoping she was enjoying staying with Nana. The second was written in childish crayon, the words, *To Dad*, taking up half the small space. The rest read, *Wish you were here. I miss you. We had ice cream for tea. Love Katy.*

Freeman slid the cards back onto the mirror and turned back to Andrew. 'Should we check the bathroom?'

Andrew led her out and switched on the bathroom light. Another immaculate room. Freeman noticed the two toothbrushes on the side of the sink. 'Anything gone?' she said and Andrew shook his head.

Freeman turned and stuck her head into the spare room before heading back downstairs. She found Katy's handbag in the living room and started rummaging. There wasn't much in it – a pack of tissues, a lip balm, an old bus ticket. She found her purse and checked inside, a library card and some loose change.

'Purse is here. Not much in it though. Would she have kept much money on her?'

'No,' Andrew said.

'No bank card either. Would she usually take that out with her?'

Andrew just paced up and down, saying nothing. Freeman wondered if he thought it was a rhetorical question. She supposed it was possible Katy took it if she was planning to go somewhere after visiting the neighbours, to the shop or something. She already knew she'd taken her phone out with her, so was that for safety or because she was planning to go out from there?

Freeman dug around some more. 'No keys,' she said and looked up at Andrew. 'Are her keys here? On a hook or a drawer or something?'

Andrew shook his head.

'So she took them with her. Locked up before she went next door.'

Andrew turned away and said, 'I should've stopped her.'

Freeman put the bag down. 'What do you mean?'

Andrew looked at the floor. 'I just wish I'd got the message sooner, wish I'd spoken to her and told her not to go. I let this happen.'

Freeman almost spoke but stopped herself. She didn't want to tell Andrew it wasn't his fault yet because she had no idea what *it* was. Katy hadn't been gone that long; it was entirely possible she could come through the door any minute. She had to agree with Andrew that it didn't look like Katy had up and left – nothing seemed to be missing – but she'd keep an open mind about it. Some people left without taking anything; depended on their reason for leaving. She just couldn't make any assumptions yet. Apart from the fact that *something* had happened in the house next door, and that Katy had been there at some point.

Freeman checked her watch, wondering where Gardner was. When she'd called him to let him know whose house she was in, he said he'd be straight there. That was almost half an hour ago. She sighed. They needed to find Katy. They need to find Lee Johnston, discover what happened in his house. And they needed to find his girlfriend, PC Dawn Lawton. But they were all gone.

Chapter 5

DI Michael Gardner kept one eye on the road as he tried Lawton's phone again. By now he knew it was pointless. She wasn't answering. The phone was switched off. Only question was why?

He thought about what Freeman had told him just over thirty minutes earlier, how he'd misunderstood. When Freeman said she was at Lawton's house, that there'd been a report of possible domestic abuse, he thought she meant Lawton was at the house, was first on the scene. He'd wondered why he was getting involved, especially as he was off duty and had just sat down to have coffee with Molly. He felt bad about it because he did like Molly but so far hadn't done much to prove it. Something always came up whenever they got together, and he wondered if she was starting to think he was stringing her along. And then there was the fact that after six dates (and yes, he cringed every time he used the term), he was still trying to work out if she was his girlfriend or not. Or if, at forty-six, it was wrong to call someone your girlfriend anyway, regardless of how many *dates* you'd been on. But then had realised that Lawton wasn't supposed to be on duty either. She'd called in sick yesterday, hadn't come in again today. So what did it have to do with Lawton? Or him?

Freeman patiently explained it again – being far more patient than usual – and once he understood what she was saying, he then understood the kid gloves. Something had happened at Lawton's house. A neighbour had reported a disturbance. Or rather a neighbour had reported his girlfriend missing; the disturbance next door was an afterthought. But from what Freeman had been told, things weren't right with Lawton and her boyfriend, Lee. Fights were frequent and two days earlier things had got out of hand.

Gardner wanted to dismiss it. He didn't want to jump to any conclusions without seeing the house, without speaking to Freeman in person and listening to what this neighbour had to say. But most of all he wanted to speak to Lawton because something wasn't right. Surely it wasn't a coincidence that the night after this apparent disturbance, Lawton called in sick. Lawton never called in sick.

Gardner felt bad for abandoning Molly in the cafe but as soon as he put the phone down he'd felt nausea rising through him and muttered something about having to leave and how sorry he was but he hadn't even bothered to kiss her goodbye or assure her he'd call as soon as whatever this was had been sorted. He'd just left her there. So if she *had* ever been his girlfriend, she probably wasn't anymore.

He hung up the phone as he turned the car onto Lawton's street. He'd been there a few times before, dropped Lawton off, picked her up once, but he'd never been inside her house. He tried not to let his mind wander to what could've happened in that house. Was there really a problem with Lawton's relationship? And if there was, how had he not picked up on it?

He pulled up on to the kerb a few doors down from Lawton's house. He could see Freeman's car further back and the crime scene van parked beside her. As he got out of the car he noticed a curtain twitch across the road. The street wasn't that wide; if cars parked on both sides there was no room for two-way traffic. He wondered if the nosy neighbour knew anything of what was going on or if they were just curious about the police presence.

Gardner walked up the path to Lawton's house; his stomach felt tight and his mouth dry. Something was wrong. He could feel it. He nodded at the officer by the door and walked into the hall. The crime scene manager, Olivia Mortimer, came towards him, her face grim. 'Freeman's next door,' she said and Gardner nodded.

'What've you got?' he asked, craning his neck to see into the kitchen.

'Not a great deal,' she said. 'Blood found in the kitchen. There was a trail to the sink that someone tried to clean up. Didn't do a great job of it though. It doesn't look like a huge amount. Best guess is it's just from the smashed frame. Upstairs in the bedroom though, there was blood on the bedside cabinet and floor. A little more in the hallway, traces in the bathroom sink though most was washed away. Doesn't look like a trail from the bedroom to the bathroom though so it could be two people or just two incidents or just whoever was bleeding managed to contain it for the most part.'

22

'Any prints?'

'A few. Looks like at least three different prints on the photo frame. We've done the doors but, until we know what we're looking at here, it's tricky.' She put her hand on his arm. Olivia knew Lawton too. Liked her. Everyone liked her. What wasn't to like? 'We'll find her,' Olivia said.

Gardner nodded and left Olivia to it. He stuck his head round the kitchen door. The place was a bit of a mess but part of that was from his colleagues. The smashed frame in an evidence bag caught his eye and he picked it up. Beneath the bloody glass was a photo of Lawton and Lee, both smiling. He stared at it for a minute until one of the crime scene guys backed into him, trying to take photographs.

'Sorry,' he said, without looking up.

Gardner put the bag down and walked outside. The air was too heavy in there with all the bodies moving around. He stood at the end of the path and tried calling Lawton again. Still nothing. He looked up at the house and wondered what was going on.

A movement in the window of the house next door caught Gardner's eye and he walked over to the neighbour's house. He could see Freeman by the window. She nodded at him and came to the door.

'Hi,' she said.

'Sorry it took so long to get here,' Gardner said and followed her inside.

'No problem.' They walked into the living room and a man in his late-thirties stood up. His face was flushed and he looked Gardner in the eye as Freeman introduced them. 'Can you tell DI Gardner what happened?'

Andrew nodded and started talking quickly. He'd probably already told his story several times, to dispatch, to the first responder, to Freeman. But he told it again, despite the emotion in his voice. Every now and then Gardner glanced away from Andrew and took in Freeman's expression, trying to work out her thoughts, whether she believed Andrew's story, whether she was picking up on any inconsistencies.

As Andrew got to the part of his story where he called the police, Gardner realised that what he'd said about Lawton and Lee was vague, that the only reason he was mentioning it was because Katy had gone over there. Did that mean things with Lawton weren't that bad or just that Andrew didn't care, not when his own girlfriend was missing. But surely he must've thought something was up with his neighbours. Why else would he be so worried about Katy going over there? Why wouldn't he just wait for her to come home? It wasn't like she'd been gone days. And even if he'd seen the blood in the kitchen, it wasn't like it was sprayed up the walls. Olivia had said it seemed like someone had just cut themselves on the glass from the frame. Cut themselves pretty badly, but still.

'You said you'd been hearing arguments for months. Had you called the police before? You or Katy?' Gardner asked.

'No,' Andrew said, looking between Gardner and Freeman. 'I mean, it wasn't that bad. Just arguments, you know. I didn't want to get involved.'

'But two nights ago it was different? Yet you still didn't call the police?'

'Well, no. But it wasn't like I thought he was killing her. It was louder than usual. It sounded like stuff was thrown, a bit of banging about; the dog was going bonkers. But then it stopped. I didn't …' He looked to Freeman for help but she kept quiet. Andrew put his head down. 'I should've done something. I know. If I'd called the police then, Katy would still be here.'

He still didn't seem concerned with Lawton's safety, Gardner thought. Was that normal? Was he just too wrapped up in his own worries to think about anyone else? Maybe so. Gardner sighed and sat back. 'I get that it's hard to know when to intervene. But you're thinking that your neighbour, Lee, could've done something to Katy, right? So, to me, that sounds like you think he's capable of hurting someone.'

'I don't know,' Andrew said. 'All I know is Katy went next door and now she's gone.'

'It is possible Katy just went out,' Freeman said. 'Remember that. What's going on next door might have nothing to do with her.'

'But what about the blood? The message she left me?'

'You said you've been listening to them for months?' Gardner said, interrupting. 'Lawton's been there a few years. You never heard anything before a few months ago?'

'We only moved in here October last year,' Andrew said.

Gardner nodded. It wasn't really what he wanted to hear. He'd rather none of it was happening at all but, if it had to, then at least if it was a fairly recent development he would feel marginally better. But for all he knew it had been going on for years. How had he not seen it?

'I've spoken to Katy's mum,' Freeman said, knocking Gardner out of his morbid thoughts. He noticed Andrew sitting forward. 'She hasn't seen her … hasn't seen her for a while. She wanted to drive over here tonight but I told her to hang on. It's early days.'

'But she's definitely not there?' Andrew said.

'No.'

'You said you didn't know your neighbours. You've never spoken to either of them?' Gardner asked, steering the conversation back to Lawton again.

'No. I see them come and go but that's it. We just hear them.'

'And when you have seen them, did anything seem odd?'

'No, not really.'

'Not *really*?'

'I mean, no. I can't say I ever pay that much attention.'

'But you listen to them fighting. Weren't you curious to see what they were like? See if either of them was injured?'

'No. It's not my business,' Andrew said. 'Why are you asking me all this? Why don't you ask them about their relationship and just help me get Katy back.'

'I *would* ask them but Lawton's missing too,' Gardner said, his voice tight.

Freeman stood up and nodded towards the door.

'What do you mean she's missing too?' Andrew asked.

Gardner ignored him and followed Freeman out to the kitchen. 'Look, you don't have to be here,' she said.

'I want to be here.'

'That might be the case, but if you're getting wound up—'

'Of course I'm getting wound up. Lawton's missing.'

'No, Lawton's just not here right now. For all we know she'll come walking through the door any minute. Same as Katy.'

'So why did she call in sick? Why is her house a crime scene?'

Freeman sighed. 'I don't know yet. But I intend to find out. But I can't do that if you're winding up the witnesses.'

'I'm just asking questions to help us find out what's going on.'

'And winding up the witness at the same time.' She sighed. 'Look, why don't you try Lawton again.'

'I've tried. Her phone's switched off.' He walked to the window and stood with his hands against the sink, head down. 'Something's wrong. I can feel it.'

He turned back to her when she didn't reply. He could tell she wanted to say everything would be fine but she knew she couldn't bullshit him the same way she bullshitted the witness. She knew as well as he did that something was wrong with all this. In fact, everything was wrong. Every last thing.

Chapter 6

Andrew sat there while the two detectives disappeared into the kitchen. He felt a stabbing pain in his gut and leaned forward to suppress it.

He'd thought when the bloke came in that he'd talk more sense than the woman copper, that he'd see what was going on and do something. But all he kept talking about was the people from next door and why hadn't he called the police before today as if he'd done something wrong. Surely that wasn't the point right now. The point was Katy was missing so why weren't they focusing on that?

He tried to listen to what was being said in the kitchen. He could hear the woman, Freeman, telling Gardner to calm down. He shook his head. He thought the bloke was in charge. At least *he* was willing to admit something was wrong. Maybe he'd do something more than look around the wardrobe and make out like Katy had just walked out.

Andrew got up and stood by the door, listening to their conversation.

'Look, I'm not saying we shouldn't be worried. Clearly something happened next door,' Freeman said. 'The mess, the blood, proves that. But it doesn't prove *what*

28

happened. Nor does it prove that Lawton or Katy are in any danger.'

'So why isn't she answering my calls? Why hasn't she been to work?' Gardner said.

'I don't know. If he's telling the truth about the arguments, maybe things did get out of hand Sunday night. Maybe Lawton went to stay with a friend or relative. If she's avoiding Lee she'd probably have her phone off.'

'And Katy? Lee? Where are they?'

'I don't know. She might have nothing to do with it. Lee might be at work for all we know.' Andrew listened as Freeman's voice got softer. 'Listen, this might sound stupid but ... Andrew brought up this guy who's been breaking into houses, attacking women. I don't think that's what we're looking at here but it might be worth considering. You know whose case it is?'

'Er ... Berman, I think,' Gardner said but sounded distracted.

'Okay. I'll speak to him. Might as well look at every angle. But so far Andrew's blamed this weirdo *and* Lee Johnston so ...' She sighed and Andrew felt a surge of anger. He didn't like this woman.

'Look, I'll get some information from Andrew and make a start calling Katy's friends, anywhere she could possibly be,' she said. 'I'll get the ball rolling with CCTV, check the bus and train station just in case. Why don't you see if you can get hold of Lawton's mum, see if she's there. You know where Lee works?'

'One of the phone shops in town, I think,' Gardner said.

'Okay, I'll get someone to check.'

'No,' Gardner said. 'I'll do it.'

Andrew heard Freeman sigh again. 'Fine. But he's probably on his way home anyway. Will be wondering why the fuck his house is crawling with cops.'

'Good,' Gardner said.

Andrew stepped back as Gardner walked past him towards the front door. 'So you think he *has* done something to them?' Gardner turned back and faced Andrew. He sensed Freeman behind him but kept his eyes on Gardner. 'You think this Lee has hurt his girlfriend *and* Katy?'

'I don't think anything yet,' Gardner said, his eyes looking past Andrew to Freeman. 'But I'm going to find out.'

Gardner walked out, slamming the door behind him. Andrew turned to Freeman and he caught her rolling her eyes.

'Mr Blake, why don't you give me a list of Katy's friends. We'll make a start there.'

Chapter 7

Gardner drove away from the scene angry. He couldn't decide who he was angriest with but he'd start with Freeman. He knew she was right, of course, that they knew nothing yet, that Lawton might not have anything to do with the blood or the mess or the fact another woman was missing. But it didn't stop him from being pissed off at her for saying so. *Something* had happened in that house and whether or not that meant Lawton was in danger, was hurt, or whether she was just pissed off too and not in the mood for work, it was still something that he thought he should've known about.

Lawton's car wasn't at the house, suggesting, as Freeman said, that she left of her own volition. Gardner disagreed with that too. Just because her car wasn't there didn't mean someone else – someone like Lee for instance – hadn't taken Lawton, and possibly Katy, somewhere after doing something to them. It would be a good cover. Make it look like Lawton just left. Freeman was already believing it. But he wasn't. He'd already asked his colleagues to be on the lookout for her car and tasked someone with trying to trace the car's movements since

Sunday night, as well as finding the contact information for Lawton's mum.

As he drove towards the town centre, past the huddles of office workers, no doubt moaning about the day just gone and how much wine they'd drink that night, Gardner wondered what he'd missed. His mind skimmed over various incidents, seemingly innocuous conversations, searching for something that pointed to what was going on in Lawton's private life.

He stopped at the lights and watched a woman pass in front of his car, her head down, looking less thrilled than the rest of the people around her that it was home time, that she could forget about whatever it was she did all day and go home and relax. He wondered what was happening in her life, what would make her prefer the dull conversations and pointless busy-work to going home.

A beep came from the car behind him and Gardner looked up to see the driver flinging his hands about, pointing at the lights. Gardner moved away slowly. He pulled in to the small road that led to the car park above the shopping centre.

He'd already checked that the phone shop where Lee worked would still be open, although he had no idea why a phone shop would need to be open later than any other shop. His phone had been bought at the supermarket, the cheapest model picked up along with a few ready meals and some cereal. He'd never stepped foot in one of these shops, and couldn't understand the point of them.

Gardner parked the car and realised his mind was wandering and he was letting it because he didn't want to think about Lawton. And yes, he was pissed with

Freeman; maybe not for suggesting that he might be jumping the gun slightly, but just for suggesting that maybe he wasn't the right person for the job. He didn't know why he was surprised; Freeman had been in Middlesbrough for five months and so far there had been no hint of her keeping her thoughts to herself. He might've been her superior but that wasn't going to stop her from voicing her opinions. Most of the time it didn't bother him, he wasn't one of those coppers who demanded that anyone beneath him called him sir. But this time it bothered him. Probably because he knew she was right. And though he might've been pissed with Freeman, he was far angrier with himself. What sort of detective misses something like this? What sort of friend?

'Fuck,' he said, slamming his palms into the steering wheel, accidentally honking the horn, making a group of passing teenagers jump. He held his hand up to apologise and one of them gave him the finger.

He waited for the group of girls to disappear, before leaving the car, and locking it. He went down the escalator to the shopping centre. It was hardly bustling. Most of the shops were already shut, some permanently, with signs pointing loyal customers to the nearest branch. He passed by a couple of stalls, one selling overpriced sweets, the other gel nails (whatever they were), and found the phone shop. It was still open and a couple of men in bright-red T-shirts stood against the counter, both intently staring at phones. There wasn't a customer to be seen.

Gardner tried to work out if one of the men was Lee Johnston. It was hard to tell from this angle and, besides, he'd only ever met the man once. Maybe twice. He recalled seeing Lee with Lawton outside the station a few months earlier. He'd interrupted their conversation and Lawton had seemed uncomfortable. Lee had seemed like a smarmy little shit. He'd wondered why Lawton was with him; just from appearance they didn't seem to fit. But who was he to question it? He remembered leaving them to it, looking back to see Lee talking to Lawton, her head down, his face close to hers. Had that been a sign? He'd assumed they'd had a tiff, nothing more. When Lawton joined him later she seemed embarrassed so he hadn't mentioned it. Maybe he should've.

He tried to remember when it was. December, when all the stuff with Emma Thorley was happening? Lee had mentioned then that he worked in the phone shop. Would he even still work there? And even if he did, what was Gardner going to do?

As much as he was pissed with Freeman, and with himself, he was even more pissed with Lee. No, he didn't have proof that anything had happened to Lawton, either in the last couple of days or in the past. All he had was Andrew Blake's word. But something had happened in that house and that was enough for him. Enough to bring Lee in and ask him some questions. But then what?

An image of Lee flashed into his mind. Him standing there with Lawton, his hand on her shoulder, his thumb across her neck … Lawton's eyes cast down.

Gardner walked into the shop. He was going to find Lee Johnston and get some answers. Whatever it took.

Chapter 8

Freeman checked her watch as she walked up to the office. 6.30 p.m. In theory she should be clocking off in half an hour but that wasn't going to happen. Not that it mattered. She had nothing to rush home for. No one waiting for her; no dinner in the oven. She wondered what would happen if *she* disappeared. Who would notice? Darren probably wouldn't. At least not until the TV went off because the bills hadn't been paid. She slumped into her chair. Maybe she was being too harsh on Darren. He probably would notice sooner. He'd run out of food long before the electricity went off. He'd definitely notice then.

She looked at the photo of Katy Jackson that Andrew had given her and again thought that no one would blink if she wasn't there when they got home. If she hadn't been in touch for a couple of hours, if she'd gone somewhere out of the ordinary. No one would think she was in trouble. But then, how many people would? She found it slightly odd that Andrew was so worried by Katy not being at home when he got in from work. Yes, there was the scene next door, which complicated things. But Andrew had gone looking for Katy as soon as he got home. Why were his first thoughts that something had happened to her?

'Hey.'

Freeman looked up from the photo just as DC Carl Harrington came up behind her, and put his hands on her shoulders. He gave them a squeeze and she pulled away from him. He walked to his desk, not missing a beat, and pulled his chair over to her desk.

If she had to describe Harrington in one word it would be letch. He was about as far away from her type as was humanly possible; as far away from any normal woman's type as far as she could tell, but that didn't stop him trying. In the short time she'd been in Middlesbrough, he'd hit on her dozens of times until eventually she'd threatened to remove his balls. His response was to claim it was all a big joke, but the majority of the flirting had now stopped. The shoulder squeezing though was apparently something he couldn't help himself with. It was some kind of sleazy tic.

She didn't particularly like Harrington but at least he was willing to make the effort with her, something not many of her new colleagues were capable of. He'd been suspicious of her too when she'd first arrived, and who could blame him, or any of them, after the way she'd ended up there. But Harrington had given her the benefit of the doubt and let her prove herself. She figured it would take the rest of them, including Lawton, a bit more time. In fact Lawton might never warm to her. Lawton already disliked her before she had good reason to. Freeman had assumed it was because Lawton had a crush on Gardner and had figured out that Freeman and Gardner had almost

... well, she wasn't sure what they'd almost done but clearly Lawton didn't approve. And then came the whole Walter James thing and Lawton's opinion was that Freeman had led Gardner down a dangerous path. And maybe she was right.

She sat back thinking it was unlikely her and Lawton would ever be friends but if Andrew Blake was right, and something had happened to Lawton, well, she was going to make damn sure she helped make things right.

Harrington leaned over the desk and picked up the photo of Katy Jackson. 'Nice,' he said, and tossed the picture back on her desk.

'You do know you're disgusting, don't you?' Freeman said. She'd seen Harrington flirt with witnesses before today. He'd never gone so far as to try and pick up a victim, at least to her knowledge, but on a few occasions when they'd been out together to interview potential witnesses, he'd turned what he assumed was charm up to eleven and she tried her best not to retch.

'What?' he said, grinning. 'I'm just pointing out an empirical fact.'

'Whatever. What's happening with the CCTV?'

'Howlett's checking out the bus station. Fatty Magoo is looking at the train station stuff.'

Freeman tried to withhold her smile but was struggling. DC Don Murphy, or Fatty Magoo, as Harrington called him, was the butt of most of the jokes around the station. Freeman felt sorry for him when she'd arrived, couldn't work out why these people found bullying the fat guy so hilarious. Murphy was big and getting bigger by the day. She could only assume he was aiming for disability because there was no way he could continue working if he continued growing. But it soon transpired that Murphy was the butt of the jokes, not because of his size, (unless you were Harrington), but because he apparently had no sense of humour whatsoever and the slightest thing got his back up. Murphy was the butt of the jokes because he was so easy.

'You think she's done a runner?' Harrington asked. 'What's the boyfriend like?'

Freeman shrugged. 'Hard to say. Seems genuine but it's early days.'

'You're so cynical,' Harrington said, smiling. 'What about Lawton? You think something's happened there?'

Freeman noticed the jokey front drop. He'd worked with Lawton for years, clearly liked her a lot. But who didn't? Even she couldn't find anything unlikeable about Lawton; the feeling just wasn't reciprocated.

'I don't know,' she said. 'Obviously something went down in the house but I don't know what. All we have is Andrew's word that things weren't right next door.'

'And the fact Lawton's missing.'

Freeman sighed. 'Well, she hasn't been to work. That doesn't mean she's missing.'

'She's not answering the phone.'

'She could actually be sick. I wouldn't want to answer the phone to you lot if I was really ill.'

'But if you were really ill, wouldn't you be ignoring people's calls from the comfort of your own bed?'

'True. But if she and Lee had an argument—'

'Then it'd be a pretty bad argument to make her leave home.'

Freeman nodded. 'And that brings us full circle. Something bad happened.' They both sat in silence for a minute or as much silence as there could ever be in the office. 'Gardner's gone to look for Lee, see if he can get any answers, find out where Lawton is.'

'Good luck to him,' Harrington said.

'Gardner or Lee?'

Harrington gave a half-laugh. 'Well, I wouldn't want to be Lee right now.'

'You think Gardner will do something stupid?' Freeman asked.

Harrington shrugged. 'I think he'll be pretty pissed off with him.'

Freeman paused before asking her next question, wondering why she was asking. 'Did they ever …?'

Harrington pulled a face. 'Not that I'm aware of.'

'But she likes him.'

'She spent the first few years here going red every time he came into the room. But as far as I know he doesn't feel the same way. He's just protective, you know.'

'How long's she been with Lee?'

'I don't know,' he said, his eyes dropping to the desk. 'A while, I think. To be honest I don't know much about her outside of work.' He flicked a paperclip across the room. 'I guess that's the problem.'

Freeman found Berman thumping one of the vending machines in the corridor. She'd never had much to do with him, hadn't worked a case with him, but he seemed like an okay guy. She didn't think he'd have a problem with helping her out and passing on a bit of information.

'I think you need to give it up and admit defeat,' she said as the big man tried to shake the machine. He turned and then shook it once more, freeing up a couple of chocolate bars with a grin. He grabbed them with a meaty hand and offered one to Freeman.

'Any news on Lawton?' he asked.

'Not yet,' Freeman said, not surprised by how quickly the news had travelled. 'But I was wondering if I could pick your brain.'

'Sure,' he said. 'About what?'

'These break-ins you're investigating. The women.' He nodded. 'I don't think this is him but the victim's boyfriend brought it up. I'm pretty sure he's just read about it in the paper and panicked but I guess it's worth considering.'

'What do you want to know?'

'Just the basics. Who the victims were, how and when, anything on the suspect.'

Berman nodded to a couple of chairs and they sat down.

'There've been two attacks, that we know of. Plus one other attempt that appears to be the same guy. First was almost two months ago. Victim was a thirty-year-old woman, lived alone. She'd just come home from work so we're talking five-thirty, something like that. She's in the bathroom, just got out of the shower, and hears a noise. Steps out into the hallway to see what is was and this guy grabs her, pushes her to the floor. Attempts to rape her but she manages to fight him off. She said she kicked him in the balls and he ran but he still managed to break her wrist and she had a fair few bruises. She called the police quickly, had a fairly good description, but we didn't find him.'

'He didn't cover his face?' Freeman asked.

'He did, with a scarf, but she saw his eyes. And he wore a hat but she could still see that he had dark hair. Also she was fairly sure of height, build and clothes. But he also wore gloves so left no prints. You'd think some guy walking around with a hat, scarf and gloves would be conspicuous in summer.'

'He dumped them, maybe?'

'Apparently not. The second attack was almost four weeks later, another woman, early thirties, lived alone. This time it was a Sunday morning. The victim had been out the night before, had just got up to get some water and paracetamol. Walked out of the kitchen and all of a sudden there's someone smashing the window and forcing his way in. He grabs her, she screams Bloody Mary. Unfortunately for our guy, the woman had brought someone home the night before. He heard the noise and came down the stairs and chased the guy. If he hadn't been in the nip, he probably would've chased him outside and caught him.'

'And did they get a good look too?' Freeman asked.

'Yep. Tall, slim, dark hair, brown eyes. Even had the same hat and scarf. Boro.'

'Well, that'll narrow things down around here,' Freeman said. 'But he's dumb enough to break into houses and attack women without checking if there's anyone else in the house?'

'Yeah. Plus he does it in daylight, which also begs the question, is he really confident or is he just really stupid?'

'You said there was another attempt?'

He nodded. 'This time the woman was home alone. She was in the kitchen, cooking. She saw someone come into the garden. He hung about there for a few minutes so she went to get the phone to call her dad. When she came back into the kitchen he was trying to get the door open. He saw her on the phone and ran off. The description matches the others *except* for the hat and scarf.'

'So she saw his face?'

'She did but so far it hasn't helped. We showed her some pictures but got nothing.'

Freeman thought about it, whether this guy could've done something to Katy Jackson. He didn't sound like the brightest spark but maybe he got lucky this time and then things got out of hand. But it didn't feel right.

'Also, the first two victims, when they were questioned,' Berman said, 'they reckoned they'd seen someone hanging around the week or so before it happened. Neighbours confirmed it too. One had actually called the police because she'd seen someone lurking on the street outside her house. I don't think it was followed up,' he said with a shake of his head.

'So it's possible he scouted things out first. He was just unlucky the second time. Picked the wrong day to go for it.'

'Except,' he said, 'the third woman, she'd recently taken in a lodger. A man in his forties. He wasn't there at the time, he was at work. But he'd been living there for over a month. If our guy had been doing research he either picked this one a long time before he tried anything or he just didn't research well enough.'

She sighed. 'Both Katy Jackson and Lawton live with their boyfriends. If he was choosing women who lived alone then it wouldn't fit.'

'But if he's just going for women who are alone at the time, or at least he thinks they are, then maybe …'

'Maybe,' Freeman said. 'But why attack Katy in Lawton's house?'

'Mistaken identity? Or he's just seeing opportunities and going for it?'

'Maybe,' she said again and stood up. 'I'll check if anyone's been hanging around recently, let you know.'

'Thanks.'

She left Berman to it and wondered if this could be part of his case, if some idiot had seen Katy enter Lawton's house alone and took a chance. But if that was the case, where was Lawton?

Chapter 9

The two phone shop guys looked up as Gardner went into the shop. They seemed to glance at each other before moving towards him, as if he was some sort of prize, a pretty woman instead of a pissed off detective. They must've been exceedingly bored.

'Can I help you?' one asked. Gardner looked at his name badge, which said Ryan.

'I'm looking for Lee Johnston,' Gardner said, showing them his ID. He saw the other man – Scott, according to his badge – back away. No sense getting involved if it's not a sale.

Ryan blinked and then said, 'He's not here.'

'But he does work here?' Gardner asked.

'Yeah.'

'Is there a manager about I could speak to?'

'Yeah,' Ryan said again but made no move to go and find said manager.

'I'll get him,' Scott said and disappeared.

'Summat happened?' Ryan asked and Gardner ignored him. A few seconds later another, older, man emerged from a room at the back.

'Can I help?' he said and walked quickly towards Gardner. 'I'm Tony Barker, the manager.'

'Is there somewhere we can talk?' Gardner asked, and Tony led him back to the room behind the counter. As he walked away he noticed Ryan watching him but Scott was already reaching for his phone from his pocket. He wondered if he was giving Lee a heads up or just instinctively reaching for his phone like most people these days.

Tony offered Gardner a seat but he chose to stand. 'I'm looking for Lee Johnston,' he said. 'Can you tell me when he's next due in?'

'Ah,' Tony said. 'Should be in tomorrow but we'll see.'

'Meaning?'

'He should've been in today but he called in sick. Didn't sound very sick to me but there you go.'

'Was he in the day before?'

'No.'

'Sick?'

'Yep.'

Gardner felt something stir. It was possible that both Lawton and Lee had been struck down by illness at the same time but he seriously doubted it. Something had happened two nights ago that was serious enough to make sure neither went in to work.

'Did Lee actually call in today or did he call yesterday and just assume you'd know he was still ill?'

'Ah, no, he called today. Store policy, have to call each day. Unless of course it's long-term. Broken bones or something.'

Tony continued to outline the sickness policy and Gardner tried to drown it out. So Lee had had chance to call in sick. Did that mean he was blowing things out of proportion? If Lee had done something serious to Lawton, or to this other girl, Katy, would he really stop and call his boss at the phone shop? He'd only known Tony for five minutes and he already got the impression that Tony wasn't a feared and respected manager. But if Lee really was ill, same as Lawton, then why the hell weren't either of them at home?

Gardner asked a few more questions before thanking Tony and headed for the door. As he looked back he saw Ryan had finally found something to do and was tidying up the displays. Scott on the other hand was now focused on Gardner, his phone still in his hand, spinning it around and around. Gardner went back in and Scott slid the phone into his pocket. He took in Scott's various tattoos and piercings and wondered when shops stopped having a dress code and when he'd started being an old fart.

'Do either of you know Lee Johnston well? Have any idea where I might find him?' Gardner asked.

Ryan stopped tidying and came over. 'Not really,' he said. 'I've not been here very long. We've only worked a couple of shifts together.' He looked over to Scott but the other man said nothing. 'You know him, don't you?'

Scott pulled a face and said, 'Not really. Don't see him outside of work.'

Gardner thought he saw Ryan frown but it was gone as soon as it came. He gathered Scott was lying though.

'What do you think of him?' Gardner asked.

'Who?' Scott said but Gardner just waited for him to answer his own question. 'He's all right, I suppose.' He shrugged and looked at Ryan again, trying to shift focus away from himself.

Gardner watched him a little longer before nodding and heading out back to his car. He tried the number for Lawton's mum that had been sent through but it just rang and rang. He called Freeman as he drove out, down the ramp and through the town centre.

'How'd it go?' Freeman said as soon as she picked up.

'He wasn't there. Phoned in sick the last couple of days.'

'There's a coincidence. Did his co-workers have anything useful to say?'

'Not really. He's been there about eight months. The two geniuses that work there had little to say. To be fair one hasn't been there long so doesn't really know Lee. The other one, Scott, said he was all right. That was about it. I think he was lying, covering for his mate. He seemed twitchy about something anyway.

'His boss, though … he was a little more forthcoming. Thinks Lee is a bit of a dick. Lazy, does as he pleases. Doesn't believe for one second he's actually ill. He's already had a few episodes of sickness but they were all single days, probably hangover related. Didn't have a huge amount of insight but hinted that Lee was a bully. I got the impression that he was bullying *him* but he didn't want to say that outright.'

'So we know he's a dick,' Freeman said. 'But that's about it. So far there's been nothing on the CCTV showing Katy leaving. But there's a lot to go through.'

Gardner sighed and pulled up outside the house. 'Seems odd that if nothing happened Lee isn't home. If he's pulling a sickie, why not stay home, play Xbox, watch telly, whatever. Why would you go out all day?'

'And why wouldn't you clear up the glass and blood from the kitchen?' Freeman said.

'So you *do* think something's happened?' Gardner said.

'*Something* has. But I don't know what. And neither do you. We need to wait on SOCO to get some answers. But finding at least one of them would help too.'

'Which is why I'm going to wait here.'

'Where?'

'Lawton's house. If one of them shows up, I'll let you know. I've tried Lawton's mum but there's no answer. Can you send someone over to the house?'

'Sure,' she said.

He hung up and settled back in the seat. One of them had to show eventually – Katy, Lawton or Lee – and maybe they'd start getting some answers. He just hoped it would be sooner rather than later because he was starting to agree with Andrew. The longer they were all gone, the more it seemed likely that Lee had done something to both women.

Chapter 10

Gardner was uncomfortable. He'd been sitting in the car outside Lawton's for over two hours and a kid across the road had been staring at him for at least an hour of that time. He wanted to get out and walk around a little, loosen up, but the kid was freaking him out. He wasn't sure if she was just bored and curious about the stranger sitting on her street or if she thought he was a paedo or something. Whatever it was, he didn't want to attract more attention by getting out and walking up and down.

He checked his phone again but there was nothing. He'd tried Lawton's phone about once every twenty minutes but each time the message was the same: this person was unavailable. Not even an opportunity to leave her a message. Same with her mum. Freeman had called back and said no one was at the house either.

Turning the radio off, he leaned back in the seat, trying to stretch a little. He was too old for sitting in cars for long periods. He should've gone home; he knew there was little point in his vigil but he also knew that if he went home he'd just sit there, staring into his phone, willing Lawton to call him back. He wouldn't sleep, he'd lie there wondering how he could've missed it and when he'd lost the ability to read people.

He tried to recall how long he'd known Lawton. Five, no, six years. A long time anyway. And what did he really know about her? Obviously very little. He'd never really taken the time to ask her about her life but then why would he? He never asked anyone else, never shared his own stuff. He'd closed himself off a long time ago, so much so that now he couldn't even see when a supposed friend was in trouble.

There'd been a few times Lawton had mentioned Lee but he struggled to remember whether she'd volunteered the information or if someone else – someone better at conversation – had drawn it out of her. Had there been clues? He remembered asking Lawton to work late a few times, remembered her leaving the office to make a call to Lee. Sometimes he thought he'd seen relief on her face when she had to stay and sift through evidence or go and talk to some poor family whose loved one had been killed. He'd wondered what Lee had planned for them that she'd rather stay at work, surrounded by grief and awfulness. He'd assumed going to a football match or a night in the pub with his mates. Not this. But what had happened when she *did* go home? Was it worse? Or was it all the same anyway, just that staying at work late gave her a little reprieve?

He knew Lawton had a crush on him, or at least had in the past, though he didn't like to admit it, not even to himself. Partly because Lawton had never said anything outright and he didn't want to be the guy who thought so highly of himself to presume such a thing. But also because it was a dangerous road to go down when he was her superior. He'd never really thought too deeply about how he actually felt about her because he knew nothing would, or could, ever happen. But when he'd got Freeman's call, panic had overwhelmed him, and a fear that something might've happened; he wasn't sure it was the reaction he'd have had for just any of his colleagues. Maybe she was more than that; a friend possibly. But if that was true, shouldn't he have seen what was right in front of him?

Gardner felt a lump in his throat. He couldn't tell whether he was going to puke or cry or whether he'd just been cooped up in the car too long. Either way, he wished that kid would stop staring and mind her own fucking business.

He turned away from the window and tried to stop the thoughts of what had gone on behind that door. They didn't know anything yet. All they had was Andrew Blake's story about hearing the fights, hearing raised voices. But he couldn't imagine Lawton shouting, screaming. Even at work, he'd seen her dealing with all kinds of arseholes, struggling and resisting, and she had a way of calming things down, getting things under control without ever once raising her voice. So why couldn't she do that at home?

Despite the hour, the air was still too warm and Gardner felt suffocated inside the car. He shoved the door open and stumbled out onto the road. He ignored the eyes on him and started towards Andrew's door. He wanted to hear it again. Wanted to know everything.

As he got to the gate he heard a car pull up behind him. He turned and saw Lee Johnston sitting there. Their eyes met and Lee looked at him with something like fury. He couldn't tell whether Lee was going to get out and confront him or run. He didn't give him the chance to do either.

Gardner ran around to the driver's side of Lee's car and pulled the door open. Lee had barely got his seatbelt off before Gardner had pulled him out and slammed him against the side of the car. 'Where is she?' Gardner shouted, holding onto Lee by the collar.

'What the fuck are you talking about?' Lee said.

'Lawton. Where is she?'

'How should I know?'

'What've you done to her, you little shit?' Lee almost smirked at this but Gardner's fists tightened around his shirt and Lee's face changed.

'Where is she?'

Gardner and Lee both looked round to see Andrew Blake running down the path from his front door, out onto the road.

'What?' Lee said. 'What the fuck's it got to do with you?'

'Katy?' Andrew said. 'Where's Katy?'

'Who the fuck is Katy?' Lee said, looking at Gardner. 'I don't know what you pair think is going on here but you're both mental.'

Gardner flipped Lee around and cuffed him although he wasn't quite sure what the hell for.

'Get the fuck off me,' Lee said, struggling against the cuffs.

'We've seen the house, Lee. The blood. Lawton's missing and so is Katy Jackson,' Gardner said.

'So?'

'So? You're going to come with me and tell me what happened,' Gardner said.

'Look, mate,' Lee said, 'I don't know what's going on here. I don't know where Dawn is. I haven't seen her. And the other lass, I don't even know her.'

'He's lying. He's done something to her. Both of them,' Andrew said, trying to get hold of Lee.

'Enough,' Gardner said, pushing Andrew away and pulling Lee away towards his car. 'Let's go.' He shoved Lee into the backseat of his car, ignoring his protests. Andrew was still loitering, shouting at Lee, demanding to know what he'd done to Katy. A small crowd had started to gather on the street and Gardner just wanted to get out of there.

As he climbed into the seat he glanced across the road and saw the little girl, still watching him. He started the car but Andrew was still standing in the road, in the way. Gardner told him to move but Andrew stood still, staring into the backseat at the man he believed had hurt his girlfriend. Gardner let the car roll forward, slowly.

Eventually Andrew moved out of the way and let them leave.

As Gardner drove away he saw the little girl in the window and she smiled and waved.

Chapter 11

Freeman thought about the information she'd received about the door to doors, which was basically nothing. No one had seen Katy at all that day – not going into Lawton's house, nor coming out – so they had no idea whether she'd been alone or with someone else. No one could verify whether Lee had been there when Katy went around, nor if he had returned at all during the rest of the day. It was a big pile of useless … *except* that one neighbour from across the street had mentioned seeing someone hanging around recently, a man who fitted the vague description of the creep who'd been breaking into houses.

It wasn't really what she wanted to hear. Not only did it mean she'd been wrong but also that it was more likely that something had happened to Katy. But it was still bothering her why this guy would attack Katy in Lawton's house. True, he could've just seen a woman and gone after her, but there was no break-in. So did he just sneak up behind her and go in at the same time as her? Or had Katy left the door unlocked? But that brought her back again to how Katy got inside if there was no one, either Lee or Lawton, to let her in. She was dizzy already.

She stopped outside the interview room beside Gardner and looked through the little window at Lee Johnston. He wasn't quite what she'd been expecting, although she wasn't sure what she had been expecting either. She guessed it was based on what she thought was Lawton's type. And as far as she knew, *Gardner* was Lawton's type. So, she was expecting someone a bit older than Lawton. Someone in a suit. Lee Johnston, if anything, looked a little younger than Lawton but that could've been the fake tan and stupid haircut. He just wasn't what she was expecting at all.

'Where'd you find him?' she asked.

'He came home,' Gardner said.

'You want me to talk to him?'

'Nope,' Gardner said and opened the door. Freeman followed him in and tried not to let the nagging feeling that this wasn't going to go well bother her too much. Gardner was a professional. Nothing to worry about.

Lee looked up at them as they filed in and he studied Gardner for a moment before turning his attention to Freeman. His face gave nothing away. If he had done something to Katy and/or Lawton he wasn't showing any signs of panic or fear. If he hadn't done a thing though, neither was he looking too concerned about being hauled in for questioning or the fact his girlfriend was missing.

'You sure you don't want a solicitor present? We can get one for you,' she said.

'Why would I need a solicitor?' Lee asked.

'Let's find out, shall we?' Gardner said.

'I am under arrest for something?'

'No, you're under caution.'

'Meaning I can leave whenever I want?'

'Exactly,' Gardner said.

Lee eyed the door and for a moment Freeman thought he was going to leave but instead he sat back in the chair, his hand rubbing his wrist where the cuffs had been. Freeman wondered if that was going to be a problem too.

'Can you tell us when you last saw your girlfriend, Dawn Lawton?' Gardner said.

Lee looked up at the ceiling. 'I don't know. A couple of days ago.'

'But she lives with you, correct?'

'Yeah.'

'So is that normal? That you wouldn't see each other for a couple of days at a time?'

Lee looked down again, his eyes meeting Gardner's. 'Well, she works long hours sometimes.'

'Is that a yes? You frequently go days without seeing each other?'

'No,' Lee said. 'It's not normal.'

'So, what happened, Lee?'

'Why were you in my house when I wasn't there?' Lee asked. 'Who let you in?'

'We had a report of a missing person. She was last known to have been at your property. When her boyfriend went to look for her, he saw a mess, blood, called the police. Officers entered the property because they had cause to believe someone's life could be in danger,' Freeman said.

Lee took a moment to take it in. 'Why was this woman at my house? Who is she?'

'Your neighbour, Katy Jackson. According to her boyfriend, she went looking for Dawn. She was worried about her,' Freeman said.

'Why?'

'They heard a disturbance two nights ago. A lot of shouting, things being thrown. Sounded like things had got out of hand. Were they right? Did you and Dawn have a fight?'

Lee sort of laughed. 'No,' he said. 'We maybe had an argument but that's it. Wasn't a fight. Not like that.'

'Like what?' Gardner asked.

'Like what she's insinuating,' Lee said.

'What am I insinuating?' Freeman asked.

'That I battered her or something. That's what you're saying, right? That I battered Dawn and then this other lass turns up and I did the same to her.'

'All we want to know is what happened that night, and to find Dawn and Katy,' Freeman said.

'Nothing happened. We had an argument,' Lee said.

'Is that something you do a lot?' Gardner asked.

'Not really. We have little fights. Who doesn't?'

'So what was different this time?'

'Nothing. I don't even remember what it was about. But she got in one of her moods and buggered off. It was nothing. She'll come back when she's calmed down. You know what she's like.'

Freeman could feel Gardner's tension, could sense he was going to react to Lee minimising what had happened. And as much as she wanted to reach over the table and push Lee's face into the desk herself, she knew it wouldn't help them. So she got in first before Gardner could get Lee's back up.

'Okay, so where did she go? Has she left before?' she asked.

Lee paused, his jaw clenching. He seemed to be weighing up his options. 'Not really.'

'Not really?' Freeman said.

'So this *was* different, then,' Gardner said.

'No, it's not,' Lee said. 'She's walked out before, in a huff, you know. She comes back.'

'Do you know where she went?' Freeman asked. 'All we want to do is talk to her and make sure this has nothing to do with Katy's disappearance.'

'I don't know where she went,' Lee said. 'She just pissed off in the middle of the night. I haven't seen her since.'

'All right,' Freeman said. 'What about Katy?'

'What about her?'

'When did you see her last?'

'I don't know,' Lee said. 'I don't know her. I wouldn't know her if she jumped in front of my car.'

'So you didn't see her at your house today? You didn't let her in? Because someone must've. The house wasn't broken into and you said yourself that Lawton wasn't there,' Gardner said.

'Well, I never let her in. I wasn't there. I was out all day,' Lee said.

'Where?' Gardner asked.

'Just out,' Lee said, smirking, and Gardner wondered if one of the idiots from the phone shop had given him a heads-up.

58

'So you think Lawton could've come back, let Katy in today?' Freeman asked.

'Maybe,' he said.

'So where are they now, do you think?'

'How should I know?'

'What time did you go out this morning?' Gardner asked.

'About half eight.'

'Okay,' Gardner said. 'We found blood in your house. Upstairs in the bedroom, hall and bathroom. Was that from the night of your argument?'

'No,' Lee said. 'I told you, it wasn't like that.'

'No? So where did it come from?'

Lee's jaw clenched and unclenched a few times and then he said, 'The dog. The stupid dog cut her paw. It was probably that.'

'Clever dog,' Gardner said. 'Managing to get from the bedroom to the bathroom without leaving a trail *and* getting up to the sink to wash it off.'

'What?' Lee said.

'We also found blood in the kitchen,' Freeman said. 'Can you tell me how that got there?'

'That the dog as well?' Gardner said.

'Look, I don't know what the fuck you're talking about. I had an argument with my girlfriend. She got in a mood and stomped off. I don't know why that's any of your business. Or why some fucking mongoloid from next door is sneaking about my house, calling the police. I don't know why I'm sitting here taking this shit when I don't have to.' Lee stood up and slammed the chair back under the desk.

'I know you weren't at work today,' Gardner said.

'Never said I was.'

'I know you weren't there yesterday either. So where were you?'

'None of your fucking business,' Lee said and walked to the door.

'It's my business when one of my friends is missing and you're the prick that's done something to her,' Gardner said, getting up.

Freeman stood up too as Lee came back towards the desk. 'Sit down, Mr Johnston,' she said, but Lee just moved around her to face Gardner, trying to go eye to eye with him despite being several inches shorter.

'I always knew she was fucking you,' Lee said, his face close to Gardner's, and Gardner launched himself at him, slamming him into the wall. Freeman tried to pull Gardner off him but there was no way it was happening so she ran out into the corridor and shouted, 'A little help in here.'

Two uniformed officers came racing in and pulled Gardner and Lee away from each other, both of whom were practically foaming at the mouth. 'Take him out,' she said, nodding to Lee. One of the uniforms shoved Lee towards the door and they left her alone with Gardner. She raised her eyebrows at him but he just shook his head and walked out.

Freeman slumped down into one of the chairs and realised the tape was still running. 'Interview terminated,' she said and turned it off.

She put her hands on her head, sat back in the chair and thought, That went about as well as I expected.

60

Chapter 12

Freeman followed Lee outside, trying to gauge whether Gardner's little outburst was going to be a problem or not. So far Lee hadn't mentioned it, hadn't started bandying around words like 'official complaint', but that didn't mean it wouldn't happen later when he'd had time to consider it an option.

'I'd appreciate it if you didn't go home tonight,' she said. 'Just in case the crime scene team need anything else.'

'Are you kidding me?' Lee said.

'No. Have you got somewhere else you can stay?'

'I'll go to my mum's.'

'Good. Can you leave me her address in case we need to find you?'

'For what?' he asked, stopping.

Freeman took a pen and her notebook out of her pocket. 'To let you know you can go home for starters.' She offered them to Lee and he started scribbling an address.

'You could just phone me to tell me that.'

'Put your number down, then,' Freeman said.

He handed the notebook back and carried on walking. The air was cooler now and she could hear the shriek of wheels on the train tracks beside the station.

'Thanks for your cooperation,' she shouted at Lee's back but he didn't bother to turn around. As she turned to go back inside she heard shouting.

Andrew ran up to Lee, shoving his face close to the other man but not actually touching him. 'Where is she?' he said, and Freeman sighed and walked over to them. 'What've you done? Where is she?'

'For fuck's sake,' Lee said and walked around Andrew, lighting a cigarette and flicking the match somewhere in the vicinity of Freeman.

'Tell me where she is. I know you've done something to her.'

'Andrew,' Freeman said, putting her hand on Andrew's arm. 'This isn't helping.'

Andrew pulled away and followed Lee. 'I know what you are. I know what sort of person you are.'

Lee stopped and turned to Andrew who seemed to shrink into himself a little now he had Lee's attention. 'Yeah? And what's that?' Lee asked.

'You knock your girlfriend about,' Andrew said.

'Is that so?'

'I've heard you. Heard the things you say to her.'

'Like what?'

Andrew looked to Freeman for help now.

'Just go home, Andrew,' she said. 'Both of you.'

Andrew shook his head. 'No. He's done something. He's hurt Katy, I know he has. That's what he does. He's a fucking monster.'

Lee laughed at that and walked away but Andrew wasn't done. He ran after Lee and this time grabbed his arm, spinning him around. 'Tell me where she is!'

Lee shoved Andrew off him and Freeman got between the two men. 'Enough,' she said as Andrew tried to get to Lee again. 'Lee, just go. Please.'

Lee stared Andrew down for a few seconds and then walked away. Freeman kept her hand on Andrew's arm until Lee had disappeared and Andrew had apparently calmed down.

'Why have you let him go?' Andrew asked. 'He's done something to Katy.'

'We don't know that.'

'Of course he has. It was his house. There was blood. Her phone was there. What about his girlfriend? What are you even doing to find her?'

'We're doing our best,' Freeman said. 'But the best thing for you to do is go home and let us do our job. You never know, Katy might show up tonight and then all you'll end up with is a pretty awkward relationship with your neighbour.'

Andrew didn't seem amused by this and Freeman regretted saying it. She sighed. She was tired and ready for home. She didn't want to spend all night trying to break up fights between various men.

'Go home, Andrew,' she said. 'As soon as we know anything we'll let you know.'

Andrew shook his head and stepped away from her. 'Katy's not coming home,' he said.

'You don't know that.'

'I do,' he said. 'I can feel it. She's never coming back.'

Chapter 13

Freeman walked up the stairs to her first floor flat and as soon as she got to the door she could hear it. She couldn't decide whether it was gunfire from a stupid Jason Statham film or gunfire from a stupid Xbox game, but, either way, it was gunfire and it was excruciatingly loud.

She slammed the door behind her as she went in, hoping announcing her arrival would persuade Darren to turn it down, but the gunfire was too loud for her to be noticed. She walked into the living room and found her brother sprawled out on the settee, enormous bag of crisps balanced on his stomach, a bottle of pop with no lid settled on the floor beside him. She glanced at the TV. It was definitely a Statham.

'Can you turn it down?' she asked but, as far as she could tell, Darren still hadn't even noticed she was there. 'Turn it down,' she shouted. Still nothing. She looked at the TV. She could just switch it off. Instead she walked over behind the settee, reached down for the pop and tipped it over Darren.

'What the fuck?!' He leapt up and Freeman expected to see the imprint of his scrawny body on the settee.

'Turn it down,' she said again.

Darren looked down at the pop dripping off him and then paused the movie. 'What the fuck, Nicky?! You could've just asked.'

Freeman couldn't be bothered to argue so she shoved the pizza box off the chair and slumped down into it. Darren stomped towards the bathroom to dry off. She looked around the room. It was what was traditionally known as a pigsty. She'd only been in the flat a few months but if the landlord ever came around for an inspection, she'd probably be out on her ear in no time. And without wanting to sound like Darren, it wasn't her fault. Her little brother had been staying with her since she'd moved to Redcar. It was supposed to be a temporary thing, just until he got back on his feet. Except Darren appeared to have no desire to get back on anything. And why would he? He was living there rent-free, had food on tap, and could sit and watch TV all day, uninterrupted, due to her long hours. Why would he want to do something stupid like find a job or his own place where there were bills to pay?

She looked at the settee and the stain forming as the pop seeped into the fabric. That'd been pretty stupid but it had felt good for at least one second so maybe it was worth it. She thought about getting up and finding a cloth to at least attempt to clean it up but as her eyes focused on the kitchen she realised that going in there would only piss her off more. There was a huge pile of dishes, a pile that every morning Darren claimed he would deal with and that every evening had just increased in size instead.

Darren came out in a fresh T-shirt. 'Bad day? Or is this how you normally treat guests?'

'You're not a guest. I'd say you were a fixture by now. And I'd say my day was about average.' She looked at the TV screen. It was frozen on some woman screaming. 'Actually I'd say my day was shitty. Someone I work with is missing. Or might be missing.'

Darren stared for a second and sat in the non-stained bit of the settee. 'Shit,' he said. 'That sucks.'

'Does for her,' Freeman said and closed her eyes. She hated this – the part where they knew nothing. And, in this case, they really knew nothing. Maybe it was worse because it was someone they knew. Or maybe that didn't matter to her. She didn't really know Lawton. She couldn't claim personal interest here, Lawton wasn't her friend. But if Andrew was right about Lee, if he really was that kind of man, then it didn't matter whether Lawton was her best friend or worst enemy. She felt a twist in her gut at the thought of what she might be going through.

Freeman had seen plenty of women come through the doors at work, seen them beaten black and blue, heard all kinds of fucked up things done to them by the men who apparently loved them. And not one of them did she feel she'd helped. Not really. And yes, it was partly, maybe mostly, a system at fault. But it wasn't just that. Someone in an abusive relationship was hard to help for all kinds of reasons. But it didn't mean she would stop trying.

She felt tears sting the backs of her eyes and thought about calling Gardner. She hadn't spoken to him since his little outburst. Maybe she should see he was okay. She wondered if he'd gone home or if he'd gone back to Lawton's to wait for her to come home. He was taking it hard. She reached into her pocket for her phone but

66

stopped. Maybe she should give him space. There was nothing she could say to him to make this better anyway.

She looked at Darren. He was sort of staring at the frozen image on the TV. He was probably waiting for her to go away so he could keep watching.

'Did you apply for that job that closed today?' she asked, and he tore his eyes away from the screen to look at her.

'Er, no,' he said. 'I didn't have the qualifications or whatever.'

'What qualifications do you need to put tins of beans on shelves?'

'I don't know. I haven't done it before. They wanted you to have experience.'

Freeman bit her tongue. She was too tired and it was pointless arguing. 'Fine. Whatever,' she said and got up.

'I'm going to find a job,' Darren said. 'You don't have to keep hassling me about it.'

'I said, fine.' Freeman found an almost-clean glass, filled it from the tap and then dug around in a drawer looking for painkillers. Her head was killing her and, as if he was reading her mind, Darren turned the TV back on and the screaming and gunfire commenced once more.

She swallowed the tablets and headed for her room. 'Night,' she said, thinking he wasn't listening, or couldn't hear anyway. And then the noise stopped again.

'You think your friend is all right?' Darren asked.

She looked back at her brother and tried to smile. 'I hope so.'

Chapter 14

As Gardner walked into the office, Freeman said, 'Morning. You look like shit.'

He tried to think of a retort but his brain was sludge and, to be honest, he thought she was probably correct. He poured himself a cup of coffee and tried not to make it obvious that his back was killing him.

'Please tell me you didn't sit outside Lawton's all night,' Freeman said as he lowered himself slowly into his chair.

'No, I didn't,' he said and took a sip. 'I left at about two a.m.' He waited for her to say something, how stupid it was or how pointless, but she kept quiet for once. Not that she needed to tell him, he was well aware of how pointless it had been. He'd sat there in the dark, staring at his phone as though he could make it ring by will alone. But the only person to call was Molly, and Gardner had ignored her, telling himself he didn't want to tie up the line in case Lawton called. When he finally went home, he'd stared up at the ceiling until it was light, wondering where the hell Lawton could be, only interrupting his panic with occasional thoughts of Molly, of how badly he'd treated her. He decided to call her back but would wait until a more reasonable hour. He was still waiting. 'Lee didn't go home,' he said.

'I told him not to. He's staying at his mum's.'

'Did you get an address?'

'Yes. If necessary, I can find him.'

Gardner gathered she thought he shouldn't go anywhere near Lee in future. He was embarrassed about the night before, for rising to Lee's bait. 'He say anything about what happened?'

'You mean you trying to throttle him whilst being recorded for posterity?' Gardner didn't respond to that so she kept talking. 'Surprisingly he didn't mention any lawsuits. But if you keep winding him up that could change.'

'How can you be on his side?'

'I'm not on his side,' Freeman said. 'But we don't know he's done anything yet. We have no evidence whatsoever. We don't even know that *anything* has happened to Lawton. I mean, she called in sick on Monday so at the very least we know she's alive.'

'The very least?' he said. 'That's reassuring.'

'Sorry. I didn't mean it like that. But you know what I mean. If she was able to call in to work then she must be okay. Right?'

Gardner almost nodded but stopped himself. 'Do we know if she called in herself?'

Freeman's face showed that she'd caught up with his own thought process. 'I don't know,' she said.

'Then I guess I'd better find out,' he said and picked up the phone, quickly putting it down when the number he dialled was engaged.

'I'm sure she'll be all right,' Freeman said but he didn't respond. 'Katy too.'

Gardner looked up and hoped that she hadn't noticed he'd basically forgotten about Katy Jackson. He decided not to push it any further with Lee, for now anyway, and focus instead on what they *did* know, what they *could* do. 'All right, so where are we?'

'Well, Katy hasn't turned up yet. Andrew was on the phone first thing. She didn't come home last night so I think we can definitely say we have a missing person. Whether anyone else is responsible for her disappearing is still unknown, as is the question of whether Lee and Lawton have anything to do with her.'

'Nothing came of the bus and train CCTV?' Gardner asked.

'Nope. Had people continue checking overnight but nothing's come up so far. Checked the ticket offices too but no one recognises her. One of the neighbours claims to have seen a man hanging around lately. I spoke to Berman last night and the description given by our witness matches his guy but that's all we have. We need the results back on the blood and prints. At least that'll tell us something. Who was there, who's injured.'

'I told them it was priority. Told them it was one of ours,' Gardner said. 'Hopefully we'll hear something today.'

'Hopefully. But they're still checking for prints in the house.'

'But if Lee's responsible, they're obviously going to be all over the place.'

'Yes, but in case you'd forgotten how this works, we need to eliminate the possibility of anyone else being responsible.'

Gardner waved her off. He could tell she was trying not to be sarcastic but it wasn't working. She was still annoying him.

'I'm going to speak to Andrew again. And I'll swing by his office, see if his colleagues can verify his story about being at work all day yesterday. Then I'll start talking to Katy's friends and family, such as they are. Andrew didn't give me much to go on. One friend, that's all he could think of.'

'Great. You focus on that side. I'm going to look at Lawton, see if I can track her down, starting with her mum. If I can get hold of her that is.'

'You think that's where she'd go?'

'No idea,' he said. 'But it's as good a place as any to start.'

'DI Gardner?'

Gardner and Freeman both turned to the young PC. He looked like he was work experience and didn't seem to know who Gardner was, looking between them, hoping for a clue.

'Yes?' Gardner said.

'We found Dawn Lawton's car,' he said.

Gardner stood up. 'Where?'

'It was down by the seafront in Redcar. Must've been there a couple of days. There was a ticket on it.' The boy looked down at his notes. 'It's been brought in to check for prints and what have you, but there was some blood inside the car. Not much, but visible from outside.' He stopped talking and looked up at Gardner.

Gardner thought he was going to be sick.

Chapter 15

Trying not to think too much about Lawton and her car and what it meant, Gardner pulled up outside Katharine Lawton's house and noticed someone kneeling down in the front garden, surrounded by tools and plastic baskets full of what appeared to be weeds but could've been actual flowers. He'd never been inclined to grow anything himself but assumed it was only a matter of time. Seemingly everyone he knew developed a sudden urge for gardening once they hit a certain age, except, perhaps, his dad who'd never developed an urge for anything but watching TV and getting annoyed at people.

He got out of the car and wondered if this woman was Lawton's mum but as soon as he stepped foot on the driveway, the woman turned and stared at him and he could see the resemblance.

'Mrs Lawton?' he said, and she stood up and brushed herself down.

'Yes?'

'My name's Michael Gardner, I work with Dawn.' He saw Katharine's face drop and he stepped forward, shaking his head. 'No, don't worry, it's not serious,' he said, dispelling any ideas she might have about it being *that* kind of visit. But then he wondered at his choice of words – it's not serious – and wondered if that was true. 'Can we go inside?'

'What's this about?' Katharine said, pulling off her gloves and squeezing them in both hands.

'I just wanted to ask if you'd seen Dawn recently, or heard from her.' Katharine looked puzzled and Gardner nodded towards the house. 'Can we?'

She came out from behind the shrubbery and led Gardner to the back door. She stood holding onto the wall as she pulled her boots off and indicated that Gardner should do the same. Without any more words she led him through to the living room and sat on the edge of the armchair, waiting.

'Mrs Lawton,' he started.

'Katharine, please,' she said. 'Is she all right?'

Gardner wanted to say yes but he didn't believe that was true. He looked at Katharine and wondered how much she knew about her daughter's life.

'We had a call last night from a man concerned about his girlfriend.'

'Lee?'

'No,' Gardner said. 'Lee and Dawn's neighbour. He claimed that his girlfriend had gone to their house that morning because she was worried about Dawn.'

'What for?'

'Well, according to him, Dawn and Lee had a big fight a couple of nights earlier. Something, he said, that wasn't entirely out of the ordinary. But this one was worse and when my colleagues entered Dawn's house, they found things a bit of a mess, some blood too.'

'Dear God,' Katharine said.

'We don't know that anything's happened to Dawn yet but we're unable to get in touch with her. She called in sick a couple of days ago, on what would've been the morning after the fight. She's not answering her phone. So I just wanted to know if she'd been in touch with you.' He decided not to mention the car just yet.

'No,' Katharine said. 'I haven't heard from her.'

'Is that unusual?'

'No. We tend to talk on the phone maybe once a fortnight. I don't see a great deal of her these days. She has her own life.' Gardner noticed a hint of bitterness in her tone. 'Have you spoken to Lee?'

'Yes,' Gardner said. 'He denied knowing where she is, but then he denied anything had really happened.'

Katharine just nodded to this and Gardner wondered if she'd understood what he was saying.

'How well do you know Lee?' he asked.

'Fairly well,' she said. 'They used to come around a lot more. I think Dawn works long hours now but, of course, you know that.'

'How long have they been together?'

'Gosh, about three years? No, longer, I think.'

'And does Lawton – sorry … Dawn – ever talk about him? About her relationship?'

'Not really. She used to a bit more when they first got together. She was smitten with him. The first time she brought him for lunch she was so nervous I thought she might keel over.' She shrugged. 'But things change. After the honeymoon period you start to settle down, things become mundane. I don't think there was a great deal to talk about. She works too hard, you know.'

'So she's never mentioned any problems to you, never gave you reason for concern?'

'About Lee?'

'Yes.'

'No, of course not.'

'You never got the impression she was scared of him, that things weren't right?'

Katharine sighed. 'No. Nothing like that.'

Gardner could sense a 'but' coming. He waited and Katharine stared out the window to the garden she'd abandoned.

'Mrs Lawton?' Gardner said, trying to get her attention back. 'If there's anything you can think of, anything at all. Any fights, arguments? Lee said she's walked out before. Has she ever come here?'

'No,' Katharine said. 'No, I didn't even know she had walked out.'

'She's never mentioned anything? Nothing that upset her?'

'There was something a while ago, and I'm talking well over a year, maybe longer. She said they'd been out for a meal. According to Dawn he was in a funny mood all night and by the time the main course was being served he'd started an argument. He was being loud and obnoxious. I don't know if he was just drunk but Dawn was obviously embarrassed by it. Even more so when he got up and left. Not only was she humiliated about being left there with all those people watching, she didn't have any money to pay for the meal. Before they left, Lee had insisted he was paying, that it was his treat. Told her to leave her purse at home. So there she was, sitting there like a fool and had to go to the manager and tell him she couldn't pay. Had to go back the next day.' Katharine shook her head. 'I thought that was disgraceful. What kind of man does something like that? I mean, she didn't even have the money for a taxi. Had to walk home.'

Gardner felt sick at the thought of Lawton being treated like that.

'Of course, she moaned about it, like she does, but a couple of days later she was happy as Larry again. He apologised and it was swept under the carpet.'

'Did you say anything?'

'To who? Dawn?'

'Yes.'

'Well, I told her not to be so stupid next time, to take some money with her.'

'And what about him? You don't think it was his fault?'

'Of course it was. He has a temper.'

'And that doesn't concern you?'

'If I thought something serious had happened, I'd be concerned. Like I said, Lee has a temper. But who doesn't? Dawn's father had a temper and when he started, I'd just ignore him. Let him stew.'

'And that's what you think is happening? That Lee just has little mood swings?'

'I know things aren't perfect between Dawn and Lee. I know that. But who has a perfect relationship?'

'I'm not talking about little squabbles. I'm talking about abuse,' Gardner said and Katharine's face changed.

'He hits her?'

'We don't know anything for certain yet. But their neighbour seems to think that's the case. The house was a mess, looked like there'd been a fight. And Dawn is missing. I think we need to consider the possibility that Lee has hurt your daughter.' Gardner let out a breath. 'I'm sorry,' he said. 'Did you ever see Dawn with any bruises? Any other injuries?'

'Sometimes,' Katharine said. 'But she said they were from work. She has to deal with some unpleasant people.'

Gardner nodded. 'What about Lee?'

'What about him?'

'How is he around you? How does he act?'

'He's always been perfectly nice to me. I just can't imagine him doing anything like this.'

Nobody ever does, Gardner thought.

'I'm sorry,' Katharine said. 'Dawn's never said a word about any of this. She might sometimes say he was in a mood again but I didn't want to interfere. What happens in someone's relationship is private. It's not my place to get involved.'

'So whose place is it?' Gardner stood up and walked to the door before he said something he regretted. 'Let me know if you hear from Dawn.'

He walked back to the car and tried to calm down. How could this woman just sit back and let this happen? She was her mother and she *knew* something was wrong but did nothing.

He dialled Freeman's number before driving away, to keep her up to date. As he waited for Freeman to pick up he wondered why he was so angry at Katharine Lawton. Maybe she really hadn't known things were so bad. Besides, who was he to talk? He hadn't noticed a thing.

Chapter 16

Freeman hung up and wondered, again, whether Gardner was the right person for this case. But it wasn't really her place to say anything. Gardner might've been a friend but he was also her superior and if he wanted in, then there was little she could do to stop him. Maybe she could go over his head but that was a last resort. If Gardner got to the point where his personal feelings really impacted the case then maybe she'd do that, but for now he was just stressed. He was wound up, virtually blaming Lawton's mum for what had happened. If what he said was accurate, it sounded like Mrs Lawton was turning a blind eye to the situation, which was, to be honest, pretty shitty, but it still didn't make it her fault.

Gardner was under the impression that Katharine Lawton was old school. That she thought what went on behind closed doors was nobody's business but those behind the doors. Freeman thought of her own mam as pretty old fashioned too but if she'd gone home and told her that a boyfriend had been treating her badly, whether that was humiliating her in a restaurant or beating the crap out of her, Lorraine Freeman would've been straight over to said boyfriend's house with a slap around the head for him and a few choice words.

But maybe that was the problem. Maybe Lawton hadn't actually told her mum what was really going on. Or maybe after her brushing off so many of the smaller incidents, Lawton decided there was no point telling her mum about the rest. As far as Freeman could tell, they could blame as many people as they wanted, and maybe they were all at fault somehow, but in the end the only real person to blame for any of this was Lee Johnston.

Freeman got out of the car and walked up to the depressing office block where Andrew Blake worked. Located on a small industrial estate, the building was one of several squat, one-storey structures with a sign above the door in an almost illegible font. She looked around the horseshoe-shaped estate and realised she didn't understand what half of the businesses there did. Several had the word logistics in their name, but offered little other clue to their actual activities. Then there was the one saying hydroponics, which could've been absolutely anything as far as she was concerned.

Andrew's office was that of a small painting and decorating business, and, as she went inside, she noticed that it could do with a bit of decoration itself. She assumed that the office was purely a base for the organisation rather than a showroom of any kind. Between the shabby interior and the location, they'd be lucky to get a single client.

She walked up to a desk in the small foyer. A phone was ringing but there was nobody around to answer it. Whoever was calling clearly wasn't getting the hint that no one cared about their call and, after about a minute, Freeman considered answering the call herself when someone finally came in from a door at the back. The woman ambled over to the phone but just as she got there the ringing stopped. She grinned at Freeman. 'Happens every time,' she said. 'Can I help?'

'I'm DS Freeman,' she said, showing the woman her ID. 'I just wanted to ask a few questions regarding one of your colleagues, Andrew Blake.'

'Is this about Katy?' the woman asked.

'Yeah,' Freeman said. 'You've spoken to Mr Blake, then?'

The woman nodded. 'Yeah, he told me this morning. It's terrible.'

'He's here?'

The woman nodded and Freeman was surprised. The way Andrew had acted the night before, she'd expected him to stay at home, waiting for either Katy to show up or for the police to come and see him.

'What's your name?' Freeman asked the woman.

'Rhiannon,' she said. 'Rhiannon Price.'

'Okay, Rhiannon. May I?' she said and pointed to a small sofa by the door. Rhiannon nodded and they sat down. Freeman noticed Rhiannon shove her hands between her knees but when she caught her eye Rhiannon stood up again.

'Should I get some tea? Or coffee?'

'No, I'm fine,' Freeman said, and Rhiannon sat down again, her eyes drifting to the door at the back.

'Were you at work yesterday?' Freeman asked.

'Yes.'

'All day?'

'Yes.'

'And Andrew was here yesterday?'

'Yes.'

'All day?'

'Yes.'

Freeman smiled at Rhiannon. The smiley woman who'd emerged earlier had disappeared and was replaced by someone much jumpier. Freeman assumed it was being asked questions by a police officer. You'd be amazed at how many people started acting strangely in the presence of the police, even when they weren't suspected of anything.

'It's okay, Rhiannon,' Freeman said. 'No one's in trouble, it's just background stuff. Nothing to worry about.'

Rhiannon smiled again and let out a breath, shaking her arms, jangling the dozen or so bangles on her wrists. 'Sorry,' she said. 'I've never talked to the police before.'

'That's okay. I don't bite.'

Rhiannon smiled again and Freeman tried to guess her age. She dressed like an ageing hippy but she couldn't have been more than mid-thirties at most.

'So,' Freeman said, hoping Rhiannon had calmed down, 'you work with Andrew?'

'Yeah,' Rhiannon said. 'There's only three of us in the office. All the painters work off-site, obviously. So it's just me and Andrew and Roy.'

'Okay. Is Roy here today?'

'Yeah. He sits out the back on his own. He's a miserable sod.'

'Yeah, there's a few of them in my office too.'

Rhiannon grinned and Freeman could see her relaxing more by the second. 'I'm supposed to sit out here,' she said, nodding to the desk at the front. 'But no one ever comes in. Or hardly ever. If any of the contractors come in they know where to find me, so they just come back. It's just nicer having someone to talk to so I go and sit with Andrew.'

'So you'd know if he went out then?'

'Yeah,' she said. 'Sometimes we'll go out for dinner, into the town, just to get out for a bit, but there's a burger van parked up at the end of the park so sometimes we just go there. It's a bit manky, but y'know.'

'So Andrew didn't go out yesterday then?' Freeman asked, confused by Rhiannon's rambling.

'No,' Rhiannon said, shaking her head.

'Okay. What about this morning? How did he seem?'

'He's upset, poor thing. I said maybe she just went out but I guess she'd have come back by now, right? And the mess next door? That doesn't look good, does it?'

Freeman gave her a non-committal smile as an answer. Clearly Andrew had been filling Rhiannon in this morning. She doubted much work had been done. Something caught her eye and she noticed Andrew standing in the doorway. He came through when he noticed her watching him.

'Have you heard anything?' Andrew said.

'No, not yet I'm afraid.' Freeman stood up. 'I'd just like to speak to Roy, if possible.'

Andrew nodded and pointed to the door he'd come in. 'Through there, there's a door on the right.'

Freeman nodded and headed in. 'Good luck,' Rhiannon said as she walked away.

She knocked on the door and a gruff voice said, 'What?', which she took as an invitation to enter. Inside the small office a man sat with his feet up on the desk. When Freeman walked in he looked her up and down and then went back to his newspaper.

Freeman was going to address him as Mr whatever but realised she hadn't asked Rhiannon what Roy's surname was so she just showed him her ID instead. Roy sat up a little straighter and dropped his feet back down to the floor.

'What's going on?' Roy asked, taking on the sudden panic displayed by Rhiannon earlier.

'I just wanted to ask you a couple of questions about Andrew,' Freeman said and Roy looked momentarily relieved but that quickly turned to confusion.

'Blake?' Roy said.

'Yes. Are you aware of what's happened?'

'No. What's going on? Has he done something?'

'No. He reported his girlfriend missing last night.'

'Shit,' Roy said and rubbed his chin.

'He didn't mention it?'

'No, never said a word.'

Freeman gathered that Roy being a miserable sod and sitting alone meant he was excluded from the office chit-chat.

'Is she dead?' Roy asked.

'I sincerely hope not,' Freeman said and took a seat opposite Roy. 'Were you at work yesterday?'

'Me?' For a moment Roy looked truly panicked, as if she'd just asked him whether he'd done something to Katy himself. 'Yeah, I was here. Why?'

'All day?'

'Yeah. From half eight to five.'

'Okay. What about Andrew? Was he here all day?'

'As far as I know.'

'But you're not sure?'

Roy shrugged. 'Tell you the truth, I don't really pay attention to Bill and Ben out there. I remember seeing him first thing when I made a cup of tea. He was definitely out there most of the day; I could hear him on the phone. Heard him and Dippy giggling away.'

'Dippy?'

'Rhiannon,' Roy said. 'Hasn't got the brain she was born with.'

'But you don't know if Andrew left at all, at lunchtime or late morning, say.'

'Couldn't tell you.' Roy scratched at his beard. 'He in trouble, like?'

'I'm just confirming a few details,' Freeman said. 'Do you know what time Andrew left? You said you were here until five.'

'He finishes earlier than me. Four usually. I assume he went normal time but I didn't check. He was gone when I came out, I know that.'

'Okay. Thanks Mr …'

'Collins.'

Freeman left Roy to get back to his newspaper and went through to the front office where Andrew and Rhiannon were still sitting. She noticed Rhiannon had her

86

hand on Andrew's shoulder but Andrew stood up as soon as Freeman came back in.

'Thanks for your time,' Freeman said to Rhiannon before turning to Andrew. 'I'll be in touch.'

Andrew nodded and Freeman left them to it. She wondered how much work would get done that day … how much work ever got done in there. As she climbed into her car she could see Andrew and Rhiannon through the small window, the hippy-dippy woman hugging Andrew tightly. She wondered whether she should be concerned.

*

Andrew watched Detective Freeman walk out and once the door had slammed shut behind her, he turned to Rhiannon who stood up and looked at him with sympathy. She reached out and pulled him into a hug. Andrew pulled away in case Freeman saw it, not wanting her to get the wrong impression.

Nothing had happened with Rhiannon. Not really. Nothing that anyone else needed to know about, at least. He wondered what Roy had to say for himself. He knew Roy disliked him, always had. Knew that he was jealous of the relationship he and Rhiannon had forged. It was always awkward when there were three people; someone was always going to be left out. He just hoped that Roy's irritation with them wouldn't translate into him making trouble.

He watched Freeman drive away and felt a little of the weight on him lift. He didn't know why but having her there, at work, bothered him. What was happening with

Katy had nothing to do with work. But he supposed she was always going to be asking a lot of questions. He had to be prepared for that.

Rhiannon had gone over to her desk, and opened up a spreadsheet. She probably thought he was angry with her but it wasn't that. He went over and leaned against the wall beside her.

'What did you say to her?' he asked and Rhiannon looked up at him.

'I just said you were here yesterday. That you were here all day.' She took hold of his hand, her bangles wiggling up her arm. 'Did I do right?'

'Yeah,' he said, and bent down and kissed the top of her head. 'Thank you.'

Chapter 17

Gardner tried to weave his way through the maze of streets that made up the newly built estate. Lee Johnston's mum lived in one of the monstrosities but for the life of him Gardner couldn't find his way onto the right road. After driving around and around for far too long he eventually stopped and asked a woman who was simultaneously pushing a pram, trying to keep control of a toddler and wrangle a dog. As he pulled up beside her and wound down the window, the woman struggled to bend down far enough to hear what he was saying. He should've picked on someone else.

When he asked for the address he was looking for she said, 'It's down there,' and nodded behind her, her hands too full to point. 'Whoever designed this place was an idiot. You go down that street and then the one you're after starts halfway down. It's no wonder we never get any bloody post.'

'Thanks,' Gardner said and drove away, wondering if he should've offered her a lift somewhere. But as he looked back in the mirror he could see the toddler throwing herself down on the pavement in a tantrum and decided that he didn't need to deal with that as well.

He finally found the right house and pulled up outside. Two cars were on the drive but neither belonged to Lee. Gardner wondered if he'd even stayed there the night before. He rang the bell and, as he waited, a black cat emerged from behind a bush to wind itself around his legs. He was about to push it away when a woman answered the door.

'Yes?' she asked and Gardner noticed she was wearing a dressing gown.

'Mrs Johnston?'

'No. Ms Weir. Bev. I'm divorced.'

'But you are Lee Johnston's mum?'

She seemed to straighten up at the mention of her son's name. 'Yes. Why?'

Gardner showed her his ID. 'Is Lee here?'

'No.'

'Did he stay here last night?'

'Yes.'

'Do you know where he is now?'

'Work, I assume. He left early.'

Gardner sighed. He doubted Lee had gone to work. Work seemed to be the last thing on his mind. 'Can I come in?'

Bev pulled her dressing gown tight and stepped back. As Gardner went inside the black cat followed and was quickly joined by two more cats who stared at him with suspicious eyes. 'I'll not be a minute,' Bev said and disappeared upstairs.

Gardner walked through to the living room and took a seat on one of the long, leather sofas. The black cat continued its inspection of his ankles while the others stared for a moment before sliding away to find something more interesting to look at. He looked at the white carpet and wondered if he should've removed his shoes but as the floor was littered with cat hair he decided it didn't matter.

When Bev still hadn't reappeared a few minutes later, Gardner stood up and looked at the photos on the mantelpiece. There were several of Bev with groups of other women, some looking a little worse for wear. But in the middle was one of mother and son. Bev clung tightly to Lee, planting a kiss on his cheek while keeping her eyes fixed on the camera. Lee grinned, not looking very embarrassed by his mum's display of affection.

'What can I do for you then?' Bev said, and Gardner turned to find her dressed and fully made up. 'Can I get you a drink?'

'No, thanks,' Gardner said and took a seat again. 'I was just looking for Lee really. You said he left early?'

'Yes. About eight. Maybe before. I was still in bed but I heard the door.'

'Did he tell you why he was staying the night before?'

'No. He just came in late last night. Brought a takeaway.'

'Is that usual? Him just showing up, staying over?'

'Not staying, no. But I see a lot of him. He drops in a few times a week. We go out to the quiz once a week. Sometimes he'll come back afterwards with a kebab but he doesn't usually stay.'

'So he didn't tell you what was going on?'

Bev looked nervous now and started playing with her necklace. 'Has something happened?'

'Lee was questioned last night. His neighbour reported his girlfriend missing. She'd been over at Lee's house earlier in the day. When police arrived at the house they found a mess, blood. Lee's neighbour is missing. As is Dawn.'

'Dawn's missing?' Bev said, and Gardner could almost see her brain whirring, trying to comprehend. 'He never said anything.' She put her hand on Gardner's arm. 'Is that why he came here? He wanted his mum? But why wouldn't he tell me?'

'Ms Weir, we asked Lee not to go home because the house is a crime scene.'

Bev pulled her hand back and sat open mouthed, her fingers looping in and out of her necklace. 'I don't understand. Dawn's left and the house is a crime scene?'

'Dawn hasn't left, as far as we know. She's missing. As is the woman who lived next door to Lee and Dawn.'

'You think they ran off together?'

'No,' Gardner said, trying not to lose patience. He wished he'd just left when Bev said Lee wasn't home. 'We don't know exactly what happened yet. But two women are missing and it appears that there was an incident in Lee's house.'

'Well, you can't think my Lee had anything to do with it.'

'Lee's neighbour, the man who reported his girlfriend missing, he told us that he'd heard Lee and Dawn fighting a few nights ago, that things sounded like they'd gotten out of hand. He claimed that it'd been going on a long time.'

Bev looked at him like he was suggesting the Pope had converted to Judaism. 'What's that supposed to mean?'

'It means that two women are missing and we're very concerned. And that I'd like to speak to your son again because I believe he could be involved in their disappearance.'

'That's not true. My Lee would never hurt anyone.'

'Not according to the witness.'

'Well, your witness is lying,' Bev said. 'Is he saying Lee hits women? Because that's ridiculous. What's he said? Lee? What did he say last night?'

'He claimed that him and Dawn had an argument and she left.'

'Well, there you go then.'

'Ms Weir, Dawn called in sick a couple of days ago. No one's seen her since and she's not answering her phone. I work with her. I know her. And this isn't like her.'

'Oh, you know her, do you? Well then, you'll know she's a moody cow. That she strings my Lee along. Tells him she wants to have kids with him but then says she can't because of her job. She cares more about that stupid job than she does about Lee.'

'And you know all this, how? Because Lee told you?'

Bev stood up now, making it clear she wanted him to leave. 'I can see things with my own eyes. She comes round here, sits there with a face like thunder. If there's anyone with a problem in that relationship, it's her.'

'I don't know if you're covering for him or if you're just *that* stupid—' Gardner said.

'Get out!' Bev screeched at him.

Gardner walked to the door, trying not to trip over the cats. 'I know Lawton and I know that unless something was seriously wrong she would've called me by now.'

Bev tilted her head to the side and stared at him. 'It's you, isn't it?'

'Excuse me?'

'You're the one she's sleeping with. Lee told me she was cheating on him. Said it was someone from work. She always denied it but he knew.'

'You have no idea what's going on between your son and Dawn. He's been abusing her for God knows how long and you just look away, believing anything he tells you.'

'Piss off,' Bev said and shoved him off the doorstep. 'I know my son and I know he'd never hurt anyone. But if he did hit her then it was because she bloody well deserved it.'

Gardner stepped back as she slammed the door in his face. He wanted to go back in, tell her what a disgrace she was, but what would be the point? He walked back to the car, and, as he climbed in, the woman with the pram wandered past and smiled at him. He tried to smile back but he couldn't quite manage it. He knew deep inside that he was right, that everything he'd said to Bev Weir was right. But it didn't help stop the feeling of shame spreading over him. This hadn't been his finest hour.

Chapter 18

Lee Johnston reversed back along the street when he saw Gardner's car parked outside his mum's house. The last thing he needed now was that prick following him about. He knew he should've come up with a better lie last night. He could've said he was at his mum's instead of saying, *Just out*, like a spaz. At least Scott had given him a heads up. Although, if the police were nosing around, he shouldn't have been calling him like that. He should've known to ring from another phone. But it was too late now; it was done. Besides, after Gardner's little outburst in the station, it was unlikely they'd bring him in again. They'd be shitting themselves in case he decided to make a complaint.

Last night he'd been lying on his old bed, thinking about what he should tell them, just in case it was necessary, but fell asleep before he thought of anything useful. He'd wondered when he got up in the morning if Gardner or one of his mates would be watching him, wondered whether it was the best idea to go out if they were onto him. Whether it was safe to go there.

He watched Gardner's car disappear round the corner and decided to take the risk. He'd come this far, he wasn't going to give up now, not because of that wanker Gardner.

Lee drove slowly to the end of the street and looked around for any sign that the pig was still hanging around, and, once he was sure no one was watching, he turned off and headed for the lock up. It was in one of the crappier parts of town so there was no security, no one concerned with who was coming in and out or what they were unloading from their cars. It was perfect really.

He was almost there when he saw him in the rear-view mirror. Lee muttered to himself, pissed off that not only had Gardner followed him but he hadn't noticed until now. He drummed his fingers on the steering wheel, trying to work out what to do. He was nearly there. Should he try to lose Gardner and stick to the plan or should he abandon it and get the hell out of there before Gardner found out what was going on? Did he really need to go there right now?

Lee put his foot down and swerved around some old biddy who was clearly too old to drive. He kept his foot on the accelerator and ignored the various horns and hand gestures from other drivers. As he looked in the mirror he saw Gardner's car being left behind.

He grinned and swung the wheel, turning the corner and barely missing an oncoming van. He could hear a siren now, maybe from Gardner's car or maybe from something else completely. But he was having too much fun to stop now and put his foot down further, bringing his speed up to seventy.

Another corner was taken too quickly and the car veered across the road, Lee almost losing control. He clipped the wing mirror of a parked car and laughed to himself as he righted the vehicle.

He could see Gardner catching up now and as he approached the turning that would've taken him off to the lock up, he knew it was too risky. He'd have to leave it, whatever the consequences. Scott wouldn't be happy but fuck him. This was none of his business really. The only reason Scott was a part of this was because of a careless conversation that meant it was easier to let the prick in on it than risk him opening his mouth.

Lee turned left and kept going, not only to put as much distance between him and the lock up as possible, lest Gardner actually do some detecting and work out that he could be hiding something there, but also because he enjoyed playing with him. If Gardner wasn't going to leave him alone, he'd lead him on wild goose chases all day long. No skin off his nose.

He almost didn't see the car pulling out until it was too late and had to swerve violently, smashing into a bin at the side of the road. It slowed him down a little, so much so that he could see Gardner's face now. He kept going, taking every corner he saw until he was back on the main road and far away from the lock up. And then, when he realised he was almost out of petrol, he pulled over, waiting for Gardner to come and get him.

He watched as Gardner stomped up to the car and pulled his door open. 'Out,' he said, and Lee undid his seatbelt and slowly emerged from the car.

'Was I driving too fast?' he asked, and Gardner shoved him against the car.

'Where were you going?' Gardner asked and Lee just shrugged.

'Just fancied a drive.'

'Where is she?' he asked, grabbing his collar tightly.

'Who?' Lee smiled.

'Lawton.'

'I've told you. I've got no idea,' he said and watched as Gardner's hand curled into a fist. 'Maybe I should've gone to the police station,' he said. 'Had a little word with someone about last night.'

Gardner's hand dropped and he let go of Lee's collar, stepping back a few feet.

'Was there anything else, officer?' Lee asked and got back in his car. He started the engine but Gardner stood there in front of him for a few seconds before getting out the way.

As he drove away, he realised that Gardner was still following him so decided to take the scenic route back to his mum's house. If Gardner wanted to play, that was fine with him. He could play all day. But it wasn't going to help Dawn or the girl next door.

Chapter 19

Freeman pulled into the car park and saw Gardner getting out of his car a few rows over. She pulled in and opened the door, shouting over to him. He turned and nodded but instead of coming over or waiting for her, he just continued walking towards the building. She locked the car and jogged after him, catching up to him as he walked into the foyer. 'Bad morning?' she asked and he answered without looking at her.

'Don't ask,' he said.

She followed him up the stairs and into the office without another word, wondering who'd upset him this time. Or who he'd upset. If he'd come across Lee again it was likely there'd been another incident.

'Blood results from the house are in,' Harrington said to her as she sat down. She reached out for the sheets of paper but Gardner took them instead, reading to himself. Harrington pulled a face at Freeman and sat on the edge of her desk. 'Blood in the kitchen is Katy Jackson's,' Harrington said. 'Blood in the bedroom and bathroom is Lawton's. Blood in the hallway is canine.'

Freeman processed the condensed information. 'Lee said it was from the dog,' she said.

'He claimed all of it was from the dog,' Gardner said, not looking up from the report. 'He lied.'

Freeman nodded to Harrington to give them a minute and he disappeared to go and try to chat up some woman Freeman didn't recognise but who looked old enough to be Harrington's mother.

'You want to tell me what happened?' Freeman asked Gardner, taking the report from him.

'With what?'

'With whoever you spoke to this morning that put you in this mood?'

'Nothing happened. I spoke to Lawton's mum and then I spoke to Lee's mum.'

'So what did Mrs Johnston have to say?'

'Bev Weir,' he said. 'She's divorced.'

'Okay. What did Bev Weir have to say?'

'That her son's an angel and would never hurt anyone.' Freeman nodded. That was probably to be expected. 'Unless of course it's Lawton in which case she deserved it,' Gardner said.

'She actually said that?' Freeman asked.

'Yep. She's about as charming as her son.'

'So she confirmed that Lee hits Lawton?'

'No,' Gardner said. 'She denied that was a possibility but said if Lee ever *was* to hit anyone it'd be Lawton because she's a moody cow.'

Freeman raised her eyebrows. 'You're right. She sounds lovely. So I'm assuming you just thanked her for her time and left before you said something you might regret?'

'Something like that.'

100

Freeman was about to ask if that was all when she spotted DCI Atherton marching into the office. He zeroed in on Gardner and asked, 'Anything?'

'No, not yet,' Gardner said, and Freeman assumed Atherton was referring to Lawton's whereabouts. From what Gardner had told her, it was only the last few months that his relationship with Atherton had been close to civil. Six months earlier and Gardner would've been the last person Atherton would've asked, but recently they'd found a little respect for each other. So far that respect had not extended to Freeman. Her DCI still harboured a suspicion about her circumstances for leaving Blyth and moving down to Middlesbrough. She often wondered herself how she'd got in so easily. Turned out another DS had retired just at the right time, and despite Gardner's insistence that this DS had gone voluntarily, the rumours and whispers Freeman had heard suggested otherwise. It was more likely the old guy was pushed. And people weren't happy about it ... weren't happy about her.

'The blood results are back,' Gardner said to Atherton.

'Lawton?' Atherton asked and Gardner nodded.

'Bathroom and bedroom. Blood in the hall was from the dog. Downstairs was Katy Jackson.'

Atherton let out a long sigh. 'Have you spoken to the boyfriend again? Johnston?'

'I went to his mother's house first thing but he wasn't there. But I spotted him parked up down the street as I left. I followed him.'

'And?' Atherton asked and Freeman got a bad feeling that whatever had happened next was what really put

Gardner in a bad mood. She just hoped it wasn't another repeat of last night.

'He appeared to be driving somewhere off towards the industrial estate. He spotted me and changed direction though so I got nothing. But I think it would be good if we keep eyes on him at all times. I think he's hiding something.'

'Like what?' Freeman asked but Gardner just glared at her. 'How do you know he was going somewhere related to the case?'

'Because he changed his mind when he saw me.'

'How do you know that? How do you know he didn't clock you from the get go? He's probably messing with you.'

'Why would he do that?' Atherton asked and looked from Freeman to Gardner. She assumed their boss had yet to hear about the incident in downstairs.

'He wasn't very helpful yesterday,' she said. 'I got the impression he was enjoying messing with us.'

'Hmm,' Atherton said. 'What about you?' He turned to Freeman.

'Andrew Blake's alibi appears to check out. I'm going to chase up Katy Jackson's friends and family. See what I can find out about her,' she said.

'Good,' Atherton said. 'Keep me informed.' He walked away and Freeman waited until he'd left the room before speaking.

'So is there anything else you'd like to tell me?'

'Like what?'

'Like should I worried about *two* complaints from Lee Johnston?'

'I wouldn't have thought so.'

'So you didn't speak to him. Didn't get in any more scuffles?'

'We spoke. Briefly.'

She shook her head. Maybe it was best she didn't know. 'You can focus on the Katy angle if you want. I'll look for Lawton.'

'No,' Gardner said, standing. 'I'll do it.'

She watched him walk away and part of her hoped that he didn't go after Lee again today. The results from the blood analysis was only going to fuel his fire and make him even more convinced that Lee had harmed Lawton. She blew out her cheeks and thought about her list of Katy's friends. Or rather, friend. Singular. She was sure Gardner had forgotten about Katy and her part in this. He couldn't see anything but Lawton and it bothered her. She just wasn't sure why.

Freeman went to put the blood results on her desk when something caught her eye. They'd found a trace of blood, Katy's blood, on the outside lock of the back door. She thought about it, about how it would've got there. It could've either come from Katy herself or whoever had harmed her. But whoever it was must've locked the door behind them. Why else would it be on the lock? So either Katy locked up behind her, after she was injured, or whoever hurt her did, meaning one of them had a key. And didn't it seem most likely that person would be Lee Johnston?

She thought about catching up with Gardner and letting him know but decided to hang on, wait until Lee was safely inside the station or at least somewhere with witnesses.

She grabbed her keys and headed out to see Katy's friend. It was only while she was driving that she realised something else. If Katy or Lee had locked up behind them when they left the house, how did Andrew Blake get inside?

Chapter 20

Freeman drove across town to the first, and only, friend of Katy's that Andrew could think of. Marie Noble had been a school friend of Katy's and, as far as Andrew knew, was the only friend she saw regularly. He wasn't sure of anyone else she should talk to, no one else he could think of that might've seen Katy recently at least. There was her mum, of course, but she'd already denied seeing Katy, and Andrew insisted that there wasn't anyone else. If there was, he didn't have contact numbers for them.

After pushing him for *something*, Andrew had said maybe she could try her old workmates at a stretch. But, again, he had no contact information, just the department in the hospital where she'd worked. Freeman wondered whether there would be any point trying the office. According to Andrew, Katy had left months ago. Was it really likely she'd choose to contact a former colleague rather than family or friends?

She arrived at a block of newly built flats, ones that had been created with jaunty angles, possibly to try and make them more appealing. The location was hardly desirable. The most exotic thing in the area was a Tesco Express, and even that looked like it had given up when she went inside for a bottle of water. Most of the shelves were empty and the staff seemed embarrassed to be there.

Freeman pushed open the external door to the flats, the lack of security fitting perfectly with the rest of the area. She climbed the stairs to the third floor and knocked at Marie's door. The woman who opened it had one small child on her hip, another stood in the hall behind her, screaming and shaking a plastic cup up and down, spilling the contents across the floor and walls.

'Marie Noble?' Freeman asked, showing her ID. The woman nodded but didn't seem to react to the presence of a police officer at all. No straightening up, no panicked expression. She just stood back and pushed the bratty toddler into the living room. Freeman followed them inside and felt a pang of sympathy for the woman. In the corner a kid's TV show played at an alarming volume and Freeman was irritated by it before she even sat down.

'Turn that off, Kayleigh,' Marie said to the toddler who just turned and poked her tongue out and ran off to another room. Marie sighed and switched it off herself before plonking down beside Freeman and depositing the smaller child on the floor. 'Sorry. It's bedlam in here.'

'Don't worry about it,' Freeman said, and heard the sound of Kayleigh thundering back into the living room. She turned and found the child with lipstick all over her face.

'For God's sake,' Marie said, reaching for the child but Kayleigh ran off and Freeman felt further conviction that her choice not to have children was correct. 'Is it always like this?' she asked Marie as the kid on the floor started crying.

'Yeah,' Marie said. 'Fortunately I only have to deal with it once a week. They're my sister's.'

'Oh,' Freeman said.

'So what's this about?' Marie asked as she picked up the baby and tried to soothe it.

'Katy Jackson. She's a friend of yours, is that right?'

'Yeah,' Marie said, suddenly looking wary. 'Why? Has something happened to her?'

'She's missing,' Freeman said.

'Oh my God. Since when?'

'Some time yesterday afternoon. I'm just trying to speak to her friends and family, see if anyone's seen or heard from her recently.'

Marie blew out her cheeks and pulled back as the baby tried to claw at her face. 'I haven't seen her for ages,' she said. 'I think the last time I saw her was my birthday.'

'When was that?'

'September,' Marie said. 'God. I didn't think it'd been that long.'

'So you haven't seen her for almost a year? What about phone calls?'

Marie sighed. 'I probably spoke to her not long after my birthday. I remember trying to call her a few times because we were trying to arrange a girly weekend away. But I gave up after a while – she wasn't replying to my messages. And then I think she rang me once, a bit later, maybe getting on to Christmas. But we never got round to meeting up.'

'Were you worried about her at all? When you couldn't get hold of her. Did you go to the house?'

'No, I've never been to the new house. I rang her to get the address so I could drop her Christmas present off but I got no answer. She left a present for me outside my front door. I thought that was a bit weird but I guessed she was busy or something; they'd just moved, I suppose. I don't know. We sort of fizzled out a bit.'

'So you don't know her new address?'

'No,' Marie said, frowning as if it was the first time she'd considered it odd.

'Okay,' Freeman said. 'Do you know anyone else I could speak to? Any other friends? You mentioned a girly weekend. Would that have been with other friends of Katy's?'

'Some of them. Lucy Maitland. She was at college with us. And Francesca Drysdale. I worked with her but she and Katy got on quite well.'

'Have you got contact details for them?'

'Sure,' Marie said and handed the baby to Freeman who froze as it stared at her with piercing blue eyes. Marie dug about in her handbag and pulled out an address book before scribbling the information down. She came back to the settee and swapped the piece of paper for the baby and Freeman let out a sigh of relief.

'Thanks,' she said. 'What about Katy's family?'

'There's just her mum. Her dad died donkey's years ago. No brothers or sisters. I don't know about other family. No one she's mentioned.'

'What about work? Do you know if she was mates with anyone there?'

'I think she was friends with a couple of them. She'd mentioned a few nights out with them in the past but I couldn't tell you their names or anything.'

'What about her boyfriend?'

'Andrew? He's lovely. Not my type but he's canny. Dotes on Katy. Wish I had someone like that.'

'Do you know him well? Did he ever go out with you and Katy?'

Marie frowned, looking like she was thinking hard. 'Once. It think it was her birthday. We went out for a meal somewhere. He couldn't take his eyes off her, bless him. But then, I don't think they'd been together that long.'

'But you were under the impression she was happy? That there weren't any problems between them?'

'No. She never mentioned anything and to me they looked like the perfect couple. Sickening really,' she said with a smile. 'Why? You think she's just up and left him?'

'We don't know yet. I'm just covering all bases.'

Marie nodded again and bounced the baby on her knee. 'As far as I know she was happy. But, like I said, I haven't seen her for a while so who knows? I just assumed she was one of them people who stop seeing their friends so much once they have a boyfriend and a house and that. She wouldn't be the first.'

Freeman thanked Marie for her time and left her to deal with two angry children. She could still hear the wailing halfway down the stairs. When she got to the car she checked the addresses Marie had given her for Katy's other friends. Lucy lived just around the corner so Freeman decided to try there first, wondering if she'd catch anyone else at home at this time of day.

She rang Lucy's bell twice but there was no answer so instead she tried the mobile number Marie had given her. It went straight to voicemail so Freeman left a message asking her to call back.

She drove the short distance to Francesca's and wondered why Andrew hadn't mentioned them, why two women Katy knew well enough to go away with didn't occur to him as good enough friends to mention talking to. Maybe he just didn't pay enough attention to Katy's social life, possibly zoning out when she talked about them. Or maybe he was just too worried to think straight.

Getting out the car, Freeman noticed a woman climbing out of a taxi, ridiculous heels in hand. She watched as the woman shuffled her skirt down on her hips and slammed the car door, before skipping over the patch of grass onto the pavement. She headed up the short path to the house Freeman had come to visit.

'Francesca Drysdale?' Freeman asked and the woman spun around, looking like she'd been caught doing something she shouldn't.

'Yeah?'

Freeman flashed her ID and Francesca stood there, open mouthed. Her mascara had long since slid off her eyelashes onto her cheek and there was a ladder in her tights. Freeman had to admire a woman who could do the walk of shame mid-morning on a Wednesday.

'Can I have a quick word? It's nothing to worry about.'

Francesca nodded and unlocked the door, tossing the shoes into a pile of other footwear and pointing to a room on the left. 'Take a seat. I'm just going to grab some paracetamol. Can I get you anything?'

'No, thanks,' Freeman said and went into the living room. A minute later Francesca followed her in and flopped onto the chair by the window.

'Sorry,' she said. 'Big night out.'

Freeman smiled at her and resisted the urge to say, 'No shit.' Instead she got straight to the point, assuming Francesca would be hoping to take to her bed shortly. 'I just wanted to ask if you'd seen Katy Jackson lately. Marie Noble told me you were friends with her.'

Francesca sat up straight. 'Katy? Yeah, kind of,' she said. 'Why, what's going on?'

'Well, she's missing,' she said but put her hand up when Francesca looked alarmed. 'She's been gone less than a day but there are circumstances that mean we're looking at her as a possible missing person. I'm just checking in with anyone who might've seen her or been in touch with her.'

'No,' Francesca said. 'I haven't seen her for ages.'

'Can you remember when?'

'God. Ages ago,' she said. 'I was sort of friends with her through Marie so we never really saw each other without her. Has Marie not seen her?'

'No, not for a while.'

'Shit.'

'Did you ever go to Katy's house?'

'No. She was a bit funny about it, to be honest; never invited anyone over. I think she was a bit weird with tidiness and that.'

'Was this the new house?'

Francesca shrugged. 'I didn't know she'd moved.'

Freeman wondered whether to continue. Clearly Francesca didn't know where Katy was now and it was unlikely she knew her well enough to give her any information that could help. She almost stood up to go but something stopped her. Francesca looked like the kind of person who'd tell it like it was.

'Did you ever meet Katy's boyfriend?' she asked.

'Andy?' Francesca said and grinned. 'He didn't like being called Andy so I did it just to wind him up.'

'So you know him then?'

'Not really. I just met him when we all went out for Katy's birthday once. Don't think I ever saw him again after that.' She picked at the hole in her tights. 'No, wait. I ran into them once in the town but he never said anything. Just stood and tutted at us because he obviously wanted to go home.'

'Did you get any impression of him when you were out that night? Did it seem like Katy was happy?'

'Yeah she seemed all right. I didn't really like him though.'

'Why not?'

Francesca shrugged. 'I don't know. Maybe that's not fair. It's not that I didn't like him, he was just a bit clingy and that. Not really my type.'

'But Katy didn't mind it?'

'I guess not. He bought her a well expensive necklace too. What else can you ask for?' she said and snorted out a laugh.

Freeman thanked Francesca and the woman walked her to the door. As Freeman stepped past her she saw the bags under Francesca's eyes and her hand shook slightly as she opened the door.

'Drink some water,' Freeman said and left her to it.

She thought about calling Gardner, checking he hadn't done anything stupid, but figured if he'd done anything *that* stupid she'd have probably heard by now. No news was good news, as they say.

Chapter 21

Having failed to get much from Katy's known friends, Freeman headed over to the hospital where Katy had worked until earlier in the year. Andrew had told her Katy took voluntary redundancy because she'd never liked her job and it was likely it would disappear shortly anyway. She wondered whether Katy had kept in touch with her former colleagues if she hadn't enjoyed her job, even if Marie had mentioned a few nights out with them.

She walked down a corridor after getting directions at the reception desk and dodged patients juggling drip stands and packets of cigarettes as if they didn't have the extra few seconds to waste getting the fag from packet to mouth. Just when she thought she was lost and was going to ask a porter for more directions, she found the place she was looking for. She went in and found a group of people sitting drinking cups of tea and staring at pictures of celebrities online.

'Excuse me,' Freeman said and only one of them tore their eyes away to acknowledge her. She showed her ID to the woman and one of the others caught sight of it and looked interested all of a sudden. 'I'm just looking for anyone who knew Katy Jackson. She used to work here.'

'I know Katy,' the woman said. 'I was her team leader.'

'What's your name?'

'Sophie Miller.'

'Is there somewhere we can talk?' Freeman asked and Sophie led her into a quieter office next door.

'Is something wrong?' Sophie asked.

'I'm not sure yet,' Freeman said, not wanting to get into the ins and outs again, not if these people hadn't seen Katy since she left. 'Did you keep in touch with Katy after she left?'

'For a little while,' Sophie said. 'She came in once, not long after she finished. Brought some cakes she'd made, had a chat.'

'Did you ever see her outside of work?'

'Not after she left, no.'

'Did you socialise with her while she worked here?'

'Sometimes,' Sophie said. 'We have nights out as a team. Christmas, birthdays. The occasional hen night. Katy came to everything for a while but then I think she got her boyfriend and she was more interested in going out with him.'

'Did you ever meet him?'

'No,' Sophie said. 'I saw him a couple of times when he came to pick her up but I never actually met him.'

'Okay. And when did she leave work again?'

'February.'

'And she was made redundant, right?'

'Well, she took voluntary redundancy. Things are changing in here; they're planning on getting rid of paper notes, making everything electronic. God only knows when it'll happen but the place is in that much debt they were looking to restructure things, hoping people would choose to go. I can't say I'd miss some of them but Katy was a loss. I have to say, I was surprised she decided to go.'

'Why was that?' Freeman asked.

'She liked it here. It's hardly the dream career any of us imagined but it's okay. Most of the people are great. And I always thought Katy liked it too. She always came in with a smile on her face, which is more than I can say for most of us. She was always cheerful, always willing to help. I was just really surprised when she said she was leaving.'

Freeman considered this, whether Andrew had got it wrong. Or maybe it was Sophie who was wrong. Maybe Katy just acted like she was happy in front of her boss when really she was dying inside every time she stepped through the door, that when an opportunity arose she grabbed onto it.

'Has something happened to Katy?' Sophie asked.

Freeman sighed. 'Her boyfriend reported her missing yesterday,' she said and Sophie gasped. 'She hasn't even been gone twenty-four hours yet so it's early days. I'm just trying to find out whether she's been in touch with anyone in the last couple of days.'

'No, I haven't spoken to her in months. Not since she came in that day.'

'What about the others in there,' Freeman asked, nodding towards the other office. 'Did any of them work with her?'

'A few of them. Should I round them up?'

'Yes, please,' Freeman said and watched as Sophie walked quickly out of the room. A few moments later three more people came in, two women, both younger than Sophie but perhaps older than Katy, and a man who looked barely out of his teens. The women took seats at the other desks in the office but the man stood by the door, his arms crossed, hugging himself tightly.

'Sophie said Katy's missing,' one of the women said and Freeman nodded.

'You all know her?' Freeman asked.

'Yes,' the woman said and glanced at the man who just looked at the floor. Freeman noticed the ID badge hanging from a lanyard around the woman's neck. Chloe Coates.

'Have you kept in touch with her since she left?'

Chloe shook her head. 'Not really. I invited her to my engagement party but she said she couldn't come. I haven't talked to her since then.'

Freeman thought she heard a bit of resentment in Chloe's voice. 'What about you?' Freeman asked the other woman whose badge identified her as Elmira Khalvati.

'I haven't seen her since she left,' Elmira said. 'We weren't really friends.'

'Okay,' Freeman said, wondering if the visit had been worth her time. She turned to the man. 'Were you friends with her?'

'Yeah,' he said, his voice deeper than she was expecting. She glanced at his badge – Dominic Archer. 'We used to have a laugh.'

Freeman noticed the two women look at each other and smile. 'And did you keep in touch after she left?'

'For a while,' Dominic said.

'Did you see her at all?'

Dominic frowned and looked at his feet again. 'Not so much. It was more like on Facebook and that. And I used to send her funny texts, you know, like jokes and stuff. Things people would send to me. I thought she'd find them funny.'

'And did she? Did she respond?'

'Sometimes,' he said. 'For a bit anyway. But then she stopped. I tried ringing her a few times because we were all going out for my twenty-first but I think she must've got a new number or something.'

'When was that?'

'March.'

'Okay. And you haven't seen her since then?'

'No,' he said, knotting his hands in front of him. 'Is she really missing?'

Freeman nodded. 'But it's early days,' she said again.

Chapter 22

Freeman got back to the station still thinking about Katy's friends and co-workers. She hadn't been in touch with any of them for months, had changed her mobile number and not informed any of her old team mates of the change. Maybe that wasn't so strange. Freeman hadn't kept in touch with any of her colleagues from Blyth. But she'd called Marie after leaving the hospital to check if she had Katy's new number and was surprised to hear that she didn't either. She tried Francesca too but unsurprisingly got no response. She was probably sleeping off the night before.

The office was busy with phones ringing and animated conversations going on in every corner. Freeman looked for Gardner but couldn't see him at his desk. She collared Harrington. 'You seen Gardner?'

'Nope. But Katy Jackson's phone info is on your desk,' Harrington said.

Freeman picked up the phone records and scanned the information for anything that stood out. It didn't take long. The only calls made or received by Katy Jackson over the last few months were to and from Andrew

Blake's mobile. Freeman felt a stab of anxiety. Something wasn't right. Maybe distancing yourself from old colleagues was normal. But real friends? Family?

She scanned the list again and on the third page there was one anomaly. Freeman looked at the number but it didn't mean anything. It was a landline, a local number. She typed it in to Google and soon had her answer. Andrew's office.

Why would Katy only call Andrew? Her friends said they hadn't heard from her in a while so, okay, maybe there was a reason for that. Maybe there was a falling out that neither Marie nor Francesca wanted to discuss. But why not her mum either, why not anything else, not even some sort of helpline for her phone or Internet or booking a hairdresser's appointment? She made a mental note to check if the landline information had been found too. Maybe Katy was making and receiving most of her calls at home. But it still felt odd.

Freeman checked the date of the start of the phone records – March – which was when Dominic said he'd last contacted Katy, when he thought she'd changed her phone. Had she been talking to other people before then? She made a note to try and get the billing information from Katy's previous phone. She wasn't sure how much it'd help, but it would be interesting to see *when* things changed, if not why.

But for now she wanted to speak to Andrew Blake again. She'd found him slightly irritating to begin with but now something was really bothering her. Was Katy ignoring her friends because she'd grown apart from them or was there more to it? Andrew insisted that Katy was happy to leave her job but her old boss suggested otherwise. Freeman was starting to get the feeling that Andrew hadn't been totally open with her.

She saw Gardner come into the office. He didn't look happy but nor did he look any more pissed off than earlier so she took it as a good sign. 'Any luck?' she asked as he sat down across from her. She assumed not. If he'd found Lawton she would've heard by now. He shook his head before running his hands through his hair and leaning back, staring up at the ceiling.

'What about you?'

'I talked to Katy's friends, such as they are, and the people she used to work with. No one's seen her for a while,' Freeman said and got up, moving to Gardner's desk where she leaned against the edge. 'I thought it was odd anyway, that Andrew could only think of one friend of Katy's, but she passed on the details of two others. I haven't got hold of one of them yet but the others both said the same thing: Katy just stopped calling, stopped seeing them. Her old boss claimed Katy loved her job whereas Andrew said she was over the moon to leave. Some lad Katy used to work with – who clearly had a massive crush on her, by the way – said she changed her number in March and never told anyone. And when I got back there's this,' she said, handing him the billing information. 'Katy only ever called Andrew, and he was the only person to call her. Not even her mum gets a look in.'

Gardner glanced at the pages. 'What about this one?' he asked, pointing to the one different number in there.

'His office.'

Gardner handed the sheets back to her. 'Bit odd,' he said.

'It's more than odd. It's fucking creepy.'

'Maybe you should ask him about it.'

'I will,' she said. 'But …'

'But what?'

'I don't know. Something's not right but I don't know what it is; something's nagging at me.'

'You think he's involved in Katy's disappearance?'

'Maybe. I know this doesn't prove anything,' she said, waving the phone info at him. 'But no one's seen or heard from Katy for a while now.'

'So what are you saying? That Andrew offed her months ago and is just reporting her missing now? Why? Besides, she left him a message yesterday, didn't she?' He reached over and took the sheets from her again, flicking to the last page. 'And she's called him every day for the last few months, usually more than once.'

'I'm not saying he's done a *Psycho* on her, keeping her corpse in the attic or something. I'm just saying that it's odd. It's like she disappeared from the rest of the world a long time ago.' She shook her head. 'By the way, did you find out if Lawton called in sick herself?'

'She did,' he said. 'But that doesn't mean she's okay. And if you're right and Andrew Blake did something to his girlfriend, then what about Lawton and Lee? What about the blood in the house?'

'I don't know,' she said. 'Clearly Katy was there, something happened to her in that house, but maybe Lee Johnston had nothing to do with it. Maybe Andrew is using him as a cover.' She showed him the blood results

122

again. 'There was blood on the lock, outside. Someone locked the door after them, after Katy was injured.'

'Lee?'

'Maybe,' she said. 'But if the door was locked by Lee, how did Andrew get in before he called us?'

Gardner sighed. 'I don't know. Lee came back? Left the door unlocked?'

'Why would he come back and not clean up the mess?' Freeman said. 'It doesn't feel right.'

'All right. So what about Lawton? If Lee's done nothing to her and has nothing to do with Katy either, where is she? And why's Lee unable to provide an alibi?'

'I don't know. I don't have all the answers yet. Or any answers for that matter,' she muttered. 'I don't know where Lawton is or what she's got to do with this. All I'm saying is that I think we should look a bit harder at Andrew Blake because something's wrong there.'

'Fine, look all you want. But Lee Johnston is up to his eyes in this. I know he is.'

Freeman watched Gardner walk away and wondered if he'd actually listened to anything she'd said. He was fixated on Lee but she wasn't sure he was really convinced that Lee had anything to do with Katy's disappearance or if this was all because of Lawton. That he didn't actually know what had happened yet didn't appear to be important. Gardner had it in his head that Lee had done something and *he* had to make it right.

Chapter 23

Dawn Lawton sat on the thin mattress, knees up to her chest, head against the cool wall. She picked at the paintwork, flakes of dirty yellow paint sticking under her nails. She caught sight of herself in the TV screen, glad that the reflection distorted her image; she didn't want to see it again. She'd already turned the mirror that hung above the dressing table around. It was the first thing she'd done when she got there. She couldn't move the bathroom mirror though, so mostly brushed her teeth and washed her face in the dark.

At the bottom of the bed Cotton lifted her head and let out a whimper, staring at Lawton with big brown eyes. She was bored and restless and wanted to go out for a walk but Lawton couldn't face it yet. She'd snuck out first thing when she knew that Hazel would be in the kitchen making the breakfasts, had walked Cotton to the end of the street and then back, hoping neither Hazel nor any of the guests would see her sneak the dog back inside.

There was a big NO PETS sign at the front desk, a sign Lawton had seen when she checked in that day. But she'd already tried a few other places who turned the old lurcher away and Lawton was getting desperate. She'd tied

Cotton up outside, gone in and booked a room, and then when the old man – Hazel's husband, she assumed – had gone back to his TV show, she'd gone and retrieved Cotton, sneaking her up the stairs to the room.

Lawton heard a noise outside the bedroom door and sat upright. Hazel had a habit of knocking on the door, wanting to come in to change the towels and sheets, even when there was a *Do Not Disturb* sign on the door. She could hear the hoover start up again and Cotton sat up, her head tilting at the noise.

As soon as the vacuuming stopped, Cotton settled but Lawton was still on edge. The knock startled her but wasn't a surprise. Cotton started crying and Lawton tried to keep her quiet before throwing the duvet over her in an attempt to keep her hidden. She knew she'd have to answer, that Hazel would just come in if she didn't. So far she'd managed to just shout through the door, telling the old woman she didn't need anything. Then she'd stood there listening as the woman muttered about hygiene as she walked away.

'I'm okay, thanks,' Lawton shouted through the door and Cotton moaned behind her. She wasn't okay, she wanted out.

'What's that noise?' Hazel shouted back.

'Just the TV.'

Lawton moved to the bed and stroked Cotton, trying to keep her quiet. She heard the key in the lock and Hazel was in before she could stop her. The old woman looked at the bed and Cotton poked her head out from under the duvet, curious at what was going on. Hazel opened her mouth, started to tell her off but the moment she looked at

Lawton she stopped. She kept her eyes on her face, on the bruises, the cuts, the swollen flesh, and took a deep breath. She seemed to deflate, the righteous anger about a dog being kept in the room disappeared and she looked like she wanted to say something but couldn't find the words. Instead she turned and went out the door before returning with a pile of fresh sheets and towels.

'You'll need new sheets with that living on there,' Hazel said, nodding to Cotton. She approached the bed and, not quite sure what to do, she reached out for the dog. Cotton ducked away from the strange hand.

'She's nervous with new people,' Lawton said and Hazel nodded and moved away, starting with the pillows.

Lawton told Cotton to move so Hazel could work, and the dog jumped down and limped across the room to Lawton. Hazel turned and looked at the dog, at the scars on her back and her legs. She said nothing, just continued changing the sheets. When she was done she went to the bathroom and cleaned the toilet and sink and changed the towels. She came back out and bent down awkwardly to empty the bin. She looked at the various wrappers from cereal bars and dog biscuits and let out a gentle tut.

'You never come down for breakfast,' Hazel said. 'It's included in the price.'

'I know,' Lawton said, her head bowed now that Hazel was right in front of her. She was embarrassed to be seen like this. She couldn't go and sit with the others in the mornings, chewing on bacon and chatting about the weather. And Cotton wouldn't like being left alone either.

'All right then.' Hazel took the dirty sheets and towels and left them to it.

Lawton put her head on Cotton's and tried not to cry. She was so grateful to the old woman for not making her leave, for not asking any questions.

Lawton moved back to the bed and tapped the mattress beside her so Cotton would join her. She watched the old girl limp across the small room and struggle to get back on the bed. She'd wondered before if the dog had arthritis or something. She was getting on a bit so maybe. But Lee didn't help either. She closed her eyes as she thought of him. She couldn't believe that she was here, sitting in this miserable place by herself. Couldn't believe she'd had the guts to go, or that she'd stayed away this long. Usually she lasted no more than a few hours, or overnight at best. But she also knew that it wouldn't last and she'd have to do something sooner or later. What that would be, she didn't know yet.

Part of her wanted to go home. She knew he'd apologise, knew things could be all right for a while. That was how it worked. No matter how bad it was, no matter how much she told herself she would end things, she always went back. After the initial pain she would remember it wasn't always that way, would feel the pull again, and want to try and get things back to how they used to be. There was always hope that it was possible.

She looked down at the bed. She'd barely slept since she arrived, reaching out across the lumpy mattress, the lack of his weight beside her too strange, even though he was often pissed off, or sometimes just pissed. Even the stink of booze, the sweat seeping into the sheets, was comforting. The familiar always is.

But then the other part of her was still in the painful period where she wanted to leave it all behind, never go back. She couldn't stay here, of course, not forever. She'd have to find someplace else, have to start anew. But to do that she'd have to go back into the real world, have to go to the people she knew. Would have to tell them what happened. And she didn't know if she could do that.

She thought about that morning, calling in to work, telling them she was sick. She'd never called in sick before, even at the worst times. She'd always managed before, always been able to keep things under control. But this time was different. She couldn't hide what'd happened. She could barely keep the tears from her voice as she told the lies. She'd claimed it was food poisoning but later thought she should've come up with something better, something that would last longer. She didn't know when she could go back. She'd have to think of something else. Unless … unless she just didn't go back. Maybe she could leave it all behind. As much as she loved her job, she couldn't go on like this.

She looked at her phone on the dressing table, switched off since she walked away. She wondered if Lee had tried to call her, if he was looking for her, if he was worried about her or just about himself. She wondered if anyone else had tried to call, if anyone would notice her absence. The tears burned the back of her eyes again and she held on to Cotton, feeling like there was no one else in the world she could hold on to.

The knock at the door made them both sit up straight. Lawton got up and answered it. She found Hazel standing there with a large tray. The old woman moved past her into the room and slid the tray onto the dressing table. She picked up a large bowl filled with water and put it down on the carpet.

'Can't have her going thirsty,' Hazel said. 'It's getting warm out there.' She picked up a plate filled with bits of bacon and sausages. 'Can she have this?' she said to Lawton before going to the bed and sitting down beside Cotton. 'You like sausages, mutt?' She held out a piece of meat and Cotton tentatively took it from her, licking her lips, immediately looking for more. Hazel put the plate on the bed and Cotton dug in.

'This is fresh,' Hazel said, getting up and pointing to another plate, this one with toast and eggs too. A glass of orange juice stood beside it, condensation sneaking down onto the tray. 'Let me know if you need anything else.' Hazel nodded at Lawton as she went to the door, turning before she left. 'There's a yard at the back if you don't want to take her far.'

Lawton smiled her thanks, not sure she could speak. The old woman left her to it and she sat at the dressing table, staring at the breakfast, a lump in her throat. She started to eat and Cotton, having finished hers, stood on the bed, staring at what could be her second course.

Lawton started to eat, taking one bite for herself and then passing a bit to Cotton. By the time she was finished she felt calmer. She wondered if she should call Gardner. She'd thought about it a lot; ever since she got there she'd wondered. She'd picked up the phone and held it in her hands until she realised she didn't know what to say to him.

Things had been weird between them lately, ever since the business with Walter James, something had changed. She knew he'd done what he thought was best but she'd seen a difference in him, a side she didn't know existed. He wasn't as perfect as she thought. And then *she* arrived. Lawton had blamed Freeman for putting Gardner in that position in the first place and she didn't want her there at all, never mind all the time. She'd tried to be civil to her but it was hard. She felt things had changed too much lately. Maybe that's why she didn't call him, maybe that's why she was here.

She finished the last of the juice and realised she was being stupid. She couldn't blame Freeman for this, for her not calling Gardner. She'd been keeping things from him long before she came on the scene. Lawton knew the real reason she kept it to herself, the reason she'd chosen to come here instead of to him, and that was because she knew Gardner would go crazy. She knew that as soon as Gardner found out what was happening she wouldn't be able to go back. She couldn't tell him because maybe all she really wanted was to go home.

Chapter 24

Freeman walked into Andrew's office, telling herself to stick to the pertinent questions and not start accusing him of anything. Nothing she'd learned about Andrew and Katy's relationship so far pointed to any criminal acts; it was just that if you put it all together it started looking rather suspicious.

She found Andrew at his desk, on the phone, presumably to a customer, although his tone wasn't the kind of friendly whatever-you-like agreeability you'd expect – more a bored, annoyance. She wondered if Andrew always spoke to clients that way or if he just had bigger fish to fry today.

Andrew wound up the conversation and muttered something under his breath as he put down the phone. 'Difficult customer?' Freeman asked but Andrew didn't respond, just typed something into his computer with heavy fingers. He finally looked up at her once he'd finished and Freeman noticed how tired he looked. She wondered why he'd bother going to work but then, she supposed, sitting at home, waiting, wouldn't help much either. 'Can we have a chat?' she said.

He got up and led her out into the front office as his phone started to ring again. He closed the door on it and took a seat on the small sofa she'd sat on before. Freeman wondered where Rhiannon was, assuming she'd gone out to get lunch, possibly from the manky burger van.

'I wanted to take a look at Katy's bank account,' she said. 'See if there's been any activity that could help us, but I'm struggling to find any accounts. I was wondering if you could help.'

Andrew paused a moment before scratching his cheek. 'She doesn't have a bank account,' he said.

'Not at all?'

'No.'

'Why not?'

'She doesn't need one. She doesn't have a job, no wages to go in. No point.'

Freeman studied Andrew as he said this; he didn't seem to find it odd at all. 'But she had a job until a few months ago,' she said. 'I assume she had an account then.'

'Yes. But after she left she closed it.'

'What about her money? She got some redundancy pay, right? I assumed that was what she'd been living off.'

'It was hardly a windfall. She couldn't live off that very long.'

'So what does she live off? She's not signing on, is she?'

'No. She lives off me.'

Freeman's brows raised at this, partly at the implication, partly at the way he said it, as if Katy was sponging.

'I pay the bills. If she needs anything, I give her the money.'

'Like pocket money?'

'No,' Andrew said, his voice sharp.

'What about any savings? Does she have any accounts like that? An ISA or whatever?'

'No. We moved everything to my account. It just makes it easier that way. Gets more interest.'

'But it's not a joint account, is it? Surely that would make it easier, save you doling out money every time she needed anything.'

'It works for us,' Andrew said.

'Does it? Because it doesn't sound very fair to me.'

'Katy's useless with money. She doesn't want to have to deal with bills and stuff. She was happy to do things this way.'

Freeman could hear the defensiveness creeping into Andrew's voice. 'What about credit cards? She have one of them?'

'No.'

'You're sure? She couldn't have got one to use for emergencies?'

'I'd know if she had.'

Freeman had a sneaking feeling that Andrew Blake knew quite a lot about his girlfriend, more than any of her friends or family these days. But did that include where she was now?

'You didn't think to mention this earlier?' Freeman said. 'When I was checking her purse yesterday, when I said her card was missing, you didn't think you should mention it?'

Andrew shrugged. 'Sorry. I guess my mind was elsewhere.'

'Katy changed her phone number a few months back, is that right?' she asked and Andrew blinked a few times.

'Yes, she changed to a better plan,' he said.

'She didn't seem to pass the new number on to anyone though, other than you.'

Andrew shrugged.

'I spoke to some of Katy's friends, some people she used to work with, to see if they'd seen or heard from her in the last few days. Apparently no one has seen her for months.'

Andrew let out a long sigh. 'Did you speak to *him*?'

'Who?'

'Dominic.'

'I did,' Freeman said and guessed she'd been right about the lad having a crush on Katy. Apparently it was common knowledge.

'Yeah, well, he was the reason she changed her phone number. Part of the reason she left work too,' Andrew said. 'He was stalking her. Did he mention that?'

'No. But if it's true I don't imagine it'd be something he'd share with me.'

'It is true. Ask anyone,' Andrew said. 'He called her all the time. He used to turn up at the old house. He's probably been to the new one too but not while I've been in. He wouldn't dare. She was terrified of him.'

'But you didn't think to mention him before now?'

'No, because it happened next door. It just seems likely it would've been Lee.'

'But you mentioned this other guy who's been breaking in to women's houses too.'

Andrew turned away from her and clasped his hands on top of his head. 'Well, I'm sorry I didn't think of it yesterday,' he said. 'But it's not my job to work out what happened. It's yours.' He turned back to her now and dropped his hands. 'I'm sorry. That was out of line.'

'That's okay,' Freeman said. 'But you need to give me the information or else I can't do my job.'

Andrew apologised again and sat down. 'I should've thought of him yesterday. Have you arrested him?' he asked, eyes wide.

'No. I have no reason to. But I will speak with him again. But what I don't understand is why Katy would stop seeing all her friends just because of this one guy. Her other colleagues, I could understand, but why everyone else?'

He shrugged again. 'She's not been very sociable since she lost her job. I think she was a bit embarrassed about being out of work … didn't think she could go for a night out without money.'

'But you would've paid for her, right?'

'Of course I would. But that's not what I mean. It's psychological, isn't it? Your confidence dips when you lose your job.'

'But Katy chose to leave,' Freeman said. 'You told me she was glad to get out.'

'She was.'

'So what about her other friends? Marie Noble told me she hadn't seen Katy for almost a year. She still would've been working then. So why did she stop seeing them?'

Andrew looked up as Rhiannon came back into the office, a couple of polystyrene boxes filled with something that smelled foul. Rhiannon looked at Freeman and something darkened her face.

'Has something happened?' Rhiannon asked, putting the lunches down. 'Have you found Katy?'

'No,' Freeman said. 'I'm just getting some more information. So if you could …'

Rhiannon took the hint and went into the other office. A few seconds later a radio was turned on and some irritating song seeped through beneath the closed door. Andrew slowly turned his attention back to Freeman. 'Sorry,' he said. 'What were you saying?'

'I was asking if you knew why Katy would stop seeing her friends all of a sudden.'

'I don't know,' Andrew said. 'I didn't know she had.'

'So she *was* going out?'

'I don't know. Maybe. We don't do everything together.'

'So it's possible she was out with someone when you weren't there?'

Darkness clouded Andrew's face and Freeman knew she'd touched a nerve. She doubted Katy went anywhere without Andrew's knowledge. She thought about the voicemail Katy had left the day she disappeared. Why call your boyfriend at work to say you're going next door? True, she could've been nervous, scared even, that something bad had happened there. But surely, in that case, you wouldn't go, not alone anyway. Had Katy been calling to let Andrew know her whereabouts in case something happened to her, or because she had to let him know her movements at all times?

'Katy doesn't seem to call many people these days,' Freeman said. 'In fact the only person she calls is you.'

'Well, if she's fallen out with her friends, who else would she call?'

'Her mum?'

'She calls her from the landline,' Andrew said. 'Gets free calls.'

'And she doesn't on her mobile? I thought you said she was on a better plan.'

Andrew sighed. 'Look, all I know is she calls her mum from the house phone. Sits there blabbering away for hours like a bloody fish wife.' He stopped and bit his bottom lip. 'I'm sorry,' he said. 'I'm just not dealing with this very well. She speaks to her mum. Often. I can't tell you why she's not speaking to her friends. Maybe she's, I don't know, depressed or something.'

'You think Katy could be depressed?' Freeman said. 'Because if that's the case, that could be important. If you think she could've done something to herself—'

'No,' Andrew said, shaking his head. 'I don't know why I said that. She's not depressed. I just … she's at home all day, alone. She says she's happy but maybe she isn't.'

'Has she said anything? Shown any signs of depression?'

Andrew shook his head. 'No. I don't think so. She's Katy. She's happy. She'd tell me if something was wrong. She didn't *choose* to leave. There's no reason why she would.'

Freeman nodded, standing up to leave. She could think of at least one reason. 'Oh, one last thing,' she said. 'You said the door was unlocked, right, when you got there? Lee's back door was open?'

Andrew nodded.

'Are you positive?'

'Yes. Definitely.'

Freeman stared at him for a few moments but he just stood there, blank. 'All right then,' she said. 'Thanks for your time.'

Chapter 25

Lawton let herself back into the bedroom, feeling better for the fresh air and the relief of not having to sneak around. Hazel had let her out the back and Cotton had enjoyed the opportunity to sniff around somewhere other than the bedroom. Hazel's husband had done a double take at the sight of a dog but Hazel had snapped at him to go and do something useful, and he didn't ask any questions about their four-legged guest. He nodded a hello at Lawton as she passed but if he'd noticed her bruises he was even better at being discreet than his wife.

So far Lawton hadn't seen any other guests, wondering if there'd be anyone who still came to this once-popular seaside resort. She knew, from coming here for work that many of these B&Bs and guesthouses weren't really in the tourist business any longer, instead catering to the needs of contractors and more likely to recently released prisoners, kids who've grown out of the foster system, and people needing somewhere temporary until they sorted out whatever misfortune had driven them there. She supposed she was one of them now.

Cotton jumped up onto the bed, staking her claim on the inside. Lawton followed and tried to make herself comfortable with the space that remained. She switched on the TV, watching the end of some banal show about people emptying lofts. It wasn't high on her list of things she'd like to spend her time doing, but at least it distracted her mind a little. She leaned back onto the pillows and Cotton put her head on her legs. She reached down and put her hand on her head, comforted by her presence.

Waking with a start she realised she'd nodded off but probably not for long. The TV screen still showed people trying to sell bits of tat. Whether it was the same people and the same tat, she wasn't sure. She pushed her hair out of her eyes, realising she needed to wash her hair. Needed to wash full stop. She got up, causing Cotton to grumble, and went to the bathroom. In the dim light coming from the bedroom she turned on the shower, pulling the curtain across a wonky rail. She started to undress, careful not to look down at her bruised skin, cautious not to move too quickly making sore parts worse.

She held her hand under the water and when it was somewhere near warm she stepped underneath. Too late she realised that toiletries weren't included in Hazel's price and had to settle for a water-only wash. Not that it mattered much. She wasn't going anywhere. Nowhere that clean hair was important anyway.

She ran her fingers through the short bob, recalling the day she went to the hairdressers, humiliated in the state she was in, trying not to cry as she asked the skinny, blonde girl with the ridiculous extensions if she could do something. The girl had wrinkled her nose and pulled at the uneven remains of Lawton's hair. She'd asked if she'd had a go herself and Lawton couldn't even respond, not trusting herself to speak. The girl just shrugged and showed her a picture in a magazine of a style she described as a pixie cut. 'You don't have a lot of options,' the girl said, fingering the hair again.

Lawton put her face under the showerhead, trying to wash the memory out of her head. She'd known that the night wouldn't go unmentioned. She'd been fairly happy, drinking with the team, even Harrington wasn't being too annoying. The only thing missing had been Gardner who was off up north somewhere, something about the Emma Thorley case. She'd wished he was there, wished she had been more important to him, even though she'd felt stupid for thinking it. And then Lee had shown up and she'd been suddenly grateful that Gardner *wasn't* there. She'd seen Lee looking around for him, checking out all the other guys from work, seeing who could possibly be a threat. But he'd played nice enough, even laughed at Harrington's jokes. But she'd known that it wouldn't go unchecked.

She'd walked home beside him, shivering in the sleeting rain, waiting for him to speak. All the way home he'd kept quiet and in some ways that was worse. She'd rather he just came out with it. But he hadn't. They'd got in, gone to bed, and nothing had been said. She'd gone to work the next day, came home. He'd asked if she'd fancied a takeaway. They'd eaten. They'd gone to bed. And all the time Lawton had felt a creeping anxiety, knowing that something was going to happen. She'd walked on eggshells for days.

It was two days before Christmas when it came. They'd just eaten, and she'd been just about to do the dishes. He'd asked her if she loved him. She'd turned, knowing this was it.

'Yes,' she'd said and he'd stared at her for a few, long seconds before holding out his arms. She'd walked towards him, to hug him, to end it, even though she doubted such a happy ending. He'd grabbed hold of her hair, twisting it in his hand until she'd felt her scalp burn. She'd screamed as he'd dragged her across the cold kitchen floor, begging as he'd picked up a knife from the sink.

She'd really thought that he would kill her as she'd cowered beneath him. He'd looked down at her like she was nothing and she'd heard Cotton whimper by the door. She'd wanted to tell her to run away but she hadn't been able to form any real words. Lee had moved the knife close to her face and tears had clouded Lawton's view. She'd felt the tug of her hair, heard the sawing sound, felt herself drop down as she'd fallen away from her hair.

'They'll think you're ugly now,' Lee had said, throwing the hair at her face and walking away.

Now, Lawton sobbed beneath the shower, hating herself for what she was, for what she let him do. For letting the thought that maybe he was right, maybe she *was* flirting too much, enter her head as a possibility, as a good reason, a good excuse for what he'd done.

She stood there until the water ran cold and then climbed out, wrapping the balding towel around herself. She chanced a look in the mirror, noticing how much her hair had grown out, wondering if she should go back to that skinny hairdresser and get her to cut it all off again. Beat him to it.

Walking back into the bedroom she sat down on the bed. The stupid TV show had finished and the local news was starting. She let her hair drip down her back as she stared at the TV.

Katy Jackson's face filled the screen. *Missing Woman*, it said. Lawton turned the volume up, listening to the report that her neighbour had disappeared. Her chest tightened as she watched DCI Atherton give the details. She'd been to her neighbour's house. *Her* house.

'We are also concerned about Katy's neighbour, Dawn Lawton, who is also missing.'

Lawton felt her stomach drop. She tried to listen, heard them say Lee's name but wasn't sure why. Did they think he'd done something to Katy? Lawton stood and picked up her phone. It was time to make a call.

Chapter 26

Harrington was waiting for Freeman as she walked back into the office. She ignored him as she picked up the information that'd been left on her desk. Katy Jackson's old phone records. She scanned the numbers, seeing more variety than her current bills showed but there was a definite petering out of different numbers towards the end of the contract. She'd find out who the numbers belonged to later but there was one that stuck out, one that appeared a lot. She suspected she knew whose number it would be but called it just to make sure.

'Hello?'

'Dominic? It's DS Freeman. We spoke earlier,' she said, wondering if Andrew had been right about the younger man. 'I was wondering if we could talk some more.'

'Er ... sure,' he said. 'I'm just coming out of work.'

'Could you hold on and meet me there? I need to speak to some of your other colleagues too,' she said, which was true, except this time she didn't want to know about Katy, she wanted to know about him. But he didn't need to know that.

'Okay,' he said.

'Great, I'll be ten minutes,' she said, knowing it was a lie. She'd never get there that quickly at this time of day. But he didn't need to know that either. She put the phone down and saw Harrington standing in front of her. 'What?' she said.

'I was looking at more CCTV near Katy's house, seeing if I could see any sign of Berman's perv lurking on nearby streets. And I saw this.' He handed her an image of a car on a street. She looked back at it and shrugged.

'What am I looking at?'

'The car,' he said. 'It looks like Andrew Blake's car.'

Freeman looked at the image again, recalling Andrew's blue Focus. The picture wasn't very clear but it could've been a Focus. Whether it was Andrew's was another matter. 'Did you get anything else? Maybe check ANPR,' she said, handing the picture back to him.

'Already did,' he said. 'Andrew lied. He *did* leave his office yesterday lunchtime. And, as this is two streets away from his address,' he said, shaking the image, 'I'd say he went home. Now, why would he lie about that?'

Freeman felt a stirring in her gut. She knew there'd been something wrong with Andrew. And now she had him. 'Let's bring him in. Question him again.'

'You want me to get him?'

'Yeah. He was at work, try there first. In the meantime I'm going to speak to Katy's ex-workmate. And then I'll drop in on her friend, Lucy Maitland. Andrew can wait here. Let him sweat it out, the lying little shit.'

Chapter 27

Freeman found Dominic hanging around outside his office, playing on his phone. He looked sheepish when she approached him and she wondered if he knew she knew.

'Is there somewhere we can talk in private?' she asked and he pointed across the corridor to the canteen. She wondered how quiet it would be in there but as they turned the corner she saw most of the chairs were stacked on the tables and the only people sitting were the kitchen staff who presumably had finished serving for the day, and a couple of old men looking sadly into plastic cups of tea.

She pulled out a seat at a table as far away as possible from the others and Dominic followed suit. He sat across from her and looked at anything but her. 'So,' she said, 'how long did you work with Katy?'

'About two years,' he said. 'Something like that.'

'You like it? Your job, I mean?'

He shrugged and continued looking past her, his fingers playing with a Boro key ring that'd seen better days.

'I've just spoken to Katy's boyfriend, Andrew, again. Do you know him?'

Dominic's eyes flicked towards her and she saw something in his face. Anger, maybe. But was he angry because Katy had a boyfriend or because he knew what Andrew would've told her?

He sat back in his seat, dropping the keys on the table, and pushed his hands under his thighs. 'Not really,' he said.

'But you've met him?' she asked.

'Once. I think.'

'Here?'

'Yes.'

'Have you ever been to Katy's house?'

He shook his head but said, 'Not really.'

'Not really? You mean you've never been inside but you have gone there?'

'I guess.'

'Why did you go there, Dominic?'

'I dropped a Christmas present off once, I think.'

'And that's it? You've never been any other time?' He didn't answer this time and his gaze went beyond her again. 'Dominic, Katy's boyfriend told me something. That you were stalking her—'

'No, it wasn't like that,' he said, animated for the first time.

'So what was it like?'

'I just liked her.'

'And did she like you?'

He shrugged. 'I thought she did.'

'But?'

147

'I'm not stalking her. I might've gone round a few times but it wasn't … it was a few times, that's it.'

'But you called her a lot,' Freeman said. 'And I mean, *a lot.*'

She saw Dominic's cheeks redden now. 'Maybe,' he said. 'But it wasn't … she didn't ask me not to.'

'But after she changed her number, did you stop trying to contact her? Have you been to the house since then?' He bowed his head and she took it as a yes. 'Did Katy give you her new address?'

'He's just saying it because he doesn't like me,' Dominic said, ignoring her question. 'Did he tell you he attacked me?'

Freeman shook her head. 'When was this?'

'Months ago. Here,' he said. 'He came to pick Katy up and we were walking out together. We weren't doing anything, just talking. He flew out of the car and pushed me against the wall. Punched me in the face. I didn't even know who he was until Katy started begging him to stop. In the end, two porters pulled him off me and he just pushed Katy in the car and then got in and left. I didn't do anything and he just attacked me.'

'But it didn't stop you from calling Katy?'

'Why should it? She shouldn't be with him. He doesn't deserve her.'

Freeman sighed. 'Dominic, can you tell me where you were on Tuesday?' He looked down again and didn't answer. She waited but it soon became apparent he wasn't going to speak. 'Were you here? At work?'

He shook his head. 'No. I was sick on Tuesday,' he said.

Freeman drove across town towards Lucy's house, her mind racing. Clearly Dominic was in love with Katy but she wasn't sure how far he'd go to get to her. After their chat she'd headed back into his office and caught up with Sophie again, this time asking her about young Dominic. His boss confirmed that Dominic had called in sick on Tuesday but seemed fine now, just as he had been on Monday. His excuse was an upset stomach, which she'd taken as meaning a hangover or just couldn't be arsed. Sophie also seemed to think he was a nice kid on the whole but it was obvious he was smitten with Katy Jackson, and there'd been more than one occasion when Sophie had had to have a word with him. He was, in her words, a bit too touchy-feely, at least for the workplace. And Katy hadn't been the first workmate he'd developed a crush on either. Freeman had come out feeling as if the lovesick young man was maybe not as innocent as he seemed. Was it possible he'd decided he was going to have Katy whatever it took?

But then there was Andrew. Not only had he been violent with Dominic, if Dominic was telling the truth, but he'd also lied about leaving his office that day. Surely he would know they would check, that they'd find out. So why lie? What could he have done that day that he didn't want them to know about?

Freeman could only think of one good reason. Plus, his colleague, Rhiannon, had covered for him. They were like two peas in a pod. If Andrew had left the office, she would've known about it. The question was, did Andrew ask her to lie for him before Freeman spoke to her, Rhiannon blindly agreeing to do so without asking why? Or did Rhiannon know what was going on, the lie already agreed the day before?

As Lucy Maitland let her into the house, Freeman tried to dampen down the thoughts swirling around her head and focus on Katy's friend. She'd already informed Lucy over the phone that she wanted to talk about Katy, that the woman was missing. Lucy had seemed shocked and agreed to talk as soon as Freeman wanted.

They walked into the kitchen where something was cooking in the oven and Freeman felt her stomach rumble. Lucy offered a drink, which Freeman declined, wishing something edible was on offer instead.

'What happened?' Lucy asked, sitting down opposite Freeman at the small kitchen table.

'We're not sure yet,' Freeman said. 'Katy's boyfriend reported her missing yesterday. She was going to their neighbour's house late morning and then she didn't come home. She wasn't there when he got in from work.'

Lucy frowned. 'But that's not very long to be missing, is it? I mean, you don't usually say someone's missing for like a day, right?'

'Right. But there were other circumstances that made things a bit more complicated.'

'What circumstances?' Lucy asked.

'Well, I can't really go into details, but it appeared there'd been an incident at the neighbour's house—'

'An incident? What does that mean?'

150

'We're not sure of the details yet, and it's a possibility that it had nothing to do with Katy anyway.' Freeman wondered how true that was. They'd found her blood in the kitchen after all. 'What I really needed from you was just to know if you'd seen her or spoken to her recently.'

'No,' Lucy said, shaking her head. 'I haven't seen her for a while. I think the last time was about three months ago.'

'Three?' Freeman asked, thinking it was a lot more recently than anyone else had seen Katy.

'Yeah, I saw her in Asda.'

'Did you speak to her?'

'Briefly,' she said. 'I'd invited her to my anniversary party. I'd sent her an invite in the post but I didn't get the RSVP. So I'd called her a few times, or tried to.'

'She'd changed her number,' Freeman said.

'Yeah, I guess. I thought it was odd she hadn't told me but I figured she just forgot or something. I knew she'd left work, someone told me that. I didn't know the details but I thought maybe she was depressed or something, about the job.'

'What makes you think she'd be depressed?'

'I don't know,' Lucy shrugged. 'I always got the impression she liked her job. If she'd lost it, I thought she'd be upset. When I saw her in the supermarket, to be honest she looked a bit down. She was usually quite fussy about clothes and stuff, spent a lot on hairdressers and her nails and that kind of thing. But when I saw her she just looked … grubby.'

'Grubby?' Freeman said.

'Maybe that's not the right word. I don't know, she just looked like she hadn't had her hair done in a while, it looked sort of lank and she looked older, I suppose.'

'So, when you spoke to her, what did she say? Was she alone?'

'No. Andrew was with her.'

'You spoke to them both?'

'Yes,' Lucy said. 'I asked how she was and she said fine. And I said it was a shame they couldn't make it to our anniversary party. She looked a bit dazed when I mentioned it. But I knew she'd got the invite. When I couldn't get hold of her on the mobile, I tried her landline number and that still worked. I spoke to Andrew and he called me back later on, said they couldn't go. Maybe she was embarrassed for not getting back to me herself.'

'Did you say anything about that?'

'No, of course not. I knew things were probably difficult with the job situation. When I called the house again later, a few times actually, she wasn't there, or that's what he said anyway. I got the impression something was wrong.'

'Wrong? How?'

'Just, like maybe she didn't want to come to the phone herself. That maybe I'd upset her somehow. Or maybe she was depressed.'

Freeman wondered if that could be true, that Katy was keeping her distance from friends because she was depressed, that she was using Andrew as a gatekeeper. Or was it more sinister than that? Had Andrew even ever told Katy about the invitation, about the calls?

'So that was the last time you saw her?' Freeman asked and Lucy nodded. 'Have you spoken to her since? Or tried to?'

'I've called,' she said. 'On the landline. I've left a couple of messages on the answering machine, I've even spoken to Andrew and left messages with him, but she never calls me back. I suppose I gave up in the end. I think the last time was maybe four or five weeks ago. I thought if she wants to talk to me, she knows where I am. I don't want to keep bugging her if she doesn't want to speak to me.'

'What about Andrew? How well do you know him?'

'A little,' Lucy said. 'He seems nice. When I call he's always polite, always makes a little joke about something, but I wouldn't say I really know him.'

'Did Katy ever talk about him?'

'Sometimes,' Lucy said. 'More when she first started seeing him. But I suppose that's normal. She seemed to think he was the best thing since sliced bread when they first got together. To be honest, it was a bit annoying to start with. She kept telling us that he'd whisked her away for a romantic weekend or something. She cancelled plans with us a few times at the last minute because he'd organised something as a surprise. After a while I think that stopped but to be fair, Phil, my husband, hasn't bought me flowers for years. Unless it's my birthday or something and then I think he only gets flowers for lack of a better idea.' Lucy smiled and Freeman noticed her glancing at a photo of her and, presumably, Phil, on a beach somewhere. 'Do you think something's happened to her?' Lucy asked.

'I don't know,' Freeman said. 'It's possible that Katy left on her own but we're looking at all possibilities for now.'

Lucy shook her head and said, 'Poor Andrew. He must be going out of his mind.'

Freeman nodded and wondered if that was true. Was Andrew worrying, wondering where his girlfriend was? Or did he already know?

Chapter 28

Gardner raced into the B&B, heading for the stairs, unclear where he was actually going, unsure what he would say when he got there. He'd been so shocked to hear her voice, to hear her say she was all right, that he hadn't really thought it through, hadn't prepared himself for what he'd find when he got here.

'Excuse me,' a woman's voice called out to him, followed by a hand grabbing his elbow, surprisingly firm considering that when he looked around at her, the woman holding onto him appeared to be in her seventies. 'Can I help you?' she said, in a voice not exactly appropriate to customer service.

'I'm here to see a friend. Dawn Lawton,' he said and wondered if she'd even used her real name to check in.

The woman looked him up and down, still holding on to his arm. 'No one here called that,' she said.

'Young woman, short dark hair,' he said but he was getting the feeling the woman was only pleading ignorant and that she knew exactly where Lawton was. He pulled out his ID and said, 'I'm a friend of hers.'

The woman looked at the ID and let go of him but the look of suspicion was still plastered all over her face. 'Hold on,' she said and moved past him up the stairs.

Gardner started to follow and the woman turned, glaring at him until he stopped.

Gardner stood halfway up the stairs as the woman pulled herself up, too slowly. He didn't have time for this. He needed to see Lawton, needed to see for himself that she was all right.

He heard a knock on a door at the top of the stairs, the woman's voice low and serious. And then he saw Lawton emerge, looking down at him, and his heart almost broke. He started up the stairs, more slowly than he'd planned, unsure of what to do. As he reached the top he could see her more clearly now, see the bruising, the sore red cuts above her eye, the swollen lip. For a moment he stood still, the woman from the B&B between him and Lawton. He saw the woman look at her and Lawton nodded, offered a small smile and the woman nodded back, walking back down the stairs, but not before eyeing him up again. And Gardner knew what she was thinking, that he was the one who'd done this. That he was the kind of man who could do this.

Unable to look at the woman any more, he turned back to Lawton and wanted to say something but felt his throat tighten. He stepped forward and wrapped his arms around her, not knowing if it was the right thing to do, if she would recoil from him. But what else could he do, what he could possibly say? All he knew was that he needed to hold on to her, to know she was okay. Even if it was more for him than her.

He rested his head on hers and felt her body shaking. He realised she was crying and held back from doing the same. He wanted to say, 'It's all right,' but he knew it wasn't. Nothing was right at all.

After a few moments, Lawton stood back, wiping her face, and led Gardner into the small, stuffy room. Gardner sat on the rickety stool in front of the dressing table, opposite Lawton who sat on the bed, stroking her dog who was about as pleased to see him as the old woman from downstairs. Hazel, Lawton had informed him, had been kind to her, letting Cotton stay, bringing them food. So far that was all she'd talked about. How much she appreciated Hazel's kindness, that she didn't know what she'd have done without it, where else she would've gone. And Gardner felt that tug again, that he was useless to her.

'Why didn't you tell me?' he asked, his voice almost a whisper.

Lawton shook her head. 'I don't know,' she said.

'How long's it been going on?'

She shook her head again, this time not answering, just lowering her head to the dog's, whispering platitudes as it whimpered.

'Dawn,' he said, needing her to talk to him, needing to understand. 'You could have told me. I could've helped.'

'No,' she said and left it at that, closing her eyes.

He could hear a TV playing somewhere, maybe in the room next door or underneath them. He wanted to say more but didn't know what. He couldn't force her to talk, to tell him what she'd been keeping secret for however long. In the end he had to look away, out of the small window that overlooked a brick wall. He couldn't look at her, at what had happened, and be unable to do anything.

'Have you got any further with Katy?' Lawton asked.

Gardner looked up, knowing that this was the only way she'd talk. He shook his head. 'Not really.' Lawton closed her eyes again. 'Can you tell me what happened?' he asked and saw her shake her head. 'With Katy, I mean. Do you know what happened?'

'No,' she said.

'You didn't see her?'

'No. I'd left by then,' she said. 'Me and Lee we … we had a fight and I left. I don't know what happened after that.'

'We found blood. In your house. In the bedroom, the bathroom.' She nodded. 'The kitchen too.' She looked up at this. 'It was Katy's blood.'

Lawton let out a breath, held on tighter to the dog.

'Katy told her boyfriend she was going to your house, that she was worried about you.' Lawton started to cry again. 'Did you know her?'

'A little,' Lawton said. 'She came round that day, the Sunday, before the argument. She was there when Lee came home. He told her to leave. That was the last time I saw her.'

'Did you argue about her?' Gardner asked.

'No. Not really,' she said, finally looking at him. 'I heard him come in. He was talking to someone. I thought he was on the phone. He sounded pissed off. But then he came into the kitchen and he had someone with him.'

'Do you know who it was?'

'Some guy from work. Lee seemed surprised when he came in and saw me and Katy sitting there. I'd said I was going to my mum's that afternoon but when I rang her she was out, staying with a friend, so I stayed in. I knew he was going to start. But then this guy started talking to Katy. It seemed like he knew her, from school I think, but I got the impression Katy didn't like him much. He's a bit of a arsehole really.'

'You know his name?'

'Scott. I don't know his surname.'

'Okay,' Gardner said and wondered if this had anything to do with Scott being skittish the day before.

'Anyway, Scott was talking to Katy, basically telling her how much he fancied her at school. It was all a bit awkward, and Lee got pissed off and told Scott to go. He said something like they'd have to sort it out later. I don't know what they were up to. Scott left but I could hear them arguing at the door and then when Lee came back in he told Katy to go too. She did. And that was it.' Lawton looked at him with sad eyes. 'Do you think Lee was there when she went round yesterday? You think he did something?'

'I don't know.'

'Have you talked to him?'

'Yes. He denied knowing her. Claimed you just had an argument and you left.'

Lawton almost smiled at this. 'I don't know if he would've done anything to her,' she said and Gardner felt sick to his stomach. Was she sticking up for him?

She stood up now, the dog grumbling as she moved. She walked to the window and Gardner could see she was in pain, holding her ribs as she walked. Lawton stared out of the window for a while and the dog looked at Gardner with frightened eyes. He wanted to go over and let it know

159

he wasn't someone to be afraid of, wanted the woman downstairs to know it too.

'This is my fault,' Lawton said and Gardner turned back to her.

'This isn't your fault, Dawn,' he said, standing up, moving beside her. 'None of this is your fault.'

'But something happened to her in *my* house. She went there for *me*.'

'We don't know what happened yet.'

'You said there was blood. You said Lee …'

He nodded. 'We know she was there. But beyond that, we just don't know anything. Except that this isn't your fault. You have to know that.'

She turned away again, looking down on the alley below the window. He wanted to keep talking, wanted her to tell him everything, but he knew he couldn't push her. 'You'll have to give a statement,' he said and saw her shoulders drop. 'Just about Katy, about what you know. The rest … it's up to you.' She didn't reply, just kept her eyes on the street below. 'You don't even have to talk to me if you don't want to,' he said, wishing he didn't feel like that was option, that that was what was stopping her. 'Technically it's not even my case. I just …' He didn't want to say the rest. That he'd only become involved for her, that he'd hauled her boyfriend in and practically assaulted him.

'Whose case is it?' she asked.

'Freeman's.'

He saw her roll her eyes, nodding vaguely. 'Can we do it here?' she asked.

Gardner looked around the small, depressing room. She couldn't stay there, couldn't be alone there another day.

'Come and stay with me,' he said, the words out before he'd really thought it through. She stepped back from the window and looked at him, the daylight highlighting the damage.

'I can't,' she said.

'Why not? It's got to be better than staying here.'

'It's not so bad,' she said.

'Please,' he said. 'I'd feel better knowing you were safe.'

She shook her head. 'What if he finds out?'

'Lee? How would he find out? And who cares?'

'I do,' she said.

He sighed. 'Please. If he's looking for you, you'll be safer there than here.' He wanted to reach out and touch her, to comfort her, but held back. She finally sighed and nodded.

'All right,' she said. 'What about Cotton?'

He smiled at her. 'I always wanted a dog.'

Gardner led the way downstairs and Hazel was waiting for him, standing up straight when she saw Lawton and Cotton following.

'You're going home?' Hazel asked, looking past Gardner at Lawton.

'No,' she said. 'Staying with a friend.' Hazel eyed Gardner up once more, obviously not content that he wasn't the enemy. 'Thank you for helping me,' Lawton said and the old woman nodded. She looked like she wanted to grab hold of Lawton too but settled for bending down to the dog and stroking her head. The dog wagged her tail at her and Gardner realised he was going to have to start supplying treats in order to get the same response.

'There's a room for you here if you need it,' Hazel said, straightening up and shifting her eyes to Gardner said, 'You better take care of her.'

'I intend to,' he said.

Chapter 29

Gardner stood back and let Freeman in, his phone ringing in his hand. He looked at the screen but declined the call and slipped the phone into his pocket. Freeman was going to ask who he was ignoring, but realised it was none of her business.

'How is she?' she asked and he shook his head. He looked tired, defeated even, and Freeman wondered how bad it would be. He led her through to the living room and Freeman saw Lawton sitting on the settee, legs curled up beneath her, an old dog beside her. She walked around and took a seat across from Lawton, taking in the damage to her face. She assumed there was more that she couldn't see.

'Hi,' Freeman said and tried to smile but it seemed inappropriate, not only to the situation but because this woman wasn't a friend. She needed to treat her like a victim, a witness. She could do that.

Lawton nodded at her and looked at Gardner who seemed as uncomfortable as Freeman felt. Why had Lawton asked to speak with her and not Gardner? Was it because he was a man or just because he was a friend?

'I'll leave you to it,' he said and walked slowly to the door as if he thought she might change her mind. When the door had closed Freeman sat forward, clicking her pen on and off.

'What made you call him?' she asked.

'I saw the news. About Katy,' Lawton said.

Freeman nodded. 'I'm glad you got in touch. We were worried about you.' She felt like a fraud saying it, even though it was true. She had been worried … was still worried. 'He's been going out of his mind,' she said, nodding to the door as if Gardner was still standing there. 'We found your car.'

Lawton nodded. 'I left it there. I didn't want to park close to where I was staying in case Lee came looking for me.' Lawton looked away and Freeman wanted to say more but Lawton changed the subject. 'Have you got any further with finding her?'

'No, not yet,' Freeman said. 'It's like she vanished into thin air.'

'Do you think Lee had something to do with it too?'

Freeman paused before answering. At that moment she really didn't know. She'd got there thinking that the two incidents were likely unconnected – what happened between Lawton and Lee, and what happened to Katy. Yes, there were links, but it didn't feel right and with everything she'd learned about Andrew Blake she was starting to think that he was the one responsible. But now, looking at Lawton, seeing the damage the man who apparently loved her had done, she had to wonder. What else was he capable of?

'I don't know,' she said. 'We're looking at a few possibilities at the moment. Do you think he could've done something to her?'

Lawton sat silent for a moment, her hand resting on the dog's back. Freeman noticed a scar on the animal's face and thought about the blood results. Lee hadn't just attacked Lawton, he'd hurt the dog too. She focused her attention back on Lawton as she started to speak.

'I don't know,' she said. 'I don't understand why he would. What reason would he have for hurting her?'

'As opposed to you?' Freeman said and felt sorry as soon as it came out of her mouth.

Lawton looked down at the carpet and Freeman thought she'd blown it, that Lawton wouldn't speak any more. She wondered how long Lawton had been with Lee, how long the relationship had been like *this*. If Lawton had never reached out before, was she likely to do so now? Or would she protect Lee despite everything?

'I don't know what he's capable of,' Lawton said, eventually, her voice catching. 'I honestly don't know why he'd want to hurt her but when I saw the news, when I saw she was missing and then they named me and … Honestly, my first thought was, *What have you done?*' She looked up now, tears settled on her eyes that fell once she blinked.

Freeman wanted to reach out, wanted to comfort her, but she didn't know how. She'd been here before, spoken to other women in similar situations and no matter how much she tried to tell them it would be all right, or that they had support, it wasn't enough. They didn't believe it enough. The fact that she knew Lawton but not really, that they were colleagues but not friends, that Lawton disliked her but chose to speak with her over Gardner, somehow made it more difficult.

'Tell me about Katy,' Freeman said, deciding the moment for comfort had passed, instead getting down to business.

Lawton wiped her face with the back of her hand and sat back on the settee, distancing herself. 'I don't know that much about her,' she said. 'I only started to get to know her these last few months. They'd been living there since the end of last year sometime, but we never spoke. Sometimes I'd see them coming in or out and she'd usually smile, but that was it. And then one day she just turned up at the door.'

'Had something happened?' Freeman asked.

'No, I don't think so. She just knocked at the door and introduced herself. I was a bit perplexed to be honest. I don't think I've ever really spoken to anyone else who lives on my street. She had a bone, a dog treat. She said she won it on a tombola and thought Cotton might want it,' she said, looking down at the dog. 'So I let her in and we talked. It was weird. When she left, I took the bone out of the bag and there was a receipt in there for it. I guess she wanted someone to talk to and thought she needed an excuse.'

'So what did she want to talk about?'

'She just told me that she'd lost her job a few months earlier and she was bored. She asked if she could walk Cotton sometime. I wasn't sure, I didn't know her or if she was responsible but in the end it didn't matter. She never mentioned it again.'

'What did she say about her job?'

'Just that she'd been made redundant and she felt a bit lost. I asked if she was looking for something else and she said not really. I don't think they were struggling for money but I got the impression she wasn't very happy.'

'About being jobless or in general?'

'In general, I guess,' Lawton said. 'She was very … she'd come in and seem down, or as if she wanted to say something. But then she'd sort of shake herself out of it and be quite cheerful for a while and then all of a sudden she'd say she had to go and rush out.'

'Did she ever mention her boyfriend, Andrew? Do you know him too?'

Lawton turned away now and Freeman wondered if she'd hit a nerve, if Lawton knew something about Andrew and Katy's relationship.

'Dawn?'

Lawton shook her head. 'I've never spoken to him.'

'But?'

She sighed. 'She never said anything outright but I got the impression things weren't great between them.'

'In what way?'

'Well, I might be wrong. I mean, she only ever came over maybe six or seven times, tops. But I started noticing that when she'd rush out, he'd come home soon after. I started wondering if she didn't want him to know that she'd been at my place. Apart from last Sunday, she never came round at weekends or on a night, only in the day when he was out. I guess he was out that afternoon. And if I saw her with him outside, in the garden or whatever, she never spoke, didn't even acknowledge me.'

'Did you ask her about that?'

'Not really,' Lawton said.

'Did Katy ever bring Andrew up in conversation? Did she ever mention anything you thought sounded odd?' Freeman asked.

'She'd say things every now and then, like she'd watched a film she really enjoyed. She'd be animated, asking if I'd seen it, and then she'd say something like, 'Anyway, Andrew said it was brainless', or something like that. It seemed like whatever she thought, he thought the opposite and she just seemed to give in as if he was always right. It was just little things, but I could see it bothered her. But then she'd just try and laugh it off. Change the subject.'

Freeman scribbled down some notes, her opinion of Andrew sinking by the second. As far as she could tell, Andrew Blake was controlling Katy, deciding who she could speak to, who she could see, what she should think. It was unlikely he knew about Katy's visits to Lawton. He hadn't said Katy was worried about her friend next door, just worried in general. He hadn't even known Lawton's name. Freeman imagined he would've put a stop to the visits had he known. So what happened that day? Katy called him to say she was going round to the neighbours. Had Andrew been so angry that he'd lashed out at her, tried to teach her a lesson and things had gotten out of hand?

'Tell me about that night, the night you left,' Freeman said.

Lawton took a deep breath. 'Katy had been round,' she said. 'She was just chatting, didn't say anything unusual,

168

just that she was frustrated by being home all day. She mentioned wanting to learn to drive but Andrew said they couldn't afford it. Then Lee turned up with his mate Scott. He was pissed off that Katy was there, told her to go home.'

'Why was he pissed off? He doesn't like you having people over?'

'I don't know. I don't have a lot of people over,' Lawton said. 'But for some reason he didn't like Katy. He'd only met her, briefly, twice, maybe three times.'

'But he said he didn't like her?'

'He didn't say it outright,' Lawton said. 'I could just tell. Usually he at least acts like he likes someone, but with her he just wouldn't speak to her other than to tell her to go home. He just glared at her. But on Sunday he'd brought his friend and this guy was talking to Katy. Lee seemed bothered by that but I don't know why. I got the feeling they were up to something but when he found me and Katy there, whatever it was, he didn't want to do it in front of us. So he told Scott to go and Katy too.

'After she'd gone he asked me why she was always there, hanging around, why we were always gossiping. He said we should get a third one and we could be the three witches. It was stupid. Like I said, as far as I know he only ever saw her there a couple of times.'

'So is that what started the fight that night?'

'I don't think so,' she said, her gaze going to the floor again. 'Maybe that started it but it wasn't really about her.' She shrugged. 'It's never really about anything. Or maybe it's about everything.'

Freeman waited. She didn't want to push Lawton and technically she didn't need to say anything about the rest of that night. If Katy had gone by then, and Lawton was gone by the time Katy returned days later, then she wouldn't have anything to offer the investigation. Gardner had told her that Lawton wasn't planning on pressing any charges against Lee so her story wasn't necessary. But Freeman felt like she needed to hear it. And maybe Lawton needed to tell it.

'He was complaining about stuff in general. I let him get on with it and I started the tea. He went for a shower and then when he came back down he started again, saying he was starving and if I hadn't been talking to Katy he could've been eating by now. And then, when I did serve it up, he said it was shit and put it in the bin … said he was going out.

'To be honest, I was glad. I was happy to have some time alone but I knew he'd probably still be in a mood when he came back so I just went to bed. I heard him come in about half-eleven. He sat downstairs for a bit watching TV. I tried to go back to sleep but I couldn't. Finally he came up and started talking. I pretended to be asleep, which was stupid. He kept talking, telling me to get up but I just couldn't,' she said, her voice wavering. 'I heard him stomp across the room and then the dog let out a yelp. I sat up in bed and he was kicking her,' she said, this fact seemingly upsetting her more than anything else. 'I got up and tried to push him away. Cotton ran out the room. She was in the hall, barking. He was obviously drunk. He said, 'That got you up.' Called me names. I tried to get out of the room but he grabbed hold of my arm, pushed me on the bed. He was just screaming at me, I don't even know what he was saying. The dog was barking, going mad. And then he just started.' She shrugged, as if it was inevitable, as if Freeman could guess the rest, that it was the standard turn of events.

'He hit you,' she said and Lawton nodded.

'He just kept punching me over and over and then he threw me into the bedside cabinet. I just sat there while he screamed some more. He threw something at me, I don't even know what it was,' she said, staring straight ahead, telling the details in a monotone voice, stating the facts like a good little police officer. 'I don't know why, but all I could think was that it was late and people would complain about the noise. I think I said that to him and he just laughed at me. I think he'd worn himself out by then. He sat down on the bed and I thought it was over. I remember touching my face, I could feel blood trickling down from my eye. I was just thinking, how am I going to explain this tomorrow? He rarely touches my face and I always felt grateful for that. It meant I didn't have to make up ridiculous reasons for it.'

Freeman felt a familiar stinging behind her eyes, in her nose. She swallowed and blinked a few times. She wasn't the one who was allowed to cry here. She had to channel the anger into something useful.

'I started to get up but then he just launched himself at me. I think I shouted at him but I don't remember. He slammed my head into the cabinet. I passed out. I don't know how long I was out, I didn't think very long, but when I came to, he was passed out on the bed. I got up to clean myself up and I saw Cotton in the hall. He'd had another go at her, I guess, because I was unconscious. There was blood. I tried to clean her up. I went into the bathroom and washed my face. And then something just snapped. I was staring at myself in the mirror, and I could hear Cotton crying, and I just snapped. I went into the bedroom, I got a few things and I left. Just like that. I drove away. No idea where I was going.

'In the end I drove to the beach. I sat there looking at the sea for a while, thinking I'd probably go back in a few hours. But I guess I fell asleep. And then in the morning I decided not to go back. I left the car and found somewhere to stay and that was it.'

Freeman looked at Lawton and in that moment she looked stronger than she'd ever seen her before. She was a good cop, capable, conscientious, but seemed to lack confidence and maybe now she knew why. But as she watched her now, she seemed in control. She said she'd snapped. Maybe now she was free.

'So what're you going to do next?' Freeman asked. 'You're not going back, are you?'

Lawton took a deep breath and said, 'I don't know. We'll see.'

Chapter 30

Freeman found Gardner loitering outside his own flat, phone to his ear, frown on his face. He stopped pacing when she came out, slipping the phone into his pocket. 'So?' he asked.

'So, we've got confirmation that Lee's a douche bag,' she said. 'But I'm not sure we've got anything that tells us what happened to Katy.' She took a seat on the top step of the stairs and Gardner came and sat beside her.

'So she didn't say she wants to press charges?' he asked.

Freeman shook her head. 'Not yet. But she did mention this guy that works with Lee. He was there at the house that night.'

'Scott,' Gardner said. 'She mentioned him to me too. We should have another word with him.'

'Can you do that? I need to get back and speak to Andrew Blake again. He should be about ready to talk by now,' she said, looking at her watch, realising she'd left him stewing a little longer than planned.

*

Gardner bumped into Scott's boss as he approached the phone shop, his mind on the message Molly had left him. She'd called several times since he abandoned her but this was the first time she'd left a message. He was expecting an angry tirade but instead she'd sounded concerned. It made him feel worse, so he was definitely going to call her back, but then Freeman came out after speaking with Lawton and once more Molly was put on hold. 'Mr Barker,' he said and the man looked up, startled. 'I'm looking for Scott. Is he—'

'He just left,' he said. 'You can probably catch him in the car park if you're quick.'

Gardner thanked him and headed back up the escalator to search for Scott. He looked around the car park but had no idea what sort of car the man drove so doubted he would find him. But as he stood there looking he saw a battered, old Mini drive past, something loud and obnoxious blaring from the speakers through the open windows. He looked at the driver and saw Scott driving away. He tried to flag him down but the man was oblivious.

Gardner got into his own car and followed Scott, hoping he could catch him and have a word. As they drove out, navigating the rush hour traffic, a couple of other cars got between him and Scott, and he doubted he'd be able to keep sight of him, never mind get his attention.

Scott turned off, heading out of the town centre and Gardner tried to keep up, following him from a distance, hoping he wouldn't lose him, wondering if he'd be better off just trying again tomorrow or finding a number and calling the man. But then Scott took another turning and headed somewhere familiar. Gardner let another car in to keep the distance and watched carefully as Scott turned into the same streets as Lee had earlier. He'd been sure Lee was heading somewhere in particular, somewhere that he didn't want Gardner to know about. Was Scott heading to that same place?

Scott had been there the night Lee and Lawton had a fight. Lee had been annoyed that Katy was there; it somehow buggered up whatever he was planning on doing. And Scott had known Katy, something that apparently annoyed Lee too.

Gardner kept his eyes on Scott's car, hoping, desperately, that this man was going to lead him somewhere, maybe somewhere he would find Katy Jackson.

The car in front of him turned off and suddenly there was no buffer between him and Scott who'd stopped at the lights. Gardner slowed down and flashed for a car to come out of a side road. But the driver of the car that was turning did something stupid and all of a sudden horns were blaring. Scott looked in his mirrors to see what was going on and his eyes met Gardner's.

The lights turned green and Scott's car didn't move for a second or so. And then, his indicator switched from left to right and Gardner knew he'd blown it again. Scott drove back across town and pulled in outside a block of flats, Gardner pulling in behind him. They both got out and Scott looked around him before wandering over to Gardner.

'Can I have a word?' Gardner said and Scott nodded.

'What about?'

'Where were you going just now?'

Scott shrugged. 'Just coming home.'

'The long way round?'

'I thought there were roadworks the way I usually come,' Scott said.

'Is that right?' Gardner stared at Scott and he had to look away. 'You seen Lee Johnston today?'

'No. He wasn't at work again.'

'And you haven't seen him outside of work?'

'No.'

'Do you ever see him outside of work?'

'Not really. Not often.'

'But sometimes?'

Scott shrugged again.

'You were at his house on Sunday. Correct?'

Scott swallowed hard. 'Er … maybe. I can't remember.'

'No? Well, let me refresh your memory. You went there with Lee, early evening. His girlfriend was there. As was a neighbour. Katy Jackson.'

Scott rubbed at his goatee. 'Right,' he said.

'You know Katy Jackson?'

'No,' he said. 'Not really. Just from school.'

'You spoke to her Sunday?'

'Just said hi,' he said. 'Why?'

'Why did you go to Lee's house that day?'

'We were going to watch a match,' Scott said.

'Really? But you left after a few minutes.'

Scott cleared his throat. 'Yeah, well. Him and his girlfriend had a bit of an argument.'

'While you were there?'

'Well, not really. But I could tell something was going on. There was an atmosphere, you know. So I left. Said we'd do it another time.'

'So you chose to leave. Lee didn't ask you to?'

'No. I just figured it was best to leave them to it.'

'And Katy was still there? When you left?'

'Yeah.'

'You seen her since?'

'No. Why?'

'Lee tell you why we were looking for him on Tuesday?'

'No. I haven't spoken to him.'

Gardner nodded. 'You got a phone number I can have. In case I need to ask anything else?' Scott looked like he was going to be sick and Gardner wondered if he should take him in.

'Sure,' Scott said and wrote down a number, his hand shaking slightly. Clearly the man was up to something. But maybe they'd be better off leaving Scott to it. If they focused on Lee, maybe Scott would think he was off the hook and lead them somewhere.

Chapter 31

Freeman told Andrew to sit and he did as he was told, looking from Freeman to Harrington as if he was trying to work out why he was there. He didn't seem too bothered by being made to wait for so long and for some reason that annoyed Freeman.

'Are you sure you don't want a solicitor present?' Harrington asked but Andrew waved him away.

'Has something happened? Have you found her?' Andrew asked.

'No,' Freeman said and looked him in the eye. 'Tell me why you lied about leaving the office on Tuesday.'

'What?' Andrew's eyes darted between the two detectives as if he didn't understand the question, as if butter wouldn't melt.

'You lied about leaving the office the day Katy disappeared. Why?'

'I didn't,' he said.

'You didn't?' Freeman said. 'So someone else drove your car from your office, to your house, that lunchtime?'

Andrew swallowed, suddenly looking more flustered. 'I didn't lie,' he said. 'I just … I was confused.'

'About what?'

'I thought you meant something else.'

'Like what? It's a simple question. Did you leave the office that day – yes or no?'

'I thought you meant did I go somewhere in particular, did I go out for something.'

Freeman glanced at Harrington. Was this really his defence? That he was an idiot?

'But you did go somewhere in particular, *for* something. You didn't just go out for the drive, did you? So I want to know why you lied. Why you thought leaving that out of your statement would be a good idea.'

'I just went for lunch,' Andrew said.

'Do you usually go home for lunch?'

'No. I ...'

'So, why did you go home that day, Andrew?'

'I forgot my lunch. Katy'd made a salad and I left it in the fridge. So I went home and got it. That was it. I'm sorry. I just misunderstood.'

'Really? So why did Rhiannon back up your story? Did you ask her to lie for you?'

'No. Of course not.'

'So why did she say you didn't leave the office?'

'I don't know. You'd have to ask her.'

'I will,' Freeman said. 'Tell us again what happened that day.'

'I've already told you.'

'No, you've told us a version of what happened. Now I want the truth. Did you see Katy when you went home at lunchtime?'

'No,' Andrew said.

'Did you go to look for her?'

'No.'

179

'But you'd already got her message, right? You knew she was going next door to see if Dawn Lawton was all right. You'd already tried calling her back and got no response. So why wouldn't you look for her when you got home? Why wouldn't you check she was okay?'

'I didn't think.'

'I don't believe you, Andrew,' Freeman said and watched as his jaw clenched and his eyes changed. It was subtle but she was looking for it. 'I think you went home that day because she'd gone next door and you didn't want her to. And when she didn't answer your calls, you went to find her.'

'No,' Andrew said. 'That's not true. I wish I had. I wish I'd stopped her going because then she'd be all right. She'd be here.'

'You said you went home to get your lunch, yes?' Freeman asked and Andrew nodded. 'Why did you plan to take your own lunch that day? You usually go out and buy lunch, don't you? You and Rhiannon?'

Andrew shrugged. 'I wanted a change. Something healthier.'

'And it just happened to be that day. And you just happened to forget it and have to go home. Which you then lied about.'

'I didn't lie!' Andrew said. 'It was a mistake. I was upset about Katy. I wasn't thinking straight and I'm sorry. But you have to believe me; everything else I've said is true. I wish I had looked for her. I really do. I just want her home. I just wish I could've stopped her going and then that animal wouldn't have hurt her.'

Freeman sat back and watched Andrew, wondering if it was all an act or just some of it. 'We found Dawn Lawton,' she said and Andrew's head shot up.

'Where? Is she …?'

'She's safe. She told us she left the house of her own accord after a fight with Lee Johnston on Sunday night.'

'But he hurt her, right? He attacked her?'

'I'm not going to discuss Ms Lawton's relationship. But what I will say is that she left on Sunday night, by herself. And at the moment, as far as I can tell, neither she nor Lee had anything to do with Katy's disappearance.'

'But—' Andrew's eyes darted around again '—but she went there. She was in the house.'

'Yes,' Freeman said. 'We have evidence that Katy was in the house next door. What we don't have is any evidence that Lee Johnston was there at the same time. What we *do* know is that you went home not long after trying to contact Katy, knowing where she was going.'

'What are you saying? That I hurt her?' Andrew said.

'I'm not saying that, Mr Blake. I'm just telling you the facts as we know them. And all I want is for you to tell us the truth about that day.'

'I've told you the truth,' he said. 'I got her message when I was at work, saying she was going next door.'

'And how did you feel about that?'

'How did I feel?'

'Yeah. Did it make you angry? Concerned?'

'Angry? Why would I be angry? I was a little concerned. I didn't want her getting involved and I'd already told her that.'

'So were you irritated that she ignored you?'

Andrew was breathing heavier now and she knew she was getting to him. She just needed to push a little further, get him to show his true colours.

'No, I wasn't irritated,' he said, sounding more than a little irritated with Freeman. 'I was slightly worried. That's why I called her back. I assumed she'd have already gone but I thought maybe if I called I could tell her to leave. Or at least check she was okay.'

'But she didn't answer the phone. So what? You were worried, wanting to see she was okay, but she didn't answer. Are you telling me that didn't make you want to go and see what was going on?'

'What do you mean?' Andrew asked.

'I mean, you said you called her back because you were worried. Are you really expecting us to believe that you just then forgot about it and only went home to collect a salad? That even if you really did go home to pick up your lunch, that you didn't think to go and check on Katy while you were there?'

Andrew let out a shuddering breath. 'I did go,' he said.

Freeman sighed. 'So you lied again?'

'No,' he said, drawing out the word. 'You're right. I probably wouldn't have gone for the salad if I'd got hold of Katy on the phone. But when I got there, she wasn't home so I went and knocked next door. There was no answer so I figured Katy had been and gone. I went back to my house, got my lunch and went back to work. That's it.'

Andrew looked flustered and Freeman saw Harrington lean forward beside her. 'You didn't try calling her again, did you? After you went home,' Harrington said. 'Why not?'

'I don't know,' Andrew said, focusing his attention on Harrington. 'I assumed she'd gone out. She wasn't next door so I thought she'd be all right. She's a grown up. Why would I just think something had happened to her?'

'But that's exactly what you thought,' Freeman said. 'When you got home that afternoon and discovered she wasn't there, you went looking for her. Even though you've just said you checked the neighbour's at lunchtime and she wasn't there, you still went back later and found a mess and reported it to police even though she'd been gone just a few hours.'

'I reported it because of the mess.'

'Why didn't you report the mess earlier?'

'I didn't see it. I hadn't gone inside earlier. I wish I had. I wish to God I'd tried harder but all I was thinking was that I better get back to work.'

'Where did you think Katy had gone that day? At lunchtime when you got home and she wasn't there and she wasn't next door? Where did you think she'd be?' Freeman asked.

'I don't know,' Andrew said. 'With a friend, maybe. Shopping.' He shrugged. 'Just out.'

'But when I spoke to you that evening you said she wouldn't have been with friends. You were adamant that she should've been home.' Andrew's teeth clenched and Freeman kept on pushing. 'When *I* suggested that as she's a grown-up, and maybe she'd just gone out somewhere, that a few hours wasn't anything to worry about, you were so sure that something had happened—'

183

'Because of what I saw next door.'

'Okay. But you were sure that she wouldn't be with friends and now you say you thought she might've been. But I think you were right the first time.'

'What do you mean?'

'I've been speaking with Katy's friends and no one has seen her for some time. She doesn't go out with them, doesn't call them. She didn't even give them her new number. In fact the only person she seems to see these days is you.'

Andrew shook his head. 'That's not true. She sees people. And I told you why she changed her number. Have you even spoken to him again?'

'I have. But you're pretty good at pointing fingers, Andrew. First Lee. Then some random guy from the news. And now Dominic Archer. And I have to say, it looks a lot to me like you're trying to cover for yourself.'

Andrew looked at Harrington, as if for help, but stared back at Freeman when he got none.

'Now, I'm not saying I'm not going to look at other possibilities, but you've not really helped yourself, have you? You've lied. A lot. *And* you've got other people to lie for you.'

'This is ridiculous! I haven't done anything to Katy. Why would I call you if I had? We were happy. Katy was happy. And all this stuff about her not seeing anyone is nonsense. She called other people. She *saw* other people.'

'Like who?' Freeman asked.

'I don't know. Her friends. Her mum. People.'

'No,' she said. 'Katy's been disappearing for a while. In fact the only person I think she's seen lately, the only person she's talked to, apart from you, is Dawn Lawton.'

'The neighbour? She doesn't even know her,' Andrew said.

'Really? Why do you think she was so concerned about her safety? Why do you think she went round there, after you'd told her not to, if she was a stranger?'

'That's just Katy. Sticking her nose in where it doesn't belong.'

'You didn't know, did you?'

'Know what?'

'That Katy had been going round to Dawn's house fairly regularly.' She watched as Andrew's nostrils flared, his chest rising and falling quickly. 'Katy had made friends with Dawn. I guess she wanted someone to talk to while she was stuck at home all day.' Andrew's hands curled into fists. 'Now, why wouldn't she tell you that? Why keep a friendship a secret from you?'

Andrew shook his head. 'You're lying. She didn't know her. This woman's lying. Maybe to cover something for her boyfriend. Katy wouldn't have gone there without telling me.'

'Well, she did. And Dawn told us that Katy was quite chatty too.'

'Where is she? I want to speak to her,' Andrew said.

'That's not going to happen.'

'I need to see her. She might know where Katy is.'

'Yeah, we already thought to ask her that. She has no idea. She wasn't there.'

'But her boyfriend was.'

'We don't know that.'

'Let me talk to her,' Andrew said. 'Please.'

'I can't allow that, Andrew.'

'I need to know what she said.'

'Who? Dawn or Katy? You think she spilled some secrets?'

'For God's sake!' Andrew said. 'Why are you trying to make out that I'm the bad guy here? I love Katy. I just want her back. That man, I know what he's like. I've heard him. I've heard what he says to her. How he treats her. Listened while he knocked her around. Why aren't you talking to him instead of me?'

'We've spoken to Mr Johnston and we will do so again if any more evidence comes to light suggesting he was involved. But at this point, the only evidence we have is that you've lied to us, more than once. So, for now, I want to talk to you.'

'Fuck you!' Andrew jumped up, his chair crashing to the floor. 'My girlfriend is missing. That man has done something to her and you want to sit here asking me about fucking salads and telling me lies about Katy. She wouldn't have gone next door. That woman is lying.'

'Sit down,' Freeman said and waited for Andrew to stop pacing. For a few more seconds he walked up and down the small room, his hands clenching and unclenching. Finally, he closed his eyes and shook his head. When he opened them he looked like he might cry.

'I'm sorry,' he said, his voice quiet. 'I'm so sorry. I just want her back.' He bent over and picked up the chair, sitting down again, head in hands.

'Why won't you accept that Katy and Dawn were friends?' Freeman asked and Andrew looked up.

'Because she would've told me.'

'She tells you everything?'

'Of course she does.'

'Do you tell her everything?'

Andrew paused just a little too long. 'Of course.'

Freeman laughed. No one tells each other everything. 'Why would Dawn lie?' she asked. 'What reason would she have for telling us that if it wasn't true?'

'I don't know,' he said. 'To protect her boyfriend, like I said.'

'Protect him from what?'

'From whatever he's done to Katy.'

'But why would Dawn protect him? He abuses her. You said that yourself. So why would she possibly want to protect him?'

'She stays, doesn't she?' he said, his voice hard. 'Maybe she's scared of him, just doing what he says. I don't know.' Andrew stood up again. 'Am I free to go?'

'Yes,' she said. 'But I'd appreciate it if you stayed.'

'I need to go,' he said and walked to the door. 'Just think about what kind of man he is, and what kind of man I am. And then decide who should be sitting here.'

'Oh, I think I know what kind of man you are, Mr Blake,' Freeman said after he walked out. 'That's what worries me.'

Chapter 32

Freeman saw Gardner at his desk as she walked into the office and asked, 'What're you doing here?'

'I work here,' he said.

'What about Lawton? Is she all right by herself?'

'She'll be fine. I think she wanted rid of me. I think I was hovering too much.' Freeman sat down across from him. 'Plus, the dog was taking up the rest of the settee. It just climbed straight on there. No invitation or anything,' he said, indignantly.

Freeman smiled at him. 'I thought you liked dogs.'

'I do. Just not on my settee,' he said, taking his glasses off. 'You've spoken to Andrew Blake again?'

'Yeah,' she said. 'And I like him even less than I did before. He did this. I know it.'

'Did what?'

'Whatever it is that's happened to Katy Jackson. He lied about going home that day. Lied about looking for her. I think he made her quit her job. I think he made her change her phone number, stop seeing her friends.'

'What about Johnston?'

'What about him?'

'You don't think he has any involvement in this?' Gardner asked.

'I'm starting to doubt it. I mean, why would he?'

'Well, it was his house for starters. And Katy was in there, we know that. Plus he's definitely up to something. Him and Scott.'

'You spoke to him again?'

Gardner nodded. 'I followed him first. He did exactly the same as Lee. Was heading the same way and then he saw me and changed direction.'

'I think someone needs lessons in how to follow people,' Freeman said but Gardner ignored her and continued.

'He saw me and panicked and went home. I asked where he was going and he gave me some cock and bull about roadworks. He's lying. And his story about Sunday didn't match Lawton's. They were up to something, I know it.'

'Something to do with Katy? Like what? And if they were already doing something on Sunday when they ran into Katy, why harm her on Tuesday?'

'Maybe she heard something she shouldn't have. Maybe when she showed up on Tuesday she saw them doing whatever they were planning on Sunday. She just got in the way.'

'Wasn't Scott at work on Tuesday?'

'I don't know. He was when I swung by on the evening. Doesn't mean he was there all day.'

'Okay,' Freeman said. 'So, maybe Lee and Scott did something. But we can't dismiss other options.'

'Like Andrew Blake, you mean?'

189

'Or, like Dominic Archer. Or even this burglar guy. We need to keep an open mind.'

'Like you're doing with Andrew Blake? Why would Andrew bother to take her next door to do something to her?'

'I don't think he would intentionally. I think Katy did go there, alone, because she was friends with Lawton. And then Andrew found out she wasn't being a good little girl, wasn't doing as she was told, and went home to let her know that. And then things got out of hand.'

'And what? He killed her? Then where's the body?'

'I don't know yet. I'm working on it.'

'And it still doesn't explain how Katy got in there in the first place. Did you ask Lawton if Katy had a key?' Gardner asked.

'She didn't. They weren't that close.'

'So how did she get in if Lee wasn't there? The door wasn't broken, no windows were smashed, which doesn't match this burglar's MO.'

'Unless he followed Katy in. She could've left the door unlocked.'

'In which case, someone had to have let her in.'

Freeman shrugged at this and Gardner wondered if she'd thought about that at all or if she was just so focused on Andrew Blake for whatever it was he'd done to piss her off.

'He still lied about not leaving work that day,' she said. 'That counts for something.'

'Maybe,' Gardner said. 'How long was he out?'

'About an hour. Maybe slightly longer.'

'And how long does it take for him to drive home from the office?'

'About ten minutes.'

'So ten minutes there, ten back.'

'So what was he doing the other forty minutes?' she said. 'He claimed he went home to get the lunch he'd forgotten. He went and knocked next door, got no answer so went back to work. That doesn't take forty minutes, does it?' She looked over her shoulder and shouted at Harrington to come over. 'When they checked where Andrew's car had been, did they check if he stopped anywhere else other than home?'

'I don't know,' Harrington said. 'The info I got just said he was seen driving towards his home address. Then heading back to the office around one. Why?'

'You heard what he said in there. He just went to get his lunch, he barely looked for Katy before going back to work. So what was he doing all that time? Find out if he stopped somewhere else, either on the way there or back.'

'Will do,' Harrington said and walked away.

She turned back to Gardner. 'So,' she said.

'So what?'

'So, doesn't this make it even more likely that Andrew is the one we should be looking at?' Freeman said.

'Lee still hasn't given us an alibi about where he was that day. He wasn't at work. So where was he? And why won't he tell us if he hasn't got something to hide?'

'But why would he hurt Katy?'

'Why would Andrew?'

'Because she disobeyed him. She went next door without his permission. You didn't see him in there when

I told him Katy was friends with Lawton, that she'd been going round for visits. He had no idea and he didn't like it one bit. He's controlling her. He's stopping her from seeing anyone else, keeping her locked up as far as I can tell, so when she had the gall to go next door he must've lost it.'

Gardner shook his head. 'Maybe. Maybe he is some kind of possessive freak but it doesn't mean he hurt her. He doesn't have any history of physical abuse that we know of. Lee, on the other hand, does.'

'So what? There are thousands of men out there with form for physical abuse. Doesn't mean any of them were responsible for Katy. Lee had no reason to hurt her. Andrew did. And the rest of what I've found out about his relationship with Katy proves it's an abusive relationship.'

'I'm not denying that,' Gardner said. 'But there's nothing to prove he hurt her physically.'

'That we know of,' she said. 'But if he's keeping her under lock and key, how would anyone know? Lawton's here every day and we didn't know about her.'

Gardner looked away. He didn't need to be reminded of that, of his lack of awareness about what was going on.

'I'm sorry,' Freeman said. 'But we don't know what goes on behind closed doors. For all we know Andrew has been just as violent with Katy as Lee has been with Lawton.'

'What did Lawton say? Did Katy tell her that? Did she get that impression?'

Freeman sighed. 'No. She said as far as she knew there'd been nothing physical. But maybe Katy wouldn't tell her that. Lawton didn't tell Katy about *her* situation.'

'She didn't need to,' he said. 'They could hear it through the walls.'

'Okay. Say you're right. Let's say that Andrew has never laid a finger on Katy, it was all mind games and control. But there's always a first time. You think he was like that from the day she met him? Of course he wasn't. He'd have been all charm, sucking her in until she was feeling secure and then bit by bit he'd have started wearing her down. That's how it works.'

'I know how it works,' Gardner said, irritated.

'Right. So he starts out Mr Charm and then slowly shows his true colours, starts thinking she's under his thumb but then finds out she went against him. So he shows a little bit more of himself. And maybe he didn't mean to go that far but things got out of control.'

Gardner shook his head. He knew that what she was saying was possible but it was also possible that Lee was responsible. He'd seen the damage he'd done to Lawton, seen what he was capable of. Why couldn't Freeman admit that it was just as likely he'd hurt Katy?

'You're too close to this,' Freeman said and Gardner looked up.

'*I'm* too close? You're the one who's obsessed with Andrew Blake and the fact that his girlfriend doesn't see her friends anymore.'

'Because it's a reason to believe he could've hurt her. We have no reason to believe Lee would do anything to Katy.'

'Apart from the fact he likes to beat the shit out of women? You saw Lawton. You really want to sit there and tell me there's no way he could've done this?'

'I'm not saying that it's not possible. I'm just saying it's more *probable* that Katy's own boyfriend did something.'

'And what about what he did to Lawton?'

'I'm not denying that either. I know Lee Johnston is a piece of shit and he deserves to be punished for what he's done to her. I'm all for that. But you need to stick to the facts of the investigation and so far we have very little pointing to him having anything to do with Katy.'

'But he hurt Lawton,' Gardner said, knowing his argument was as weak as his voice.

'I know. And maybe that's the point. He hurts Lawton. That's what he does. But he doesn't just lash out at random women. He's just like Andrew. With the rest of us he can be all charm. He knows when to act like a good little boy. Lee doesn't hurt Lawton because he *loses* control. He hits her because he wants to be *in* control.'

'So maybe he wanted to control Katy too. We don't know what's gone on between them. You said it yourself: we don't know what happened. So why aren't we pushing at him some more to find out?'

Freeman sighed again and shook her head. She was losing patience, he could see that, but he wasn't going to stop trying to convince her. 'We've tried pushing him,' Freeman said. 'Remember that? You pushed him really well. So well in fact that you pushed him into a wall. And did he react? Did he lose control and push you back? No. Because that's not who he is. If Lee Johnston was so out of control that he'd just lash out at anyone, you should've noticed by now.'

Gardner felt like he'd been punched in the stomach. He could feel his face drop and Freeman looking like she'd actually thrown a punch.

'I didn't mean—'

'Don't,' he said. 'You're right. I should've noticed what was going on.'

'That's not what I meant,' she said, but it was too late. He'd gone.

Chapter 33

Gardner stomped up the stairs to his flat, trying to get the frustration, the anger, out before he went in and faced Lawton. He'd got as far as the car park at work when he'd wanted to go back and tell Freeman she was wrong, that this wasn't his fault, but he knew it would be a mistake and had forced himself to get in the car and go. But leaving hadn't helped calm him down. He was furious with Freeman. She might've tried to backtrack but he'd got the picture. She thought he should've noticed something was wrong with Lawton a long time ago. She thought he'd missed the signs and had allowed it to go on when he could've been doing something to help.

The more he thought about it, the more wound up he got, the more he wanted to call Freeman and say, *Fuck you, you didn't notice either*. But he knew that the real reason he was so angry was because she was right. He *should've* noticed. He'd met Lee before, didn't like him, got the impression he was an arsehole. But why hadn't he noticed what was really happening? And why hadn't Lawton trusted him enough to tell him?

He shook his head. Now he was trying to blame Lawton for this? The only person to blame was himself. Freeman was just being honest. Brutally honest, but still. And maybe she was right about him being too close to this. But just because he was close didn't mean he wasn't right. It didn't mean that there wasn't the possibility that Lee was responsible for Katy's disappearance.

Gardner walked into the flat, stopping by the door, listening for the TV, trying to work out if Lawton was still in the living room. He couldn't hear anything so took a breath and went inside. The settee was vacant. No Lawton. No dog. He went to the spare room and listened at the door. He thought he could hear something. He knocked gently but there was no reply. He pressed his ear to the door and thought he could hear a low snore. Maybe she was sleeping. Or maybe it was the dog. He considered going into the room but decided against it. If she wanted to talk to him she'd come out.

Gardner walked away, wondering again why she didn't want to talk to him. Why she didn't feel she could confide in him after all these years. He wondered what she'd said to Freeman, how much she'd opened up. Freeman had only told him a little, only things that pertained to the investigation into Katy's disappearance. But what else had Lawton told her? Maybe nothing. But maybe something. Something she didn't want him to know.

He was pleased when the phone started ringing, pulling him out of his thoughts. The fact that it was the landline too – that it wasn't work related, wasn't some more misery – made him relax for a moment until he realised that hardly anyone called him at home these days. For a second he hoped it was Molly, that he hadn't blown it by abandoning her and then ignoring her calls since. But then again, was he really in the mood to speak with her now?

'Hello?'

'Hello? Who's that?'

'Dad?' Gardner said.

'Who's that?'

'It's Michael, Dad. You called me.'

The line buzzed for a moment and for a fleeting second Gardner wished he hadn't answered. He never came off the phone with his dad feeling better than before he'd spoken to him. Norman Gardner only ever called to complain about something or someone and he wasn't in the mood.

'Michael?' Norman said. 'I … I …'

'Dad? What's going on? Are you all right?'

'Am I what?'

'Are you all right?'

'Of course I'm all right. I was looking for someone else.'

'Who?'

'What?'

'Who were you looking for?' The line buzzed again. 'Dad?'

'What's for lunch?' Norman asked.

'For lunch? Dad, are you sure you're all right?'

'I'm fine. I haven't got time for this.'

The line went dead and Gardner stared at the handset for a moment. What the hell was that? He tried to call his dad back but the line was engaged. He tried his brother but there was no answer, not even voicemail.

'Shit,' he muttered and tried his dad again. This time it just rang and rang. He hung up and sat down, wondering what to do. His dad was 180 miles away. He tried to recall the last time they'd talked. It wasn't recently; they didn't have that kind of relationship. It was maybe a month, probably longer. He'd been fine then, hadn't he? As fine as he ever was. Miserable, curmudgeonly, but fine.

He tried calling again but still got no answer, not from his dad or his brother. He pulled out his mobile and found his brother's landline. It rang a few times before his sister-in-law, Karen, answered.

'Hello?' she said.

'Karen, it's Michael. Is David there?'

'No, he's out at football,' she said and then he heard her shout at one of the kids. 'Should I get him to ring you later?'

'Yeah,' he said, quickly adding, 'Have you seen Dad recently?' so she wouldn't hang up.

'Haven't seen him for a few weeks but David spoke to him last week I think. Why?'

'He just rang me. He sounded confused.'

'Confused?' Karen said and then shouted another order at the kids.

'Yeah, he didn't seem to know he'd rung me, asked what was for lunch and then hung up.'

'That sounds weird,' she said. 'He was all right last week, I think. David didn't mention anything.'

'Do you think you could go round and check on him? I tried calling back but there's no answer.'

Karen sighed. 'I'm sure he's all right.'

'Probably. But I'd feel better if you could check,' he said and she sighed again. 'He's only round the corner, Karen.'

'And I've got three kids to look after. I can't just leave them here while I go off on a wild goose chase.'

'He could be ill,' Gardner said. 'It's not much to ask to go and see he's all right. If I wasn't at the other end of the country I'd do it myself.'

'Look, David will be back in an hour. I'll send him round. But I'm sure he's fine. The home help would've said something if he was ill.'

'Since when has he had a home help?'

'Since his fall.'

'What fall?' Gardner said, feeling his stomach drop.

Karen faltered a little, her voice softened. 'A couple of months back. Didn't David tell you?'

'No, he didn't.'

'He had a fall. The postman saw him lying in the hallway and called an ambulance. He was fine. Just a bit of bruising really. But they got him some support, a woman comes in once a day.'

'Once a day? That's it? What about the rest of the day?'

'I don't know what to tell you. They won't give him any more help.'

'Well, aren't you and David going round? You said you hadn't seen him in weeks. Why aren't you going in every day, seeing he's all right?'

'Because we have lives, Michael. It's all right for you to say we should go every day ... you're up there, you don't actually have to do anything. But we have jobs and kids. It's not that easy.'

'He lives two minutes away.'

Karen sighed again. 'I'll tell David when he comes in.' And then she was gone.

Gardner put the phone down, his anger levels rising again. He squeezed the bridge of his nose and took a breath. Why the hell hadn't David informed him that their dad had had a fall? And more to the point, why wasn't he doing anything to help him?

He tried calling his dad again. That's all he could do, keep trying. He stood up and paced back and forth while the phone just rang and rang. Eventually he gave up and threw the phone. It bounced off the edge of the settee and skittered across the floor, landing by the door causing the dog to squeal and run away.

Lawton stood there watching him and he opened his mouth to apologise. He didn't want to be another person to scare her and the dog.

'I didn't mean to interrupt. I just wanted to get a drink,' she said.

'No, it's fine,' he said and she walked past him to the kitchen, careful not to stand on the phone, and, it seemed, careful not to get too close to him.

She went back to her room without another word and he wondered if that's what he was. Another man who scared her. Someone she might've once trusted, might've confided in, but was now just someone else to possibly be afraid of. Because how did you know?

Chapter 34

Gardner had spent the night awake, his mind going over the past few days, the past few hours, trying to make sense of things, trying to stop feeling so angry. His brother, David, had called back a couple of hours later than Karen had promised and assured him that he'd been to see their dad and everything was fine. Gardner had railed at him about the fall he kindly hadn't informed him about, and David had ranted back that Gardner didn't know how hard it was trying to deal with the old man, and they went back and forth until David put the phone down and Gardner couldn't be bothered to call back.

He got up at five, deciding lying there any longer, with just his thoughts for company, was probably going to give him an ulcer. He'd walked to the garage around the corner, bought a pint of milk, some bread, and some overpriced tins of dog food, and then walked back, not feeling any better.

Lawton was still asleep when he got back but the dog had come out to see what was going on, possibly when she heard the sound of food being prepared. She loitered in the doorway, cautious not to get too close to Gardner. In the end he emptied a tin of the meat into a bowl and slid it across the floor at her. She sniffed it suspiciously and backed away so he finished frying the bacon and cut up a slice, putting that on top of the dog food. That seemed to do the trick and the dog wolfed the lot down.

Gardner watched her eating and for a moment forgot about all the crap that was going on. As she finished eating, he bent down and reached out for her. She still looked unsure so he offered another piece of bacon and she tentatively stepped closer, taking the meat from his hand.

'Good girl,' he said and she gave a little wag of her tail in appreciation.

Content that not *everyone* was against him, he left the dog on the settee and went out, careful not to wake Lawton. He'd planned on going over to Lee's mum's house and hauling him in again. Despite what Freeman thought, he knew they needed to speak to Lee again. Even if they'd found Lawton, Lee still hadn't given them an alibi for Tuesday and Gardner believed there was a reason for that. But as he drove towards the house where he was clearly unwelcome, he realised that Lee was unlikely to go anywhere with him and that he was even less likely to be able to keep his thoughts about Lee to himself, which would only fan the flames of the situation. Instead he turned around and headed to work.

He found Harrington at his desk when he arrived and asked him to call Lee and politely ask if he'd mind coming in and answering a few more questions. When Harrington came off the phone, he was surprised to hear that Lee had agreed to it.

When Lee arrived an hour later, he looked less obliging on seeing Gardner and rolled his eyes. 'I hope you're going to keep him on his leash,' Lee said to Harrington.

For a second, Gardner considered leaving them to it, letting Harrington conduct the interview, which was probably the sensible option for all concerned. But he needed to ask his own questions, needed to prove that Lee was involved in this, that he had something to do with Katy as well as Lawton.

'You don't have to speak with DI Gardner,' Harrington said. 'You're here voluntarily. You can leave whenever you like.'

Lee just shrugged and sat down. 'Whatever,' he said.

'Where were you going yesterday when I saw you?' Gardner asked.

Lee smiled and sat back. 'I told you. I was just going for a drive.'

'When you're off sick?'

Lee shrugged. 'I'm not that kind of sick.'

'Why did you lie about being at work on Tuesday?' Lee didn't answer this time, just stared at Gardner. 'Well?' Gardner said and Lee just shifted his eyes and stared past him. 'Tell us again what you were doing Sunday night until the evening of Tuesday, after Katy Jackson had been reported missing.'

Lee sighed and sat back. 'Me and Dawn had an argument—'

'Why? What about?'

'Nothing, really,' Lee said.

'So arguing about nothing led to you kicking the shit out of her?'

Lee's face changed now, the smarm gone, irritation starting to surface. Maybe Freeman was wrong about the control. 'I didn't kick the shit out of her.'

'No? So why was there blood all over the room?'

'I don't know. We had an argument; things got thrown. That was it. When I got up the next day she was gone. Took the dog with her.'

'Did you try to stop her leaving?'

'No. I didn't even know she'd gone until morning.'

'Why not?'

'I was asleep,' Lee said.

'Okay. So you got up on Monday and Lawton was gone. You didn't look for her, didn't try calling her? You weren't concerned that she'd left?'

'Not really.'

'What about Katy Jackson?'

'What about her?'

'Did you see her that day?'

'No.'

'What about the next day. Tuesday. Did you see her that day?'

'No.'

'No? She didn't come to the house?'

'Not while I was there,' Lee said.

'And what time were you there?'

'I don't know. I left early.'

'So you didn't see her at all. You didn't let her into your house?'

'No, why would I?'

'So how did she get into the house, Lee? She didn't break in. Lawton wasn't there to let her in. So how did she get inside?'

'I've got no idea.'

'It doesn't worry you that this woman was in your house while you weren't there. That she somehow managed to get in.'

Lee sighed. 'There's a spare key,' he said.

Gardner paused. 'Katy has a key?'

'No,' Lee said. 'Why would she have a key? I'm just saying there *is* a spare key. If she was so bothered about getting in she could've found it.'

'You didn't mention this before.'

'Didn't think about it before.'

'Where's it kept? This spare key.'

'Under a big plant pot near the fence in the back garden.'

'Could you be more specific?' Gardner asked.

'A blue and white pot. A big, heavy one. You can't miss it.'

Gardner looked at Harrington, wondering how likely it was that Katy would know where the spare key was. It was possible Lawton had told her but Gardner didn't really want to believe it. They still had nothing to prove Lee was in the house with Katy, other than the fact she hadn't broken in. So if she hadn't broken in …

'What did you think of Katy?' Gardner asked.

'What?' Lee said. 'What do you mean?'

'I mean, what did you make of her? What was your opinion of her?'

'I didn't make anything of her. I don't know her. Never met her.' Gardner sat back now, knowing he'd caught Lee in another lie. He waited for Lee to say something else. 'What?' Lee said. 'I don't know her. I told you that already.'

'You're lying,' Gardner said.

Lee just shook his head. 'Whatever,' he said and stood up. 'Are we done here?'

'Why don't you want to admit you know Katy? Was there something going on between you? Something you don't want Lawton to find out about?'

Lee turned, the irritation bubbling up some more. Gardner wondered if he could push him so the irritation turned to anger, that the anger would turn to letting something slip.

'I don't know her.'

'That's not what Lawton told us,' Gardner said and saw Lee's face change. He came back to the table, standing above Gardner.

'You found her?'

Gardner hadn't wanted to tell Lee that Lawton had come forward, didn't want him to know she was safe with him. But he needed something to push Lee, to make him talk.

'Where is she?' Lee asked.

'She told us you didn't like Katy. That the night you had that big fight, the night she left, Katy had been there and you came home and told her to leave.' Lee sat down again and Gardner could almost see his brain whirring. 'She also told us Scott was there too. That you and him came home, bickering about something. That you didn't seem pleased to see her and Katy there. What were you doing? What did Lawton and Katy get in the way of?'

'Nothing,' Lee said.

'But you were annoyed Katy was there. More annoyed when Scott spoke to her. Why was that? You like her more than you're letting on? Jealous?'

'No.'

'So what happened?'

'Nothing happened. I came home. Brought Scott. He wanted to borrow something.'

'What?'

'A DVD.'

'And did he get it?'

'No. I couldn't find it.'

'So?'

'So, nothing. He went home. I asked Katy to go because I wanted to get my tea. If her and Dawn thought I was being arsey then ...' He shrugged.

'That's not how Lawton tells it,' Gardner said. 'She says you didn't like Katy at all. Why didn't you like her, Lee? What did you have against Katy Jackson?'

'Nothing!'

'Come on, Lee. Lawton told us.'

'She's lying.'

'Why would she lie?'

'I don't know. To get back at me.'

'For what?'

Lee's jaw tightened and he started shaking his head. 'I'm not saying anything else until I see her.'

'That's not going to happen,' Gardner said.

'I want to speak to her.'

'Not going to happen,' Gardner said again. 'You're not going anywhere near her.'

'Tell her,' Lee said. 'Tell her I want to talk to her.'

'No.'

'I'm not leaving until I speak to her. I'm not saying anything else. I'll only talk to her.'

'But you don't have anything to tell us,' Gardner said. 'You claim you don't know Katy. Didn't see her at all. Why would we bring Lawton in for you to tell her nothing?'

'Because I do know something. But I'll only talk to Dawn,' Lee said and crossed his arms. 'Let me see her and I'll tell you everything.'

'You can't even tell us where you were on Tuesday.'

'I was looking for Dawn,' Lee said and Gardner rolled his eyes.

'How convenient.'

'What?'

'Now we've found her and know she's all right, or at least relatively all right, you suddenly want to use her as an alibi? I don't think so.'

'It's true. I was looking for Dawn.'

'Really? Was your mate Scott looking for her too? Because you both seemed to be going somewhere in the same direction until I stopped you.' Lee's mouth twitched. 'Why not tell us you were looking for Dawn the first time we asked where you were?'

'Because I knew you'd kick off if I said I was looking for her.'

'She's your girlfriend,' Harrington said. 'Looking for her would've been perfectly understandable. Or it would've been if you'd told us that straight away. But now it just sounds like you're backtracking.'

'Why would I do that?' Lee said.

'Because you're hiding something,' Gardner said. 'You and Scott are both hiding something.'

'So let me talk to Dawn and I'll tell her what I know.'

'No.'

'I told you about the keys, didn't I? I can tell you other stuff. But not until I see Dawn.'

Gardner and Harrington left Lee alone and walked to the office. 'He's full of shit,' Harrington said. 'He doesn't know anything.'

'Maybe,' Gardner said.

'Come on. He's full of it. He just wants to see Lawton.' Harrington waited while Gardner picked up the phone, tapping it against his hand. 'You're not going to let him see her, are you?'

'No,' Gardner said. 'But I think he does know something.'

'So how are you going to get him to talk?'

'I'm going to speak to Lawton myself, see what else she can give us that might encourage him.' He picked up the phone and then looked back to Harrington. 'Did anyone check the back garden for a key before?'

'Not sure.'

'Find out. If not, get someone to go and have a look. See if he's bullshitting or not.'

Gardner dialled and waited for Lawton to answer, not letting his nerves get the best of him when she didn't answer straight away. Lee was here, out of harm's way. There was nothing to worry about.

'Hello?'

He breathed a sigh of relief when she picked up. 'Hi, it's me,' he said. 'How's it going?'

'Fine,' she said. 'Has something happened?'

'No,' he said. 'I was just checking in.' He paused, not sure how to say it.

'What's wrong?' she asked.

'Nothing,' he said. 'We've brought Lee in again. He's denying knowing anything about Katy, denies knowing her at all, but won't say any more.' He paused again. 'He wants to talk to you.' He heard Lawton let out a breath. 'I've told him that's not going to happen but I thought, maybe, you could give us something to—'

'I'll talk to him,' Lawton said and Gardner felt unsettled again.

'No,' he said. 'You don't need to do that. Just give us some more information we can use.'

'I don't know what else I can say. I'll talk to him.'

'Lawton,' Gardner said.

'It's fine.'

'No, it's not. It's far from fine.'

'Do you think he knows something about what happened to Katy?'

'Maybe,' Gardner said. 'But we can find out without you having to see him.'

'But what if you don't?' Lawton said.

Gardner sighed. 'I don't want you talking to him.'

'It's up to me. I want to.'

'Why?'

'Because I feel bad about Katy. She was in my house and maybe Lee did have something to do with it. If I can help, I want to.'

'But—'

'It's fine,' she said. 'I'll be there in half an hour.'

Gardner tried to argue some more but she'd already gone, her mind made up. He put the phone down and slumped in his chair. He shouldn't have called her, shouldn't have let her know Lee was there. Certainly shouldn't have let Lee know they'd found her.

Harrington came back in. 'No one checked before, someone's on their way over.' He looked at Gardner expectantly. 'What did Lawton say?' Gardner sighed and Harrington said, 'She's going to talk to him?'

Gardner nodded.

'You think that's a good idea?'

'No. I think it's a very bad idea.' He rubbed his hand across his face. 'Let's just hope we get something useful out of it.'

Chapter 35

Freeman parked outside of an office building a few down from Andrew's. She'd already seen his car there, so knew he was at work. But she wanted to go in without giving him a heads up. She didn't know what she expected to find him doing but she felt the need to do it anyway.

She'd already considered the possibility that Andrew and Rhiannon were more than friends; they were certainly more than just work colleagues. No matter what Andrew had claimed about a misunderstanding, she knew he'd lied about leaving the office that day and so had Rhiannon.

She walked along to the office and went in, closing the door gently behind her. There was no one in the front office but this time the phone wasn't ringing off the hook. She walked through towards the door that led to the second office, the one Rhiannon preferred to sit in with Andrew. She leaned against the door, listening for the sound of them talking but could only hear a muffled noise. She opened the door, knocking as she did, and found both Andrew and Rhiannon in there – him sitting on the edge of his desk, her standing in front of him, her arms around

213

him, his head on her chest. When Andrew saw Freeman he pushed back and his face flushed.

'I shouted but there was no answer,' Freeman said. 'Can I have a word?'

Andrew stood but Freeman shook her head and said, 'No. With Rhiannon.'

Rhiannon looked to Andrew for answers but he just kept his eyes on Freeman.

'Won't take long,' Freeman said and held the door for Rhiannon.

As they walked back into the front office, Freeman guessed she had her answer, that something was going on with Andrew and his workmate. But was it a full-blown affair or was he just using her to cover for him? Was she part of all this or just one more victim of Andrew's charm?

Rhiannon sat down on the small settee but Freeman stayed on her feet and she could see it made Rhiannon worried. *Good*, she thought, *you should worry*.

'Why did you lie to me?' Freeman asked and Rhiannon looked about ready to cry already.

'I didn't lie,' she said in a small voice.

'You told me Andrew didn't leave the office and that wasn't true.'

Rhiannon's eyes went to the door to the back office, maybe she was hoping Andrew would come out and tell her what to say again. Freeman wondered if Andrew had already warned her, had told her he'd been found out and that she should prepare another story.

'I didn't think he had left. I guess I was mistaken,' Rhiannon said.

'It's a small office and you usually sit with Andrew, eat your lunch together, so how could you not notice he was gone for an hour?'

'I don't know. It was busy that day. I guess I just didn't realise. But he only went out to get his lunch from home. Maybe it's because he didn't offer to pick anything up for me, maybe that's why I got confused.'

'So you *do* know where he went,' Freeman said.

'What?'

'You just said Andrew went home to get his lunch. How do you know that if you didn't even realise he'd gone?'

Rhiannon swallowed and looked to the door for help again. 'He just told me.'

'Today?' Freeman asked and Rhiannon nodded. 'So he came in this morning and told you we found out he was lying. So he was prepping you?'

'No! He just told me that he'd done something stupid, that he'd got confused and said he hadn't left when he had. But he didn't mean to lie.'

'Just like you didn't mean to?'

Rhiannon was crying properly now and Freeman wondered if she should pull back a little. This woman might not have anything to do with Katy's disappearance, might not have done anything wrong at all. Maybe she was just stupid enough to believe Andrew was a good guy.

'Did Andrew ask you to lie for him?' Freeman asked her.

'No,' she said. 'He wouldn't do that. He wouldn't lie about anything, certainly not this. And neither would I.'

'But he did lie. And so did you. And call me cynical, but I don't believe that it was a mistake. Maybe you *didn't* realise he went out. I could possibly believe that. But he outright lied. And I think he asked you to lie for him.'

'No, he didn't. I swear,' Rhiannon said. 'He's a good person. He loves Katy. He just wants her back.'

Freeman looked at Rhiannon. She'd heard that before, those same words. Only last time it was from Andrew himself. So not only had he asked Rhiannon to lie for him, he was telling her exactly what to say, as if he was controlling her too.

*

Andrew came out of the back office and stood at the window, watching as Freeman walked to her car. He heard Rhiannon come up behind him, waffling on about something or other, sniffling, but he wasn't listening. He had other things on his mind. He needed to keep on his toes. Needed to keep everything straight, what he'd told them, what he hadn't.

He slid his hand into his pocket and as his hand touched the warm metal, he jerked his hand back. He'd forgotten it was there. Andrew walked away from Rhiannon, into the small toilet cubicle at the back of the office. He could hear Roy whistling. Didn't know why he was in such a good mood. He pulled the key out of his pocket and turned it over in his hand. There was still a bit of blood on it and he picked at it with his fingernail even though it made him uncomfortable. He knew he should get rid of it. Really he should've come clean and told Freeman about it, say he'd found it, give her at least part of the truth. But that would've led to more questions, more suspicion, and he didn't want that. And now it was too late. He needed to stick to his story.

He turned the key over in his hand. He should go and throw it down a drain. But he just stood there, feeling its weight in his hand. He didn't want to let it go. Who knew when it would become useful again?

He looked around the small room. He knew taking it home would be stupid. But maybe he could keep it here. Just for emergencies. Maybe for when this had all blown over. He spotted the curled-up linoleum under the toilet. He bent over and pushed the key underneath, trying to press down the flooring over the top. He doubted anyone would find it there. Roy would be too lazy to bend down for anything. The cleaner never bothered with proper cleaning. And Rhiannon? Well, he could always count on her.

Chapter 36

Gardner drummed his fingers on the desk. She would be there any minute and he wasn't sure he could go through with it. But it wasn't really his decision to make, it was hers. He just hoped she knew what she was doing.

'Did you ever meet him before this?' Harrington said and Gardner looked up. 'Lee. Did you ever see him with Lawton?'

'Only briefly. I spoke to him here, just outside.'

'And?'

'And I thought he seemed a bit of a tit. Couldn't see him and Lawton together at all.'

'But you didn't get the impression something was wrong?'

Gardner thought about that day. He saw Lawton and Lee, decided to go and say hello, even though it looked like they were deep in conversation. He thought Lee's friendliness was as fake as his tan. But had he thought something was wrong? He remembered leaving them to it. Remembered looking back over his shoulder. Lee had his hand on her neck. It could've been a protective gesture. But he recalled feeling uncomfortable, assumed they'd had an argument. He'd asked Lawton if she was going with him on the lead he had, offered her an escape from whatever was going on, even though she had no reason to go. But had he thought something was really wrong?

The hand on her neck. Not protective. Possessive. Controlling. Threatening. And he'd missed it. Somewhere inside of him he'd known something was wrong. Why else would he have given her an escape route? So why hadn't he kept looking, harder?

He looked back at Harrington and said, 'No. I didn't know anything was wrong.'

'Me either,' Harrington said. 'That night we went out for her birthday, just before Christmas, he turned up at the pub halfway through the night. We'd been having a right laugh and then he showed up and spoiled things. I didn't really think at the time. I just assumed that Lawton changed a bit around him because that's what people do, act differently with different people. Even we changed a bit, I thought because he wasn't one of us, but now..? It was like the mood changed, you know. He didn't do anything, but something changed. He was chatting with everyone but when I think about it now, he never properly laughed or anything. Just watched everyone. And he kept asking about you.'

'Me?' Gardner said. 'What about me?'

'Kept asking where you were, why you weren't at the party. I said you were working, some case up in Blyth. He let it go but then I heard him ask a few other people. I think he thought something was going on with you and Lawton.'

Gardner felt a stab of guilt. He knew he had nothing to feel guilty about. Nothing had ever happened between him and Lawton, never would. But the idea that he could be the cause of some fight they'd had made him sick. He felt his throat close up.

He tried to remember seeing her the day after he'd run into them outside the station. Had there been any clues that something had happened that night? He couldn't think, couldn't remember what happened that day. Why would he? It was just another day.

Harrington was still talking about that night but Gardner wasn't listening. He turned his face away, embarrassed by the wave of emotion washing over him. He'd felt bad about missing her birthday, had apologised profusely afterwards, telling her there was no way he could've gotten away from what was going on up north. But now he was glad he hadn't gone. That he hadn't caused more problems for her. He remembered talking to her, apologising. She'd accepted it, hadn't seemed too concerned. Had she been relieved? He tried to remember, tried to see her face as he'd said he wished he could've been there.

The scarf. He'd given her a scarf as a gift, part birthday present, part apology. She seemed happy but had she kept it? If so, what had she told Lee? He assumed she wouldn't have told him who it was really from.

He got up and went to the toilets, walking quickly, ignoring Harrington's voice behind him. He couldn't keep doing this. He was questioning everything, wondering if something he'd done had caused her to suffer, if some little thing was a hint about what was going on … something he'd been oblivious to.

He closed the cubicle door, sat on the closed toilet seat and started to cry.

Chapter 37

Gardner made his way back to the office to find Lawton had arrived and was sitting at his desk being talked at by Harrington. He felt like he'd failed her again. But maybe that wasn't fair. Harrington had been surprisingly sensitive about everything, had shown real compassion for Lawton. Something Gardner didn't think his oversexed colleague was capable of.

She looked up as Gardner approached and Harrington stopped talking, looking slightly relieved that Gardner had returned and he no longer had to think of small talk, more safe subjects to discuss with her. 'I'd better get back to the CCTV before Freeman comes back,' Harrington said.

'Yeah, you'd better,' Gardner said, managing to cut himself off before he said what he was thinking, that Freeman would kick his arse if he hadn't done as she asked. He was convinced Harrington was scared of Freeman, which amused him to no end, but he caught himself in time before saying it in front of Lawton. Before all this had happened, he would've thought Lawton would find it as funny as he did. That the mighty Carl Harrington was actually scared of a tiny woman. But now? It just seemed in bad taste.

Gardner waited for Harrington to disappear before sitting down with Lawton, hoping he could convince her not to go through with talking to Lee. 'How're you feeling?' he asked and she shrugged.

'All right,' she said but didn't look it. As people came in and out of the office they stared at her, offering small smiles, pitying looks.

'Let's go and talk somewhere else,' Gardner said and she nodded, gathering her jacket and bag. He led her into an empty interview room, preparing his case as they sat, working out the best way to tell her this was a mistake. But she got in first.

'I wouldn't be here if I didn't want to do it,' she said and he tried to speak but she kept going. 'I know you don't want me to see him. But I have to.'

'No, you don't.'

'If it'll help find Katy, I do.'

'He's just using that as an excuse to see you.'

'So you don't think he knows anything?'

Gardner sighed. 'No, I think he might know something. But I don't know if whatever that is will be worth you going in there. And maybe he won't tell you anyway. He just wants to see you. To know he's won.'

Lawton shook her head. 'I don't care. I have to try,' she said and stood. 'Shall we?'

Gardner took Lawton along to where they'd left Lee and asked her one last time if she was sure. She nodded and they went in. Lee looked up as they entered, his face changing from boredom to pleasure. A smile spread across his face and Gardner wanted to wipe it off him.

'All right, Dawn,' Lee said.

223

'Sit down,' Gardner said to Lee as he moved towards Lawton. Lee glanced at Gardner before doing as he was told.

'Where've you been?' Lee asked Lawton.

'Just get on with telling us what you know about Katy Jackson,' Gardner said.

Lee shook his head. 'No. Not you. Just her.'

'Not a chance,' Gardner said.

'That's what we agreed to.'

'No. You wanted to see Lawton. Here she is. Now tell us what you know.'

Lee ignored Gardner, just stared at Lawton and Gardner was surprised that she held his gaze.

'It's all right,' she said. 'I'll talk to him.'

'I'm not leaving you alone with him.'

'It's fine,' she said and finally looked away from Lee to Gardner and nodded. Gardner sighed. He could see Lee's smug expression from the corner of his eye, which made him want to leave even less. But Lawton nodded again so he went to the door.

'You've got ten minutes,' he said and left the room, rushing down the corridor to keep an eye on things from the monitors that showed what was going on in each interview suite. He watched as Lee leaned across the table and took Lawton's hands. She flinched but didn't pull away.

'How are you?' he asked her.

'Fine,' she said.

Lee moved his hands further so that he had hold of her wrists and Gardner felt his stomach tighten. 'I'm sorry, Dawn,' Lee said. 'You know I didn't mean it, don't you?'

Lawton had her head down but Gardner could see her head move, nodding in agreement.

'How's Cotton?' Lee asked.

'She's fine.'

'Good.' Lee licked his lips, his eyes never leaving Lawton. 'Are you coming home?'

Lawton didn't answer immediately and Lee sat further forward, his hands tugging her wrists, jerking her forward. Gardner could hear his own breath, shallow, nervous. He needed to stop it.

'I don't know,' Lawton said.

'Why not? Where are you staying? With him?' Lee said, nodding to the door.

Lawton shook her head. 'No,' she said. 'A B&B.'

'So come home,' he said, his hands moving back down, his fingers entwining hers.

'Maybe,' she said. 'In a few days.'

'Why a few days?'

'We can't even *go* home. It's a crime scene.'

Lee dropped her hands. 'Why was she even there, Dawn? How did she get in my house?'

Lawton shrugged. 'I don't know. You didn't let her in?'

'Of course I never let her in. Is that what you think? Is that what he's telling you? That I did something to her? He's lying. I never even saw her. He's trying to get between us. He knows I wasn't there.'

'You said you knew something.'

Lee laughed. 'I don't know anything about her.'

'Lee,' Lawton said and shook her head. 'Why did you tell them you don't know Katy?'

225

'I don't.'

'You've met her. A few times,' Lawton said.

'Not the same thing.'

'Did Scott say anything about her?'

'Like what?'

'I don't know. He knows her. He was talking to her. I just wondered if he mentioned anything about her later.'

'I haven't seen him since then.'

'You didn't seem happy he was talking to her.'

Lee smirked. 'Jealous?' Lawton sat further back in her seat and looked at her hands on the table in front of her. When she didn't respond, he went on. 'I just wanted to get something sorted with Scott but I couldn't do it with her sitting there. I was just a bit pissed off about it.'

'What were you going to do?'

Gardner noticed Lee glance up at the camera and smile. 'It doesn't matter,' he said. 'Let's just say I told her to piss off because she was in the way. Not coz I fancy her.' He smirked again and reached for Lawton's hand.

'I didn't think you did,' Lawton said. 'You didn't even like her.'

Lee sat forward, his face angry. 'Is that what you've been telling them? Is that why I'm here? Coz of some shit you've been spouting about me hating her?'

'I haven't—'

'I don't know her.'

'All right,' Lawton said. 'But you've met her and you're just going to make things worse if you lie about it.'

'I just wanted to see you,' Lee said, his voice dropping again. 'I have a right to see you.'

Gardner felt the anger surge through him. He knew Lee wouldn't talk. That it was just an act to get Lawton in there. He turned to leave, to put a stop to it, when Lee spoke again.

'Did you take the money?' he said.

Gardner turned back to the screen. Lawton looked confused. 'What money?' she said.

'The money in the tin, in the kitchen.'

'No,' she said.

Lee reached out for her again. 'It's all right,' he said. 'I get it. You needed a break. That's fine. Just pay it back, whenever.'

'I didn't take any money,' she said.

'Dawn, please don't lie to me.'

'I'm not lying. I didn't take it. I didn't even know there was money there. What was it for?'

Lee stared at her until she looked away and Gardner knew there'd be nothing more. He headed back down the corridor. An officer in uniform stopped him halfway and he tried not to appear too annoyed.

'I checked Lee Johnston's back garden. No spare key that I can find,' the officer said.

'Okay, thanks,' Gardner said, unsurprised, and continued walking to the interview room where he found Lee with his arms around Lawton.

'All right, we're done here,' Gardner said and Lawton tried to pull away but Lee held on. 'You're done,' he said again and Lee finally let go. 'You can leave,' he said to Lee. 'I'll let you know when I want to speak to you again.'

'Are you coming?' Lee said to Lawton.

'No, she isn't,' Gardner said, answering for her.

Lee looked from Gardner to Lawton. 'Did he tell you he hit me?' he said. 'In here. Right in front of the cameras.' Lawton looked at Gardner and he felt embarrassment sweep over him. 'I could put a complaint in about that,' Lee said.

'Go home, Lee,' Lawton said. 'I'll see you later.'

Lee smiled at her. 'I know you will,' he said and winked before walked away.

Chapter 38

Freeman was just about to buy some lunch when Harrington called. She moved away from the counter and found a quiet corner to talk to him. 'Yeah, what's up?' she said as she answered the phone.

'I found something else on your man,' Harrington said. 'He did go somewhere else that day.'

'Where'd he go?' she asked, feeling a little buzz, wondering if they had him, if he'd taken Katy somewhere, either dead or alive.

'He went to the retail park close to his office first.'

'Before he went home?' she asked.

'Yeah. We've got him turning off into the car park at 12.05 p.m. and then leaving at just after 12.25. You can see him park in front of B&Q but the footage doesn't show if that's where he went. I'll have to speak to the management of the park, see if their footage gives us more.'

'What else is over there?'

'Carpet shop, furniture place, pet shop, and a shoe shop.'

Freeman wondered what Andrew could've gone for, what he wouldn't want them to know about. They didn't have any pets so that was probably out. And she couldn't see him shopping for carpets or furniture in such a short amount of time. So that narrowed it down. But was his visit to one of those shops the reason he lied or was it just that he didn't want her to know he'd gone home?

'I'll give them a call, see if we can find him on the CCTV,' Harrington said.

'Did we check his bank transactions when we were looking for Katy's?'

'Yeah,' he said. 'I don't think there was anything from any of those stores though.'

'Any cash withdrawals?' She could hear Harrington shuffling about.

'Not that day,' he said, eventually. 'Took out £150 from a cash machine the night before.'

'That's quite a lot of cash,' Freeman said.

'And makes it harder to find out what he bought.'

'Listen, I'm close to the retail park. I'll go over there now, see what I can find.'

'All right. You're the boss,' he said.

Freeman got her lunch and carried it back to the car, wondering what Andrew had stopped off for that day and why he hadn't mentioned it. If forgetting to mention his trip home really had been a mistake, which she doubted, then surely being found out would make him pipe up with the whole truth, unless he had something to hide.

She drove towards the retail park, stuffing fries into her mouth as she drove. Harrington said he'd parked close to B&Q. She couldn't imagine the place would be packed at lunchtime on a weekday so surely he'd park closest to the shop he wanted to go in. So that's where she'd start.

Finishing the greasy food, she wiped her fingers on her trousers and got out, walking towards the DIY store. She hated those places. She'd spent hours following her dad around them on a Saturday afternoon as a kid, bored out of her mind. She'd sworn that she wouldn't be one of those people when she grew up. She had yet to spend a bank holiday putting an Ikea shelving unit together and she hoped she never would.

Freeman looked around at the dozen or so people milling about, trying to work out who was staff and who the customers were. She eventually collared an employee who looked about as happy to be there as she was and asked to speak to the manager. The woman sighed and said, 'Hang on,' before sauntering off leaving Freeman by a display of carpet cleaner.

'Can I help?'

Freeman turned and found a man striding towards her, all smiles and enthusiasm. 'Hi, I'm Alistair Burgess, the manager.' Freeman showed him her ID and he faltered a little.

'I was hoping to take a look at your CCTV footage from Tuesday,' she said.

'Oh, sure,' he said, although he didn't sound it. 'This way.' Freeman followed him through the store, taking in all the things she would never, ever buy. 'Is this to do with shoplifting? There's been a lot on the park recently,' Alistair said.

'No,' Freeman said, an image of someone running off with a roll of carpet slung over their shoulder coming to mind. 'I'm just trying to trace someone's movements. We know he came into the park on Tuesday lunchtime. I think he might've come here but I need to make sure. Do you have a camera at the door?'

'Yes,' he said. 'If you have an approximate time, they shouldn't be too hard to find.'

He unlocked a door by pressing numbers into a keypad and walked in, holding the door for Freeman. There was a small set up on a desk in the corner, a couple of monitors showing some very dull activity live in the store. For a second Freeman felt a little uncomfortable, memories of last Christmas coming to mind, of her making the biggest mistake of her life. Or one of them. She decided to let the manager work the controls.

'So, Tuesday, you said?' he asked, taking a seat at the desk.

'Yes. Just after noon.'

She watched as his fingers moved quickly, bringing up different screens. 'Right,' he said after a few minutes. 'I'll play it from just before twelve.' He got up and moved out of the way so Freeman could see more clearly. She watched the footage. For the first five minutes no one entered at all. She heard Alistair clear his throat behind her before saying, 'We're usually busiest at weekends,' as if she was there about the crime of slow business.

Finally someone went into the store at 12.06 p.m. but it wasn't Andrew Blake. She let the excitement settle down and kept her eyes on the screen. At 12.08 p.m. someone else entered and this time the excitement was warranted. It was him.

'That's him,' she said and Alistair leaned forward, looking to see the customer the police were interested in.

'Can we follow him?' she asked and stood up, allowing the manager to work the controls again.

'There he is,' he said, pointing to the screen. 'Aisle twelve.'

'Which is?'

'Security and alarms. That kind of thing.'

Freeman leaned forward, trying to see what Andrew was doing. He stood looking at the shelves for a couple of minutes, picking things up, inspecting them and then returning them to the shelf. He walked up and down a few times.

'Can you get any closer?' Freeman asked.

'Sorry,' he said.

'What sort of thing would he be looking at?'

'All sorts. Smoke alarms, security lighting, home alarms, that kind of thing.' Alistair squinted at the screen. 'I'd say, from where he is in the aisle, he was looking at CCTV.'

Freeman had to admire a man who knew his business so well, even if it was a very dull business. 'CCTV? For home use?'

'Yes,' he said. 'Some people just use dummy cameras as a preventative measure. But you can get functional ones too.' He turned and looked at her, his face flushing. 'But you already knew that. Obviously.'

They watched as Andrew picked something up and walked down the aisle, heading to the checkout. At least she knew he bought something, even if she didn't know what yet. 'Can you see what it is?' she asked but he shook his head.

'But I can find out,' he said. 'I can check what was bought at that time on that till.'

'Excellent. Thanks.'

'I'll be right back.'

Freeman sat and waited for him to return, again feeling uncomfortable left alone in the room. She knew it was stupid. She was the only reason there'd been a problem before and she certainly wasn't going to repeat her mistake. But she still couldn't help feeling unsettled and hoped he would come back quickly.

She heard the door being unlocked and stood up, feeling claustrophobic in the small room. 'Did you find it?' she asked and he nodded.

'He bought a wireless CCTV system. One you can view remotely, from your phone or whatever.'

Freeman felt a surge of something but couldn't decide if it was excitement or nausea. She thanked the manager, who grinned like he'd won a prize, and left the store. Why would Andrew need a CCTV system? And why would he decide to go and buy it then? And more importantly, why didn't he want her to know?

As she walked back to the car she felt a little stupid for her earlier thoughts. When she heard B&Q she immediately thought of garden spades and heavy duty bin bags. The thought had crossed her mind that Andrew had gone for supplies necessary for burying a body. But this?

She already knew that Andrew was controlling Katy, keeping her from friends, from work. He'd gone home that day, allegedly to get his lunch, but Freeman believed he was going to check up on Katy. She'd dared to go somewhere without his permission and so he was going home to make sure she didn't do it again and had bought a CCTV system that would allow him to watch her even when he wasn't there. Only Katy wasn't there when he got home. So what did he do?

Freeman rested her head against the back of the seat, realising it definitely was nausea and not excitement she was feeling. Andrew was planning on filming his girlfriend's every move, keeping an eye on her to make sure she never left the house again without him. But she was still out when he got there, still disobeying him. So had he gone next door and found her, taught her an even bigger lesson?

Chapter 39

They drove home almost in silence but Lawton could feel Gardner looking at her, his unasked questions hanging heavy in the air. As soon as they'd left the interview room she wanted to go home, or maybe not home, just somewhere that wasn't the station. She couldn't stand the looks from her colleagues, pity and incredulity. It seemed like everyone knew by now and maybe she should've been grateful that her situation, the possibility that something had happened to her, had affected so many people. That they'd worried about her and moved her to the top of the queue of missing people even though she wasn't really missing, just not where she was supposed to be.

She'd watched Lee walk away and she just wanted to get out of there but Gardner held her back, told her to wait. She wanted to argue at first, thinking he was making her stay, wanting to ask her more questions, finish up some paperwork on the failure of their little experiment. But she was wrong. He just didn't want Lee to be there when they left, didn't want him to see where she was going. As if waiting half an hour would stop him. He was pretty good at waiting, at searching her out. If he hadn't been so drunk that night, hadn't passed out on the bed, he would've known she was leaving, would've followed.

She wondered if he'd been looking for her the last few days. Gardner said he hadn't been to work but couldn't account for his movements. Maybe this time she'd beaten him, had found a hiding place he didn't think of. Whenever she'd left before, somehow he could tell what she was thinking, where she'd most likely go. But this time he didn't find her. Maybe she could've stayed there forever. Maybe she should've.

She thought about his lies about Katy. Was it really possible he'd done something to her? The idea made her shiver. She thought about his question about the money, as if he really thought she'd steal from him. And then she thought about the way he held her hand. Maybe he was sorry. Maybe the attitude was about Gardner, not her. She knew how he felt about Gardner, even though it was ridiculous. Or maybe it wasn't. She couldn't deny she'd once had feelings for him. Maybe Lee was right to suspect her.

'Lawton?'

She turned to Gardner, unsure of what he'd said. 'What?'

'I said, are you all right?'

She nodded and looked back out the window, realising they were back at his flat. She looked around, trying to see if Lee was there, lurking. She couldn't see him but that didn't mean anything. He was good at hiding too.

Lawton followed Gardner up to the flat and he opened the door, letting her in first. She walked into the living room and found Cotton on the settee. The dog's eyes moved as she walked across the room but she didn't get up. She wasn't one for big welcomes.

'Tea?' Gardner asked and she nodded again, thinking he was building up to it. She could tell he had a million questions that he wanted to ask but she wasn't sure she could answer any of them. She had been in the room when other women had been questioned and so far she had yet to hear an answer to the big question, *Why do you stay?*, that made sense, that satisfied anyone, either the person asking the question or the person answering. The answers were always different but if you dug deep enough they were the same.

She sat down beside Cotton who grumbled at her space being invaded, and Gardner brought out two cups of tea. He slid hers onto the table but she didn't touch it. She just waited for the inevitable.

'Do you keep a spare key out the back?' Gardner asked and Lawton had to take a moment to think, it not being the question she was expecting.

'No,' she said.

Gardner made a noise, a kind of a hmmm, and she waited for him to say something else. 'Why?' she asked when he didn't.

'Lee told me that Katy could've used the spare key.'

Lawton frowned. 'He used to have one,' she said. 'Kept it in case he forgot his and I was at work, but I asked him to get rid of it. I didn't think it was safe.' Gardner nodded and she could tell that he hadn't believed Lee anyway. 'It's possible he kept it though,' she said and Gardner looked disappointed. 'It's not like he listens to me.'

'Someone checked earlier. There's no key. And how would Katy know it was there. Especially if you didn't even know,' Gardner said.

Lawton sighed. She didn't know why Lee would lie about the key. But then why did he lie about anything? They sat in silence for a few minutes and then Gardner said, 'I'm sorry,' once most of his tea was gone.

'For what?' Lawton said.

'For making you come in.'

'You didn't make me. You told me *not* to do it.'

'I shouldn't have told you he was there, that he wanted to see you.'

'Why? Because you knew that I wouldn't be able to resist seeing him? Because I'm too weak to say no?'

'You're not weak, Dawn.'

She had to laugh at that. 'I had to see him eventually.'

'Why?'

'Because he's my boyfriend. Because I live with him.'

'You don't have to.'

She shook her head, frustrated at his lack of understanding, at her need to try and explain.

'You don't have to,' Gardner said again. 'Now we know, now *I* know, I can help you.'

'It's not always like that though. That's the thing.'

'It's like it enough,' Gardner said. 'You can't go back there. Look at what he's done to you.'

'I know what he's done.' She closed her eyes, wanting to shut it all out. Maybe she should've stayed at the B&B, at least there she only had to answer to herself. 'If I didn't think he loved me, I wouldn't be there,' she said and Gardner had that look he got when some suspect was bullshitting him. He wasn't buying it and maybe he was right to. Did she really believe it herself anymore or was she just so used to saying it to herself that it was an automatic response?

She remembered when she'd first moved in with Lee. Or rather he'd moved in with her. Just five months into the relationship and already things were serious. He'd made her laugh, doted on her. She'd loved coming home to him. She'd introduced him to some friends, they thought he was great, a keeper. She'd introduced him to her mum and he'd charmed her over Sunday lunch. And then one morning as she'd put make-up on, he'd stood behind her, staring through the mirror. She'd smiled at him but it hadn't been returned. He'd asked why she was wearing make-up. She'd shrugged. Sometimes she liked to, other days she didn't bother.

'But why?' Lee had asked.

She'd shrugged again. She didn't know. 'It depends on how I feel that day.'

'Who are you seeing?'

'I'm not seeing anyone. I'm going to work.'

'Who are you working with today?'

She'd turned away from the mirror to face him. Why was he so bothered about her make-up?

'Who are you working with?' Lee had said again, his voice sharper.

'Dave,' she'd replied.

Lee had walked away without another word, leaving her there, confused. She'd kept thinking about it while she was at work. On the way home she'd stopped to see her mum. She'd mentioned it to her, feeling slightly stupid for being bothered by it.

'He's probably just jealous,' her mum had said. 'It's nice, isn't it?'

Lawton hadn't say so but she hadn't thought it was nice. She hadn't liked it, hadn't liked being made to feel like she'd done something wrong. 'Dave's fifty-three. He's got six kids,' Lawton had said and her mum laughed.

'Maybe just make a bit more effort with Lee,' she'd said. 'Maybe he's just insecure. His last girlfriend probably cheated on him.'

Lawton had gone home and Lee had been in a good mood. He hadn't mentioned make-up or Dave or anything that night or the next. Everything had been good for a while and she'd forgotten about that morning until it had happened again, weeks, maybe months down the line. She'd mentioned Dave, something he'd done, something stupid. It was supposed to be funny, a way to make Lee laugh like he made her laugh. But just the mention of Dave's name had made the atmosphere change. Lee had stood up, spat in her face, and called her a whore. She hadn't told her mum. She hadn't walked away. She hadn't mentioned Dave again.

'He doesn't love you,' Gardner said. 'It doesn't matter if he hits you all the time or once a year. It's enough. It's too much. Just stay here. As long as you want. Or we'll find you somewhere else. Whatever you want. Just don't go back there, Dawn. Don't go back to him.'

'Stop telling me what to do,' she said and stood up. Gardner looked taken aback. She hadn't meant to shout but she didn't need it. 'I can decide for myself.'

She walked away, to the bedroom, closing the door behind her. She would decide for herself. She kept telling herself that. She would decide for herself.

Chapter 40

Freeman headed back to the station for a check in with DCI Atherton and was already five minutes late. When she got to his office she found Gardner and Harrington sitting in the chairs across from Atherton. They all looked up as she went in and she had to make do with standing up, leaning against the wall. Atherton made a point of looking at his watch before beginning.

'So,' he said. 'Katy Jackson.' He stared at the three detectives and when no one spoke, unsure where the question was, he continued. 'Do we know what we're looking at yet? Missing person? Murder? Abduction? Did she leave by herself? What are we thinking?' His eyes darted around the room and finally settled on Freeman so she guessed she was to go first.

'An all ports alert has been issued in case Katy tried to leave the country but I doubt that's likely. Her boyfriend claims she doesn't have a passport but considering everything I've learned about him and their relationship I thought it was possible she could've got one without his knowledge. But I've checked. And she doesn't.

'Her information had been distributed to all local police forces and along with the appeal you'd expect something by now if she was out there. And we found out something else about Andrew Blake,' she said. 'Before he went home on Tuesday, he stopped at B&Q. Guess what he bought.'

Gardner and Atherton shrugged, obviously not in the mood for games. 'Well, I have to admit, my first thought was he was stocking up on tools to bury his girlfriend. But it turns out he was buying a CCTV system so he could keep tabs on her,' she said.

'Nice,' Gardner said.

'Yeah. It's just a shame the creepy little shit didn't buy it sooner. If he'd already put it in we might've had more clues about what happened.'

'So, what does it prove?' Atherton asked. 'Apart from him being a creep?'

'Well, I think that he was pissed off that she dared to go out. He's been slowly alienating her from all her friends, from any outside contact. I think he couldn't get hold of her that day and got angry, went and got the CCTV and went home to show her who's boss. But things got out of hand.'

'So you think we're now looking at a murder investigation?' Atherton asked.

'That's how it feels to me,' Freeman said.

He nodded but said, 'We don't have enough to say definitively, so for now it's still a missing person. As far as the media and public are concerned at least,' Atherton said.

'We're searching the local area for a body,' Freeman said, 'whether through accidental death or otherwise. But if Andrew Blake is our main suspect, which I believe he is, then I'm not sure how far afield the search should go.

We know he lied about leaving the office, that he *had* gone home that day, that he did have opportunity to kill or hurt Katy. But we've retraced his steps the rest of that day and the days following her disappearance. At no point has Andrew had the opportunity to move a body. Garden's already been searched, as has Lee Johnston's.'

'So what other options do we have?' Atherton asked.

'We're looking at Lee Johnston harder, tracing his movements too, although so far we've found no evidence of him moving Katy's body, *but* he did have more opportunity than Andrew,' Gardner said and looked at Freeman. 'He also claimed that Katy could've found their spare key. Lawton claims they don't have one so I sent someone over this morning to check. Guess what? No key.'

'Someone could've taken it after they let themselves in,' Freeman said.

'Maybe. But there's no trace of Lee for most of Tuesday and he can't provide an alibi. It was his home where the attack took place, plus we already know what he's capable of.'

'And now we've got this other guy too,' Harrington said.

'Right,' Gardner said. 'Lee's workmate, Scott Hill. He was at the house with Lee when Katy was there. He knew her previously. And both have been spotted driving somewhere in the same vicinity until they realised they were being followed.'

'Driving where?' Atherton asked.

'I don't know. I'm still trying to figure that out.'

'But you think this Scott could be involved somehow. That he and Lee were in it together?'

'I don't know,' Gardner said. 'I checked and Scott was at work all day Tuesday so any involvement he had was secondary. He can't have been at the house on Tuesday morning when Katy vanished.'

Atherton sat back and steepled his hands. 'So basically what we're saying is Andrew Blake had the motive to kill her and Lee Johnston the opportunity?'

'Technically Andrew had the opportunity to kill her when he went home that day. He just didn't have time to move the body,' Freeman said.

'But Lee had opportunity for both. And he could've had motive. He didn't like Katy, according to Lawton. In fact, I'd say he doesn't like women at all. I don't think he necessarily had to have a personal issue with Katy,' Gardner said.

'And why would Andrew even call the police if he'd done something to her?' Atherton asked. 'Why draw attention to himself?'

'To cover it up? If he reported her missing then no one would wonder why she's not around anymore,' Harrington said.

'But if she's been isolated from her friends and family as much as Freeman suggests, who'd notice? Wouldn't it be better to keep his mouth shut? Are we even considering the idea she could've left by herself?' Atherton asked.

'She certainly had reason to,' Freeman said. 'But I don't think it's likely. She left without taking anything with her at all. Plus Andrew kept all the money, she couldn't have gone far without any. And we've checked buses and trains and taxis and got nothing. I don't see it happening. Not with the evidence left in Lee's house too.'

'But we're forgetting the other possibilities,' Harrington said.

'Which are?' Atherton asked.

'Firstly, this creep breaking into women's houses. We have a witness who's seen some guy hanging around the street who fitted the description given by the victims Berman spoke to. Plus there's that guy she worked with,' he said, looking over to Freeman.

'Dominic Archer,' she said. 'Has a major crush on Katy. Had been calling her a lot until she changed her number. Was also pretty touchy-feely at work, according to his boss. And it wasn't the first time either.'

'Alibi?' Atherton asked.

Freeman shook her head. 'Called in sick the day she disappeared.'

'So he's obsessed with her and has no alibi,' Atherton said. 'Why aren't we pushing him as hard as Johnston and Blake?'

'I've spoken to him a couple of times but Andrew seemed more likely—'

'Bring him in again,' Atherton said and turned to Harrington. 'Can you see to it if DS Freeman is *too busy*?'

Freeman bit her tongue.

'What's this Dominic Archer look like?' Gardner asked.

'Er, tall, slim build. Dark hair,' she said.

'And what about this guy breaking into houses?'

Freeman pulled a face. 'You think Archer's the guy breaking into houses? Why?'

247

'You said Katy's not the first woman he's been obsessed with. And that this guy attacking women watches them first, chooses them. Maybe he's not just obsessed with one woman at a time.'

'But none of the others were taken. Most weren't even injured,' Freeman said.

'Maybe they were practice.'

They all looked at each other but no one spoke for a while.

'I thought you were convinced Lee did it,' she said, finally.

'He's where I'd place my bet, but if we're considering other options ... does Dominic have alibis for the other dates, the break-ins?'

'I don't know,' she said.

'Find out,' Atherton said, looking at Harrington and then picked up his phone, which she'd come to understand meant *Go away*.

They all left the DCI's office and Freeman was even more frustrated than when she'd arrived. She couldn't help thinking that some of that frustration was anger, or guilt, about how she'd left things with Gardner the day before. She caught up with him and said, 'Can I have a word?'

Harrington took the hint and left them to it. Gardner looked tired and not especially pleased to see her. She tried to remember the last time they'd had a laugh together. It seemed that these days they just got on each other's nerves more than anything else. Perhaps if she'd stayed in Blyth their relationship might've developed in a more agreeable way, but as it was, working together seemed to just bring home how different they were.

'I'm sorry about yesterday,' she said, and Gardner just sort of shrugged as if it didn't matter. 'I didn't mean it the way it sounded. You aren't the one at fault here. No one noticed what was happening.'

'But you were right. *I* should've noticed,' he said.

'No, you shouldn't. That's how this works. Nobody notices, no one thinks it's happening to someone they know. That's how they get away with it. You're not to blame. And if you are, we all are.'

Gardner shook his head. 'She won't talk to me.'

'She will. When she's ready.'

'I just keep making it worse. Pushing her.'

'So don't,' Freeman said. 'Let her do it in her own time.'

'I want to. But she keeps saying it's not like that all the time, or he loves her. It's … frustrating.'

'I know.'

'I told her not to go back. To stay with me or find somewhere else.' He sighed. 'I shouldn't have done that.'

Freeman agreed but kept her mouth shut. Gardner looked up, obviously waiting for her to say something.

'It's all right,' he said. 'You can say it.'

'Okay. No, you shouldn't have said that. She already has someone to tell her what to do. She doesn't need you to do it too, even if you think it's for the best. Even if it *is* for the best. You can't push her.'

'I just don't get it,' Gardner said. 'We see it all the time, these women who're trapped because they have no way out. No money or place to go, or they have kids and-'

'But that's-'

Gardner put up his hand to stop her interrupting. 'I know it's not always that way. Sometimes it's other reasons. But isn't it usually because no one else knows? Even if they have money and family and whatever they need to get out, they don't because it's a secret and that keeps them there. But Lawton? We know now. It's not hidden. So why..? Why isn't she..?' He stopped talking and Freeman put her hand on his arm. He was trying to find reason was there wasn't any.

'I just feel useless,' he said.

'I know. Me too.'

They were quiet for a moment before Gardner brought things back to safer ground – the investigation. 'How well does Andrew know Lee?' he asked.

'Not at all, according to him. Why?'

'Well, I was thinking about what Atherton said in there. If Andrew had opportunity and motive to kill Katy, and Lee had opportunity to move the body ...'

'That they did it together,' Freeman said, thinking about it. 'It's possible, I suppose.'

'So how's Scott involved? I keep thinking about what Lee and Scott are hiding. They were going somewhere they didn't want me to know about but still felt the need to try and get there even after the police were snooping around. So what would be so urgent?' he said.

Freeman thought about it. 'Katy? She could be alive. They're keeping her somewhere.'

'Exactly,' he said. 'They need to go to her to keep her alive.'

'The CCTV,' Freeman said. 'If they're in this together, maybe the CCTV is to monitor her wherever she's being held.'

They looked at each other and Freeman wondered if he was thinking the same thing. Were they going way out on a limb with this? The lack of anything solid, the various loose ends, were they trying to tie them together when they really had no connection? Trying to find reason where there was none?

'But why would they do it?' she asked. 'And why would Lee help Andrew do this to his girlfriend?'

'Maybe they *are* friends. He lied about knowing Katy. Maybe they're lying about knowing each other.'

'Andrew put on a show outside the station Tuesday night, demonstrating how much he hated Lee. Maybe that was another cover,' she said. 'But why point the finger at Lee at all if they were both involved?'

'I don't know.' He sighed. 'Maybe Andrew panicked. Maybe he knew there was more evidence pointing at Lee and decided to give his buddy up.'

'So why wouldn't Lee fight back a little? You really think he'd just sit back and take it?'

'Maybe we should speak to them both again.'

Freeman nodded. 'You speak to Andrew this time,' she said.

'Why?'

'Because I want to know what feeling you get from him. He has a problem with women. I want to know how he reacts to a man. Maybe he'll open up to you a little more, give us something we can use.'

251

'All right,' he said. 'But before you speak to Lee, I want you follow Scott. I'm not sure Lee would risk going wherever they're going again just yet. But Scott might. And he doesn't know you. He won't think he's being followed. Let's find out what they're all up to.'

Chapter 41

Gardner arrived at Andrew's house unsure about how to approach him. Freeman might've been right that the man had problems with women but Gardner didn't know if she was expecting Andrew to confess in some sort of women-are-all-bitches bro-fest or if he'd just be less guarded with him, perhaps assuming that all men understood a little bit of controlling behaviour when it came to their women folk. Either way, Gardner hadn't quite decided how to play it, deciding to wait and see how Andrew reacted to him being there.

He walked up the path and hearing a car door slam behind him, he turned. Behind him, Lee Johnston locked his car and started up his own path, facing Gardner as he reached the door, a smirk crossing his face. Gardner wanted to go over and wipe it off his face, wanted to go and press him some more about how well he knew Andrew Blake but he knew he had no cause and, even though he thought that Lee would put a complaint in about him eventually anyway, he'd rather it came later instead of sooner, so he turned away from Lee and knocked at Andrew's door.

'Mr Blake, I'm DI Gardner,' he said, showing his ID when Andrew opened the door.

'Yes, I remember,' Andrew said. For a moment he looked scared and Gardner wondered if it was guilt, that he was thinking they'd figured him out and had finally come for him, or if he thought something had happened, that they'd found Katy.

'Can I come in?' Gardner asked. Andrew stepped back and as Gardner went inside he looked back, noticing Lee was still standing there, watching. He saw the look Lee gave Andrew before he closed the door.

They went through to the living room, Andrew's hands shoved deep into his pockets. 'Has something happened? Have you found her?'

'No,' Gardner said. 'I just wanted to ask you a few more questions. I know you've already spoken to my colleague DS Freeman a few times.' Gardner caught the beginning of an eye roll but Andrew turned away, perhaps aware of his reaction. Maybe Freeman was right and Andrew had issues with women. Or maybe it was just Freeman.

'I've already told her what I know,' Andrew said. 'She thinks I was lying to her because I forgot to mention going out for lunch on Tuesday. But it was a misunderstanding.'

Gardner nodded. 'It happens,' he said, and Andrew seemed to relax a little.

'Please,' he said, 'sit down.' Gardner sat and Andrew followed, nodding at the adjoining wall as he did so.

'He's allowed back in then. It's not a crime scene anymore?'

'I guess not,' Gardner said, pleased that Andrew had brought Lee up, giving him an easy segue into what he wanted to ask. 'How well do you know Mr Johnston?'

'I don't,' Andrew said.

'Not at all?'

'No. I've never spoken to him. Not before all this. But I suppose I know things *about* him.'

'Like what?'

'I've been listening to him for months. The way he treats that woman is awful. I can't stand people like that. Bullies. He should be locked up.'

'But you never went to the police,' Gardner said.

Andrew looked confused for a second as if he didn't understand why that would be an option.

'Why didn't you do something if it troubled you so much? Why did you tell Katy to keep out of it?'

Andrew's jaw clenched. 'Because it's none of our business. And if she'd wanted help she would've asked for it, wouldn't she? Just because I think something is wrong, doesn't mean I can do anything about it.'

Gardner bit his tongue, knowing he needed to keep on Andrew's side if he was going to get anything. But he was already agreeing with Freeman on the fact that Andrew was a wanker.

Andrew sighed. 'I do feel bad about it,' he said, maybe sensing he'd said the wrong thing. 'But she's all right, isn't she? Dawn?' He paused and when Gardner didn't respond he continued trying to justify himself. 'The reason I didn't want Katy going round there was because I didn't want her to get hurt. I knew what he was like, heard what he did to his girlfriend and I didn't want Katy

255

involved. But maybe she was right to go. Maybe I should've stepped up and done something and then none of this would've happened. If I'd gone round then maybe …' He bowed his head and Gardner thought he could hear him crying, wondered if it was an act.

'Dawn Lawton told us Katy had been going round before that day. That she'd been talking to her for a while. You didn't know about that?'

Andrew looked up. His eyes were red but there was no sign of any tears. 'No,' he said.

'Why wouldn't Katy tell you about that?'

'I don't know,' Andrew said. 'Maybe this Dawn didn't want anyone to know. Maybe she was telling Katy stuff about her boyfriend and asked her not to tell anyone. I don't know, maybe that's why he did something to her. He thought she knew something.'

'Like what?'

'I don't know. About how he was with Dawn.'

'But you knew that already. It's not like he was being careful to hide it from what you've said.'

'No. But I'm not a woman. He couldn't have hurt me. And anyway, maybe it wasn't that. Maybe it was something else, something worse.'

Gardner realised that Andrew was grasping at straws. Whether that was to cover his own behaviour or just because he was so convinced Lee had hurt Katy but didn't know why or how, he didn't know.

'Did you see Lee at all that day? Either before you left for work or at lunchtime when you came home?'

'No.'

'Was his car there? Outside the house?'

'It was in the morning. He'd parked too close to me, it was hard getting out.'

'What about lunchtime?'

'I don't think so,' Andrew said.

Gardner thought about the theory that Andrew and Lee were in this together. That they were denying knowing each other would back that up, they wouldn't want anyone to know they were friends if they had done this. But why was Andrew so keen at pointing the finger at Lee if that was the case? Surely he'd be trying to make them look the other way, at someone else, at the break-ins. He even mentioned them himself that first day. So why focus on Lee now? It didn't make sense. And despite Andrew's personality and lack of transparency with the police, the only thing they were sure of was that he didn't have the time or the opportunity to get rid of Katy's body. So maybe he'd been right about focusing on Lee. Lee hadn't provided a good alibi for his whereabouts the day Katy disappeared and, if Andrew was right, he was still at home that morning after Andrew had left for work. It was entirely possible Lee had been at the house when Katy turned up. The only thing that he couldn't work out was why Lee would hurt Katy. Like Freeman said, it wasn't like he was lashing out at women en masse. There had to be a reason. Was Andrew right? Did Katy know something about Lee? Something more than his violent tendencies with Lawton. Something about him and Scott perhaps?

'You didn't know about Katy's relationship with Dawn Lawton,' Gardner said. 'Do you think it's possible that she had a relationship with Lee Johnston too?'

257

'What do you mean?' Andrew said, visibly tensing up.

'Do you think she knew Lee better than she'd claimed?'

'You mean was she cheating on me?'

'Not necessarily,' Gardner said. 'But I suppose it's a possibility.'

Andrew stood up. 'She wasn't cheating on me. She wouldn't.'

'I'm not saying she was, I'm just—'

'He hurt her. You know that as well as I do.'

'So he must've had a reason to.'

'Because it's what he does,' Andrew said. 'I've heard him. I know what he's capable of.'

Gardner sighed, knowing he was getting nowhere. He wasn't getting Andrew to tell him anything he wouldn't tell Freeman. And he wasn't getting him to admit to knowing Lee.

'Did Katy ever mention someone called Scott?' Gardner asked and could see Andrew's hackles rise again.

'No, she didn't,' he said. 'Who is he?'

'He works with Lee. He was at the house on Sunday when Katy was there. Apparently he knew her. They talked for a while.'

'She didn't mention it,' Andrew said and Gardner could see the man's knuckles turn white.

Gardner knew he wasn't going to get anything more. He was tired and not thinking clearly, maybe not asking the right questions. If he was being honest with himself, he didn't care as much about Katy Jackson as he should've. All he could think about was Lawton and trying to help her. But she wasn't the missing person anymore and maybe there wasn't anything he could do for her anyway. Perhaps Andrew had been right. If she wanted help she'd ask for it. No matter how much he wanted to tell her not to go back to Lee or that she should press charges, he couldn't push her. Couldn't make her do anything. Freeman was right too. She already had someone to do that for her.

Gardner almost stood up to leave but he decided to give it one more shot. Even if he couldn't get anything from Andrew that would help Katy, maybe there was something he could get to help Lawton.

'Tell me again everything you heard next door,' Gardner said. 'Everything you know that Lee did.'

When Andrew had finished, Gardner felt drained, feeling useless again that he hadn't noticed, that it'd been going on so long right under his nose, that he hadn't been able to help. But that was going to change.

'If it came to it, would you testify to all of that?' Gardner asked and Andrew nodded.

'Yes, I would.'

Gardner thanked Andrew and left, thinking maybe he did get his answer after all. After everything he'd just told him about his neighbour, the fact that he'd help make sure he went down for it, Gardner seriously doubted Andrew and Lee were friends.

Chapter 42

Andrew let DI Gardner out and went back inside, the words swirling around his head. Was it possible that Katy had been seeing Lee behind his back? He didn't believe it, didn't want to believe it. But she had obviously been lying to him. He knew that much. She hadn't told him about this Scott or her little visits to see Dawn. When Freeman had told him about that he'd been furious. He thought about the days he'd come home from work and asked Katy what she'd done that day and she'd say nothing. Done the ironing. Done the dishes. Made the tea. No mention of sneaking out next door, having secrets with someone else.

He swiped his hand across the mantelpiece, sending the photo frames and the knick-knacks flying. The sound of the glass shattering pleased him and he stepped forward into the debris, his foot resting on her face. He remembered the day that picture was taken. He'd given her the gold necklace she was wearing and she'd been thrilled. She always was materialistic. And then a few days later she'd left it on the edge of the bathroom sink where it could've easily slipped in, slithered down the drain. It annoyed him how careless she was. So he took the necklace away. She spent days searching for it. He could see how worried she was every time he mentioned it, but still she lied. It bothered him how much she lied and he remembered each fib, saving them up. And when she said it was in the jewellery box upstairs when he knew it was actually around Rhiannon's neck, he should've known then that he couldn't trust her.

Andrew went into the kitchen and poured himself a drink, trying to calm his nerves. He wondered if he should be worried about Gardner's visit. Freeman hadn't really troubled him. Not really. But now she was sending someone else to needle him. He tried to recall everything the detective had said but his mind was getting stuck on his accusation about Katy. He gulped down more wine and closed his eyes, counting back from ten. When he opened them, things were clearer. Where Freeman was obsessed with him and what she thought she knew, Gardner seemed more interested in Dawn and maybe that was an opportunity.

Gardner was upset by what had happened to Dawn Lawton. He knew her. She was a copper too. So was it just because she was one of them? Or was Gardner's interest more personal?

Andrew thought about the things he'd heard through the walls. Sometimes he'd sit on his and Katy's bed with his ear to the wall, listening to the screamed words from next door. It bothered him at first, made him uncomfortable. But it soon became addictive. He wanted, needed, to hear what was going on. His own private little soap opera. He didn't approve of it, but it thrilled him nonetheless.

He remembered several arguments he'd overheard. Lee accused her of cheating on him all the time. He was obsessed. And she always denied it but who knew if that was true? Andrew wondered if Gardner was the one she was sleeping with. That would make sense, would be why Gardner was so set on getting Lee, on getting Andrew to testify against him. But if he *was* sleeping with her too, wouldn't he have noticed? Wouldn't he have seen the bruises as he undressed her?

Maybe he just *wanted* to sleep with her. Maybe it was someone else she was actually seeing. Maybe she slept around. Or maybe Lee was just paranoid. Some men are.

Andrew finished his drink and as the dregs slipped down his throat he had a thought. When Freeman told him she'd found Dawn, that she'd been telling tales about Katy, he knew he had to speak to her, find out what she'd been saying. But Freeman wasn't going to let that happen.

Now, maybe, there was another way.

Chapter 43

Freeman sat and watched as Scott took another call and stood in the street in front of the supermarket, speaking at an obnoxious volume. At least it meant she didn't have to get out of her car to hear him and risk letting him see her. Unfortunately, his conversation, or at least his side of it, was made up entirely of 'yeah, mate' and an irritating high-pitched giggle. She was starting to lose patience.

When he finally put the phone down and headed inside, she wondered if she should follow. Her first instinct was to stay put. What could he get up to inside anyway? But then if he was buying supplies to take to, say, a woman being held against her will, then she wanted to know about it.

She waited for Scott to disappear through the sliding doors and got out, walking quickly into the shop but keeping a distance. She picked up a basket but put nothing in it. Scott went straight to the beer aisle and picked up a couple of four packs of lager and then headed to the checkout. Unless they were keeping Katy on a strict diet of Foster's, this was a waste of time.

Freeman put her basket down and walked back to the exit, glancing over her shoulder once to make sure Scott was following. She got in her car and waited for him to drive away, hopefully to somewhere more interesting.

She could see he was on the phone again and let out a long sigh, slowly losing the will to live as Scott giggled and said 'yeah mate' over and over again. She almost wished she'd taken on Andrew Blake again. Even with all his lies she'd have still got more than this.

She wondered how Gardner had got on, whether Andrew had been any more forthcoming with him. She was still thinking about the meeting earlier and wondered if they were any closer to solving this. Not really. If anything they were further away. She was still sure that Andrew was the one responsible. He had the most reason to harm Katy and had done nothing but lie. But the evidence wasn't stacking up and she couldn't help focusing on the question, why would he call the police if he'd killed her?

Of course, Gardner was still convinced Lee was responsible and even though Freeman couldn't see *why*, maybe that didn't matter. There was plenty against Lawton's boyfriend, as well as his mate Scott. And then there was Dominic. She felt a tightness in her stomach as she thought about Gardner's theory that he could be the man breaking into houses. Was he capable of that? And if so, how had she missed it? So he didn't look the type, but who does? Monsters don't go around advertising the fact. They disguise themselves as people. You only had to look at Lee and Andrew to realise that.

Scott paced up and down in front of his car and Freeman realised she couldn't hear his voice anymore. Had he just realised how dickish he was being or was he now talking about something he didn't want the entire car park to overhear?

He hung up and got in the car and Freeman followed him out, wondering if this was it. She followed him a mile or so and watched as he swung into a tight space opposite a pub.

'Shit,' she muttered. Was she going to have to sit there all night as Scott got wasted? She watched from further down the street as he finished up a cigarette and tried to decide whether she should go inside after him or just call it a night. He obviously wasn't going anywhere near this mystery place Gardner was so sure about. But why go and buy a load of tins if you're on your way to the pub?

She kept her eyes on him in the rear-view mirror and as someone emerged from the pub, Scott flicked his cigarette onto the road. The two men did one of those weird handshakes that involved most of their body parts and then they spoke with their heads close together.

Freeman considered getting out of the car. It seemed like this might be a conversation she wanted to hear. But by the time she'd thought about it, the two men had stopped talking and the man from the pub slipped something into Scott's hand. She tried to see what it was but was too far away. Scott put it into his pocket and nodded at the other man before getting back in his car.

Drugs? she wondered. Is that what was going on here? But was Scott buying or selling? She waited for him to pass her and then pulled out, driving slowly to give him space to trip himself up.

Ten minutes later she was turning into an industrial estate in a part of town where she considered it wise to lock the car doors. She slowed down some more and let Scott get ahead. She could see him looking around, and wondered why he was only looking for a tail now.

She pulled out her phone and stopped at the side of the road. She noticed Scott looking in her direction and hoped he hadn't clocked her, that he thought she was lost or just taking a call.

He sped up a little and turned right. She knew that the road he'd gone down led to a park that contained small businesses that didn't need big showrooms or couldn't afford premises in any of the more central business parks. She also knew that Andrew Blake's office wasn't too far away. She felt her stomach knot again and wondered if she should call Gardner; maybe she was about to find something she couldn't deal with alone.

Thirty seconds after Scott had turned the corner, Freeman followed and saw him pull up outside a storage container. She got out of the car, knowing she could go no further in it without being seen. She crept along the edge of the fence until Scott had unlocked the door and gone inside.

Freeman moved quickly towards the container, listening for any sound of a struggle, any sign of life other than Scott. All she could hear was him moving around, his feet heavy on the metal floor.

She put her hand on the door, about to open it, when Scott emerged. She didn't know who was more shocked. Him, probably. His face paled and he glanced over his shoulder at what he'd been trying so hard to hide.

Chapter 44

Gardner left Andrew's house convinced that the man he'd just spoken to was not friends with Lee Johnston. The possibility of them working together, the ideas he and Freeman had been bouncing around, didn't make sense. But he had also come away with the feeling that Andrew Blake wasn't telling them the whole truth.

He got in his car and started the engine, trying to decide whether to call Freeman now and tell her that their theory was likely a bust, or to wait until morning. As he sat there, he noticed the little girl on her bike who'd been watching him a few days earlier. She was driving in circles at the end of the driveway, but her eyes never left his car. He wondered if this street was considered safe, if people let their kids out on their own because they knew their neighbours.

His eyes went past the girl to the window of her house. He noticed a woman sitting in the window, watching the kid play. He turned back to Andrew's house. If the kid's mother sat there often, watching her daughter play, maybe she'd seen things across the street that could be helpful.

Gardner turned off the engine and got out of the car, crossing the street. The little girl stopped moving and stared at him.

'Hello,' she said.

'Hi,' Gardner said and looked up and saw the girl's mother watching, getting up from her chair as she saw a strange man talking to the little girl. 'Is that your mum?' he said, pointing to the window and the girl nodded.

'Can I help?' the woman said, racing out the door, coming towards him, suspicion all over her face. She stopped behind the girl and put an arm across her, pulling her towards her legs.

Gardner showed the woman his ID. 'I just wanted to ask a few questions, if that's all right,' he said.

The woman seemed to relax a little and nodded. She took the girl's hand and led her inside. 'Go upstairs and play, Megan.' The girl made a groaning sound, the kind only kids can make when something is totally unfair, but she did as she was told and stomped up the stairs.

'It won't take long, Ms …'

'Wood,' the woman said. 'Kelly.'

She led him to the living room and they sat. Gardner noticed both seats were by the window, perfect for seeing what was going on.

'Is this about the girl from over there?' Kelly asked, nodding across the road.

'Yes. Do you know her?'

'No,' she said. 'I've seen her about. Never spoken to her though. Didn't even know her name until all this happened.' She stared across to Katy's house for a second before looking back to Gardner. 'I already spoke to someone,' she said. 'I didn't see anything. Wish I had. I mean, I wish I could've helped.'

'That's okay,' Gardner said.

'Is it this weirdo that's breaking into women's houses?' she asked. 'Because Kim next door said she'd seen someone hanging about. If it's him, I think you should tell us. I live alone, just me and Megan.'

'We don't know that what happened to Katy has anything to do with that, but I promise if I hear anything, you'll be the first to know.' She didn't seem very comforted by this and Gardner understood why. But he knew there was little he could say that would help. 'I wanted to ask you about something else.'

'Okay.'

'Do you know either Katy's boyfriend, Andrew, or the couple from the house next door?'

She shook her head. 'Not really. The boyfriend, I've just seen him about. Like Katy. Never spoke to him. The others. I don't know really. The bloke is a bit funny.'

'In what way?'

'I don't know. I just thought he always looked a bit creepy or something. Always looks like he's in a bad mood. The woman. She's all right. A copper, isn't she?'

'Yes.'

'She speaks sometimes. Not a lot. Sometimes Megan goes and talks to her. She likes the police,' she said, smiling.

'Have you ever seen them together? The two men, I mean.'

'Don't think so,' she said. 'Not that I can think of.'

Gardner sighed. He knew it was highly unlikely he'd come over and be told that Lee and Andrew were best buddies, but at least he'd tried, and if nothing else, he'd got something from his visit to Andrew, a possible witness if Lawton decided to press charges against Lee.

'I see him in the house sometimes though,' Kelly said.

Gardner shifted his attention back to her. 'Who?'

'The boyfriend. The missing girl's boyfriend.'

Gardner was confused. 'What do you mean? You see him at home? Doing what?' He wondered if Kelly had witnessed Andrew doing something to Katy, if he had been violent before.

'No,' she said. 'Next door. I've seen him there before.'

'He goes to their house?' Gardner said. 'What for?'

Kelly shrugged. 'I don't know.'

'Does someone let him in or do they just talk on the doorstep?'

'No, he goes inside. I don't think I've seen him actually at the door but I've definitely seen him inside the house. Upstairs sometimes.'

Gardner felt a jolt. 'With Lee? The man from next door?'

'I'm not sure,' she said. 'I'm pretty sure he's been there when the bloke's been out. At least his car hasn't been there.'

'So he was there with Lawton? The police officer?' Gardner said, feeling his stomach drop.

'Maybe. I just know I've definitely seen him in there. Quite a few times I'd say.'

Gardner thanked Kelly and she walked him to the door. Megan was sitting at the top of the stairs and waved again as he got to the door. But this time Gardner didn't wave back. He had other things on his mind.

Chapter 45

Andrew looked out the window and saw Gardner leaving the house across the street. Why would he be going there? Maybe he was looking for more dirt on Lee. He certainly had it in for him. He ducked behind the curtain as Gardner got to his car and waited until he heard the door slam before looking back. This was his chance. He got up and grabbed his car keys. He didn't know where Dawn was but it was likely Gardner would visit her soon enough and he needed to see her, find out exactly what she'd told the police.

At the end of the road, Andrew panicked, thinking Gardner had seen him, so he slowed down, putting a hundred yards between them. He felt ridiculous, like some spy in a film. But he needed to see Dawn and this was his best chance.

He followed Gardner across town, stopping at the supermarket first before moving on. Andrew wondered at the logic of his plan, if it was a waste of time. He couldn't follow him all the time. And if he got caught ...

Gardner pulled in to a small car park in front of a block of flats. Home, Andrew assumed, and wondered if he should come back in the morning, try and follow him again.

And then he saw her. Dawn was walking along the edge of the building, her skinny dog pulling her to sniff the edge of a flowerbed. Gardner waved as he got out of his car and they walked back into the building together. Andrew waited, watching the windows of the flats, hoping to catch a glimpse of them, finding out exactly where he could get to her. But after a few minutes it became obvious that he wasn't going to see them again. But it was a start.

He sat there and thought about all the times he'd been in the house next door, all the times he'd sat at the table, trying to understand what went on in there, why she was there. All the times he'd touched her things, the smell of her clothes. Maybe there would be no more times. Maybe it was over.

He looked up at the window and started his car, wondering what she'd be saying to Gardner, how much he should be worried. But now he knew where she was, approximately at least, he could see her, talk to her. Find out exactly what she'd said.

Chapter 46

Gardner opened the door and let Lawton and the dog in first. In the living room, she turned the TV off that'd been playing to itself. 'Don't turn it off on my account,' he said but she shook her head.

'I wasn't really watching it,' she said. 'Have you eaten? I made some pasta if you want some.' She stood up and went towards the kitchen and Gardner wondered if he should say something or let it go. Things were already difficult; did he really want to start accusing her of things that he knew, deep down, had to be untrue?

'You all right?' she asked and he nodded.

'I've just spoken to Andrew Blake again,' he said. 'I guess I'm just wound up.'

She went into the kitchen and started heating things up and finding plates and cutlery and for a second he felt like a normal person with a normal life and wondered if this was what he wanted, even if it wasn't with Lawton. Or maybe even if it was. It was almost nice. And then he had to go and spoil it.

'How well do you know Andrew Blake?' he asked and she put down the plate she was holding and looked at him.

'I don't,' she said. 'Why?'

'No reason,' he said but knew it was too late.

'No, there must be a reason why you asked.'

'It was just …' He scratched his cheek.

'Just what?'

'Nothing. It doesn't matter,' he said.

'If I knew him, I'd have told you.'

'I know.'

'So why are you asking me? It feels like you're accusing me of something,' she said and when he didn't respond she moved past him and headed for the bedroom.

'I'm not accusing you,' he said, but it was too late. The door was closed.

He looked at the pasta and decided he wasn't hungry anymore and turned the oven off. He went back into the living room and sat down, staring at the phone. He was already in a bad mood so he thought, why the hell not?

'Hello?'

Gardner could hear the TV playing in the background, some kids cartoon by the sound of it. He heard his brother bellow at someone to turn it down but the order went undone.

'Hang on,' David said. Gardner waited, listening to movement. He was leaving the TV behind, he guessed. 'Right. Go,' he said and Gardner resisted the urge to tell him he was an amazing douche bag.

'It's me,' Gardner said and his brother sighed.

'Yes, I know. Caller ID is a wonderful thing,' David said.

'How's Dad?'

David let out a long breath and Gardner couldn't decide if it meant he was annoyed at the question, that his own brother had the gall to call him twice in one week about their father, or that something was wrong with Norman and that David was at the end of his rope.

'Have you called him?' David said and Gardner assumed it was him David was pissed off with.

'Not today,' Gardner said.

'Well, don't you think you should try him first. He could tell you himself how he is.'

'Not if the last time I spoke to him is anything to go by. He was confused. Didn't know who he was talking to or what he was talking about.'

'Was he pissed?' David asked.

'Why would he be pissed?'

'Well, he was always partial to a few brandies.'

'At Christmas. He's not an alcoholic.'

'I'm not saying he is. I'm just saying he could've had a drink. That might be why he was off.'

Gardner shook his head. David could be an absolute twat at times. There was a knock at the door and Gardner sighed and told David to hang on. He expected it would be another pizza delivery for the wrong address, what would've been the third this month, but instead Molly stood there, bottle of wine in hand. He felt his stomach drop, and his first thought was, *Not now*. But he tried to arrange his face into something slightly more welcoming.

'Hi,' she said and then noticed the phone in his hand. He beckoned her inside and she kissed his cheek before going through. He followed her in, half-listening as David asked if he was still there, and half wondering what the hell he should say to Molly.

'Yeah, hang on,' he said and motioned for Molly to sit down and that he'd not be long. She smiled and went off into the kitchen, presumably to find glasses. Was she really okay with things? Or was she pouring herself a glass of wine in preparation for battle, like his ex-wife used to do?

'Hello?' David said, impatiently, and Gardner turned his back on Molly, trying to focus on one problem at a time. He rubbed his eyes, trying to remember what he'd been saying before Molly arrived.

'Oh right, you think he's a drunk,' he said, finally. 'So you think he was drinking when he had his fall too?'

'Look, if there was anything wrong with Dad we'd know about it. He was in the hospital. They would've noticed.'

'Yeah, because they have all day to sit with him and see what gibberish he's spouting. You're the one who's down there.'

'But I don't see him every day, do I?'

'And why don't you? He lives two minutes away.'

'Jesus,' David said. 'Are we really going to have this argument again? We can't go there every day. We have lives, kids. There's a home help who goes in. If there was a problem she'd have said something.'

'Really? You think some woman on minimum wage, who sees dozens of people in one shift, is really going to know or care if something's up? She won't be trained to see it.'

'And I am?'

'But you know him. You know what he's like. You should be able to see if something's wrong.'

'And I've told you there isn't anything wrong. It was an off day.'

277

'And what if there are more off days?'

'What do you want me to say?'

'I want to know that you give a shit and that you or your wife or even one of the bloody kids are making the effort to visit him and see he's all right.'

'Fuck you,' David said. 'If you're so concerned about him, then you come down here and sort him out yourself. You never come. But you're right about one thing. I *do* know him. And I know nothing's wrong. You speak to him once in a blue moon and suddenly you're the expert. You're such a self-important shit.'

Gardner listened to the dead air and realised David had hung up. He put the phone down and realised Molly was watching him. 'Hi,' she said again and handed him a glass of wine. 'Something wrong?' she asked.

'Just my brother. He's an arsehole,' he said and took a swig of wine, embarrassed that Molly had witnessed it all.

'I've been trying to call you,' Molly said. 'I was starting to wonder if I'd been dumped.' Gardner felt his stomach tighten. He put his glass down.

'I'm sorry,' he said. 'Things have been difficult at work. But that's not an excuse.'

'I'm willing to forgive you. On a number of conditions,' she said, grinning, and moved closer, pressing herself against him.

'Oh. Excuse me.'

Gardner stepped away from Molly and she turned around as Lawton came out of the bedroom. The two women looked at each other for a second and then Molly stuck out her hand. 'Hi, I'm Molly,' she said. Lawton shook it and smiled shakily.

278

'Dawn,' she said. 'I was just getting some water but I can get out of your hair if—'

'No, it's okay,' Gardner said and Molly looked at him, probably for an explanation about the strange woman living in his flat. 'Er, Molly, Dawn's a colleague. She's staying with me for a while.' Molly nodded but it wasn't much of an explanation. He looked at Lawton and wondered if he owed her one too or if it was obvious anyway.

'Nice to meet you,' Lawton said and went back into the bedroom as Molly turned back to him, eyebrows raised.

'So,' she said. 'Another woman.'

'It's not like that.'

Molly grinned again and took a gulp of wine. 'You didn't think to mention her earlier?'

'I didn't—' Gardner was flustered and couldn't tell whether Molly was actually pissed off or just pulling his leg. 'It's just … it's complicated,' he said. 'But not in that way. Look—'

The phone rang again and he wanted to ignore it but it kept ringing and ringing and when he saw it was David again he wondered if something was wrong. 'Hang on,' he said to Molly.

'I'm sorry,' David said as he picked up the phone and Gardner thought hell must've frozen over for his brother to apologise. But he wasn't going to argue or be a child about it. And not just because Molly was listening.

'I'm sorry too,' Gardner said. 'Look, I know it's difficult. And I know he can be a pain in the arse at the best of times. But something was wrong. Maybe just

279

speak to his GP, try and get him to do a house visit if Dad won't go.'

David sighed. 'He won't like it. He'll go berserk.'

'Maybe. But if it's for his own good, then so be it.' Gardner sat down again, feeling utterly exhausted. 'He might not think he needs help but maybe he does.' He waited for David to say something but he was clearly done. 'What about a home?' he said, hating the idea as soon as he said it. But what other choice was there?

'A home? An old folks' home?'

'He is seventy-eight. It's not like he's not eligible.'

'But can you imagine him in a home? He'd torture them. He'd probably get kicked out in a week.'

Gardner smiled at this. David was right. Norman Gardner would kick up such a fuss. He'd make mincemeat out of the carers.

'It's not ideal,' Gardner admitted. 'But if there is something wrong, dementia, whatever, then he needs care. You said yourself, you can't do it. I can't do it. Maybe speak to him about it.'

'Me?' David said. 'It's your idea. Asking the doctor to go round is one thing but there's no way on earth I'm telling Dad I'm shipping him off to a home.'

'It's just an option. And it might not be necessary. Speak to the GP first; maybe see if they can assess him. We'll take it from there.'

'And if they do nothing? Or find nothing? Then what?'

'Then we'll think of something else.'

'Or we could leave him alone.'

Gardner rubbed his eyes. David wasn't taking anything he'd said on board. He doubted he'd even make the call to the GP. 'He needs help, David.'

'If he needed help, he'd ask for it.'

'No, he won't,' Gardner said. 'Some people can't.'

'Well, that's up to him, isn't it? If you can't help yourself, why should anyone else bother.'

Gardner didn't know how to respond to that. He knew his brother was a tool but still. He had no interest in helping anyone, least of all their father.

'Look, I've got to go,' David said. 'Do what you want. But I'm not sticking my nose in until he asks me to.'

'Thanks a lot,' Gardner said and hung up. He turned to apologise to Molly but she was gone. He ran to the door but there was no sign of her in the corridor so he went down the stairs hoping to catch her even though he knew it was too late.

His phone started ringing again – Freeman this time. He almost answered but as he stood looking around the car park for Molly, he decided he was too tired. He was tired of all of it. If it was important, he'd know about it sooner or later.

Chapter 47

Andrew arrived at the flats early the next morning, parking beside a SUV that blocked the view of him for anyone coming into the car park. At 7.30 a.m. he saw Gardner leave but Dawn wasn't with him. He got out of the car and walked towards the entrance to the flats, hoping she would come out sooner rather than later to walk the dog.

By 8.15 a.m. all he'd got was a few funny looks as he loitered by the door. He wondered if he should go inside, take advantage of someone coming out and holding the door for him. But he decided that hanging around inside would look more suspicious and, besides, it was warm outside already. Just a gentle breeze to keep him cool.

Finally at 8.45 a.m. the door opened again and the dog wriggled out, pulling Dawn behind her. Andrew moved quickly.

'Dawn?' he said and she looked up, shocked to see him. She pulled the lead, trying to get the dog back inside but Andrew was faster. As Dawn got back into the building, he held onto the door. 'I just want to talk,' he said.

She pulled the dog down the corridor but Andrew followed her inside so she stopped, he assumed because she didn't want him knowing which flat she was staying in. But that didn't matter to him as long as he got what he wanted, and he could get that right there in the hallway.

'Please,' he said. 'I need to talk to you.'

'Leave me alone,' she said.

'I just want to talk. I need your help,' he said.

'With what?'

'Katy.'

He saw her soften slightly, weighing up her options. As far as he was concerned she didn't have any options. She was cornered. She could go to the flat but he'd just follow her.

'Why didn't you tell me you knew her?'

'Why would I?'

Andrew sighed. 'The police said you'd talked to her. That she used to come round.'

'Sometimes,' Dawn said.

'What did she say? Did she talk about me? About us?'

'No,' she said but he could tell she was lying. Why else would Katy go there?

'She saw you that day, before you had that big fight, didn't she?'

'Briefly.'

'Was that why you fought with him?'

'No.'

'Was Katy sleeping with Lee?'

Dawn looked shocked, hurt by this. If Katy was sleeping with Lee, Dawn didn't know. That wasn't the reason they argued.

'What do you want, Andrew?' she said.

'I want to know about Katy. About what she told you, what you've been telling the police.'

'Why?'

'I need to know,' he said, stepping closer, making her move back so she was even more penned in. 'What did you tell them about me?'

'I didn't tell them anything.'

'Don't lie to me. You've been telling them things. Lies.'

'I haven't lied about anything.'

'So she lied then. Katy told you things that weren't true.'

'Like what? Like the fact you don't let her see anyone.'

'That's not true.'

'Really? So why didn't she tell you about visiting me? Why would she panic if it got too late, if she thought you might come home and find her somewhere else?'

Andrew stepped forward again but the dog growled this time, a low rumbling sound. He didn't think it looked like a real threat, didn't look the kind to rip your legs to shreds, but its teeth were bared and he decided not to take the chance.

'That's not true, Dawn. I don't know why she'd tell you that. Maybe she was trying to get you to talk to her, about your situation. She was like that. She always wanted to know what was going on next door. She used to sit listening when you were arguing.' He put his hands out, palms open to the dog, trying not to be a threat. It stopped growling, showing a bit of interest in him. He crouched down, hands still out, and the dog tentatively moved towards him.

'That detective, the one you're staying with, he asked me yesterday if Katy was seeing Lee. He thinks something was going on between them, that that was why Lee hurt her.' He was stroking the dog now, had managed to soothe it. 'I just want to know the truth,' he said. 'I just want Katy back.' He looked up at Dawn now, eyes pleading. 'Please help me. Tell me what happened.'

'I don't know what happened,' she said. 'I wasn't there.'

'But what about the days you *were* there. What happened then? Did she see Lee? Did you get the feeling something was going on?'

'No.'

'Have the police asked you about that?'

'No.'

'What about me?' he asked. 'Did they ask you about me?' He stood up straight now, closer to her than before.

'They asked if I knew you. I said no.'

'What else?'

'Nothing.'

'They didn't ask about me and Katy? About the lies she told you. You didn't pass that on to the police?'

'I told them what I know, what Katy told me.'

'And what else did she tell you?'

'Nothing. She didn't say anything about you. She just wanted someone to talk to.'

'And what did you tell her? Did you encourage her to come round? To go behind my back? Is that why she was so concerned about you? You were best friends?'

'I barely know her.'

'Did you tell her to leave me?'

'She didn't leave. Something happened to her.'

'Why? Because of you?'

Dawn tried to walk away then but he stopped her, blocking her in. 'She went round there that day because of you. Something happened to her because of you,' he said, his face close to hers.

'It's not my fault,' she said, but her voice was feeble and he knew she didn't believe it. She blamed herself. She was weak and he could work with that. He could get her to say what he wanted to hear.

'If it wasn't for you, she'd be all right. If she'd just listened to me and done what I said.' He put his hand on her arm and she flinched. 'Just tell me what she told you. What you've told the police. Tell me everything and maybe we'll find her. She'll be at home. Safe.'

Dawn pushed his hand away. 'With you? She wasn't safe with you.'

'Just tell me what you know!' he said, slamming his hand against the wall beside her head. The dog lunged at him, baring its teeth and he jumped back.

Lawton shoved past him, not as pathetic as he'd assumed. 'I know who you are, Andrew. I should've seen it sooner. You're just the same as him.'

Andrew grabbed her arm. 'I'm nothing like him,' he said. She pulled away, grabbing her phone from her pocket. 'What're you doing?' he said but she already had the phone to her ear.

'Gardner,' she said. 'Andrew's here. He—'

Andrew didn't hear the rest. He walked quickly back down the corridor, punching the door release button, rushing out into the heavy air. Stupid bitch, he thought.

Chapter 48

Gardner was staring into space when Freeman spoke. 'You're alive then,' she said and Gardner turned to her. 'I tried calling you last night. Several times.'

'I know. I'm sorry,' he said. 'What was up?'

'I arrested Scott Hill last night,' she said and Gardner almost dropped his coffee. Freeman rolled her eyes and said, 'Don't get too excited. It had nothing to do with Katy.'

'So what was it? Did you find what he was hiding?'

'Yep. An awful lot of mobile phones,' she said and Gardner felt his heart sink.

'Phones?'

'I've since discovered that the very shop Scott and Lee work at was robbed a couple of weeks ago. I spoke to their boss who didn't seem very surprised Scott had been arrested. If you ask me, he knew all along who did it but was too scared to say anything. He's still not talking now. But at least we've solved the mystery of where Dumb and Dumber were going to all those times.'

'Has Lee been arrested too?'

'No,' she said. 'Scott's refusing to tell us anything. Denying anyone else was involved. But I guess we can cross them off our list of suspects now.'

'Why?'

'Because we know all their sneaking around and suspicious behaviour was about a load of stolen phones, not Katy,' she said.

'Not necessarily,' Gardner said. 'Just because Lee's guilty of this, doesn't mean he hasn't done anything else.'

'Come on,' Freeman said and shook her head, 'you're grasping.'

'What if Katy found out about the robbery? What if she overheard something she shouldn't have? Maybe *that's* Lee's motive.'

Freeman sighed again. 'I guess it's possible,' she said but he could tell she didn't believe it.

'So you still think Andrew is our guy?'

'I do,' she said and shrugged. 'But Harrington spoke to Dominic Archer again last night. I'm starting to wonder if you're right about him. He has no alibi for the two attacks in the women's homes. The first one, he was at work that day but the attack didn't happen until five-thirty p.m., which left him plenty of time to get there. Second was on a Sunday but Dominic says he can't even remember where he was. The third is where we fall down though. He was at work at the time and we've got half a dozen people verifying it.'

'So what makes you think it could be him?'

'Well, the third incident was different anyway. Slightly different MO. Berman showed the victim a picture of Dominic Archer and she's sure it wasn't him. So, it's possible we're barking up the wrong tree. But it's also possible that the third attempt wasn't the same guy at all. Which means we're still looking at Dominic.'

Gardner processed what he'd been told. True, it looked more likely that Andrew Blake or Dominic Archer was responsible for Katy now, but he still wasn't willing to discount Lee altogether. His other crime might account for some of his movements and his lies, but there were still too many questions unanswered.

'Did you have any luck with Andrew last night?' Freeman asked as she made herself some coffee.

Gardner shook his head. He knew he should've called her the night before and told her it was a bust but after speaking to Kelly Wood and then his clumsy attempt at speaking to Lawton, he wanted time to think about things. It was more than likely Kelly was mistaken, or that if Andrew *had* been there it had been with Lee instead. But it made him uncomfortable nonetheless. He'd rather just ignore it but knew that wasn't an option. Knew he'd have to tell Freeman, even if it meant nothing.

'What?' he asked, when he caught Freeman watching him.

'I don't know. You look … weird. What's going on?'

'Nothing,' he said, but she didn't look convinced.

'Did Andrew say something last night?'

'No,' Gardner said. 'Same old rubbish. Denies knowing Lee. But …'

'But what?'

'I decided to go and talk to the neighbour opposite them. Kelly Wood. See if she'd seen Lee and Andrew together at all.'

'And?'

'She claims to have seen Andrew in Lee's house. On more than one occasion.'

'*In* the house?' Freeman said.

'Yep.'

'Lying little shits.'

Gardner let out a breath. 'Thing is, she claims, or thinks, that Lee wasn't there at the time.'

Freeman frowned. 'Meaning?'

Gardner raised his eyebrows.

'Lawton? She thinks he was there with Lawton?'

Gardner shrugged.

'Have you asked her?'

'Not directly.'

'Don't you think maybe you should?'

Gardner said nothing.

'If you don't, I will,' Freeman said.

Gardner's phone started ringing and he felt relieved. He knew Freeman was right but he didn't want to make himself even more of the bad guy than he already felt. He picked up the phone. 'Hello?'

'Gardner,' Lawton said. 'Andrew's here.'

Chapter 49

Gardner realised he was driving recklessly as Freeman put out her hand to steady herself on the dashboard. Lawton said Andrew had fled once he realised she was calling him but he wasn't taking any chances. Andrew could've still been there, waiting, and he wasn't going to let anything happen to Lawton again. Freeman had insisted on coming too but he wasn't sure whether it was to try and catch Andrew in the act so she could arrest him, or if it was to prevent *him* from doing something to Andrew, something he might later regret.

He pulled up right outside the flats instead of the car park and strode up to the door, not waiting for Freeman to catch up. In the end she managed to just get to the door in time before it closed.

'Lawton?' he called out as soon as he opened the front door. She appeared in the doorway to the living room, the dog at her heels. 'You all right?'

She nodded. 'I'm fine. It was more to make him go away than anything else. I don't know if he would've done anything. He was just wound up.'

'How did he find you?' Freeman asked and Lawton shrugged. Freeman looked over to Gardner, he could see what she was thinking – had Lawton invited Andrew there? – but he refused to believe it.

'Did he hurt you?' Gardner said.

'No. He grabbed my arm—'

'He assaulted you?' Gardner said and Lawton rolled her eyes.

'What did he want?' Freeman asked and indicated for them all to sit down. But Gardner didn't want to sit so he paced while the others sat.

'He was asking what Katy had told me, what I'd told you,' Lawton said. 'He seemed concerned about what I knew.'

'About him?'

'I guess. About their relationship. About what happened to her.'

'He thinks you know what happened?' Gardner asked, looking from Lawton to Freeman.

'Do you reckon he's thinking you know *he* did something to her or just that you know who else, meaning Lee, did something?' Freeman said.

'I don't know,' Lawton said. 'He kept saying he needed to know what'd happened. He tried to blame me for it. But he was mostly bothered by what I knew, or according to him, what I thought I knew.'

'So is he covering his tracks or actually trying to find out what happened to her?' Freeman said, sighing.

'He's trying to cover something,' Lawton said. 'I just don't know if it's killing Katy or just his behaviour leading up to her disappearing.' She turned to Gardner

293

now. 'Did you tell him you thought Katy was having an affair with Lee?'

Freeman looked surprised at this.

'I asked him if he thought it was possible, trying to get a reaction. Trying to see how well he knows Lee really,' Gardner said.

'But do you actually think it's a possibility?' Lawton asked.

'I've got no idea. Do you?'

Lawton let out a long breath. 'I... I doubt it.' She looked away. 'Anyway, I'm not sure I could see Katy going for him, or anyone else. She was too ... cowed by Andrew. I don't think she'd try anything like that.'

'So does Andrew believe it?' Freeman said. 'Or was he just trying to get to you? Trying to get you to spill whatever you know about Lee.'

'I don't know,' Lawton said.

'Dawn, one of your neighbours told Gardner something yesterday,' Freeman started and Gardner tried to intervene but she held up her hand. Lawton looked up at him, questioning. 'She told him that she'd seen Andrew in your house. On several occasions.'

'What?' Lawton said. 'When?'

'I don't know. But a few times.'

'With Lee?'

Freeman looked to Gardner. 'No,' he said and sat down across from Lawton. 'She said she thought Lee was out at the time. She insinuated that ...'

'That what? That he was with me?' Lawton said, shaking her head. 'And you believe her?'

'I don't—'

'So you think what? That me and *him* are having an affair now?'

'No.'

'How could you think that?' Lawton said.

'We don't think anything,' Freeman said. 'We're just telling you what she said. And maybe she's wrong. Maybe Lee *was* there. But ...'

'But what?' Lawton said.

'Why was Andrew so desperate to see you? Why did he come here?'

Gardner watched the tears form in Lawton's eyes. He knew he shouldn't have told Freeman. It was bullshit. Plain and simple. 'It doesn't matter,' he said.

'Of course it matters,' Lawton said. 'You think I'm keeping things from you. You think I'm lying and that I know what's happened.'

'No,' he said.

'You know we had to ask you,' Freeman said. 'We have to take everything seriously, consider everything.'

Lawton nodded but Gardner could see she wasn't appeased. 'We just want to know why he came here,' he said.

'And I've told you. He wanted to know what I'd said to you. Other than that, I don't know.'

'Okay,' Gardner said and turned to Freeman. 'Either way, I want to speak to him again. Even if he's got nothing to do with Katy, he's going to answer for this. He's got no right coming over here.'

'I'll speak to him,' Freeman said.

'No, it's fine.'

'Is it? Are you going to talk to him the same way you talked to Lee?'

Gardner wanted to tell her to back off but she was right. If he spoke to Andrew right now it was highly likely he'd end up throwing him into a wall too. 'Fine,' he said. 'I'll stay here with Lawton.'

'I don't want to stay here,' she said quietly and they both turned to her. 'I don't feel safe with him knowing where I am. And if he does know Lee like you say, he could've told him where I am too. I'm going back to the B&B.'

'You'll be safe here,' Gardner said, not wanting to have failed her again. 'I'll stay here all day myself if I have to.'

'No,' she said. 'I want to go.'

'But—' he started but Freeman interrupted.

'You can stay at my place,' she said and Gardner wasn't sure whether he or Lawton looked more surprised. In fact Freeman looked a little surprised herself as if the words had fallen out of her mouth without her knowledge.

'I can't do that,' Lawton said.

'Yes, you can.'

'She'll be by herself there too,' Gardner said.

'No, she won't. Darren's there. He barely leaves the house.' She turned to Lawton. 'He's my brother. He's irritating but harmless.'

I wouldn't say that, Gardner thought, but didn't want to voice his opinion out loud.

'Just come over, see what you think. If you can't bear listening to Darren's drivel all day, we'll find you somewhere else. Who knows, maybe his endless wittering will take your mind off things,' Freeman said.

Lawton glanced at Gardner before letting out a sigh and nodding. 'Okay. Thanks,' she said. 'I'll go and get my stuff.' She clicked her tongue and the dog followed her to her room.

Once she was out of earshot Gardner spoke. 'You really think leaving her with Darren is a good idea?'

'They'll be fine. He'll either ignore her and focus on daytime TV or else he'll gibber on about nothing all day. She might get annoyed with him but she won't be in danger.'

Gardner blew out his cheeks. Leaving Lawton in the care of Darren Freeman. Hadn't she been through enough?

Chapter 50

Lawton followed Freeman up the stairs to her flat and wondered if she was doing the right thing. She didn't particularly want to stay with her but it was a kind offer and – unless she went back to the B&B, which, despite Hazel's kindness, was still depressing – she had little choice. But she was nervous about how it would work. She and Freeman barely spoke unless it was work-related and even then they usually found a way around it.

They walked in and Lawton could hear a TV playing loudly and Freeman muttered something before storming off towards the noise. Lawton kept a tight hold of Cotton's lead, hoping she wouldn't get scared again finding herself in a new place and be unable to control her bowels. She'd already done it in Gardner's kitchen but fortunately it was tiled flooring, easy to clean, and so he was none the wiser.

The deafening sound of the TV stopped and Lawton heard a man's voice. 'I was watching that.'

She assumed it was Darren, Freeman's brother. She'd never actually met him before but she knew enough about him to be wary. She wasn't particularly looking forward to staying with him. Wasn't sure why Freeman or Gardner would think he was the best person to leave her with, unless, of course, they were thinking he would act as bodyguard in case Andrew or Lee showed up. Or maybe they just wanted to keep an eye on her for other reasons.

'What're you doing here anyway?' Darren asked and Freeman nodded to the doorway as Lawton walked in.

'This is Dawn. She's going to stay here for a while,' Freeman said.

He turned and looked at her and said, 'Oh.'

Lawton wasn't sure what she'd been expecting from Darren Freeman but it wasn't the man in front of her. Darren was short, maybe her height, and skinnier than her or Freeman. She knew he was about thirty but he looked and sounded ten years younger.

'Is that your dog?' Darren asked.

'Yes. Cotton,' Lawton said and Darren came around the settee to stroke her. 'She's a bit nervous of new people.'

Darren nodded but bent down and stroked Cotton's neck. She didn't seem to mind.

'How come she can bring a dog but I'm not allowed one,' he said to Freeman.

'Shut up,' Freeman replied and walked over to them. 'I'll show you where you can sleep. I'll have to change the sheets.'

Lawton followed Freeman and as they got to the door of the bedroom she heard Darren shout, 'My room?'

'It's not your room,' Freeman said. 'They're both my rooms. And anyway, you spend all day on the settee. You can spend the night there too.'

299

They went into the room, leaving Darren muttering to himself. 'I can sleep on the couch,' Lawton said. 'I don't want to take his bed.'

'Don't worry about it. If he thinks he always has dibs on the bed, he might never leave.'

Lawton watched as Freeman stripped the bed of the sheets and she caught a whiff of something stale. Freeman clearly smelt it too and walked to the window, pushing it wide open. Lawton could hear seagulls circling outside. 'I'll do the bed but I'd maybe wait a while before you settle in here,' Freeman said. 'Give it chance to breathe.'

'Thanks.'

Freeman left the room and Lawton put down her bag. She needed some clean clothes. She thought about asking to use the washing machine but decided not to intrude any further. She stood looking out of the window, which overlooked the High Street. It wasn't very busy; there wasn't much noise. She turned as she heard Freeman come back in, a pile of clean sheets in her arms. Freeman started making up the bed.

'I can do it,' she said. 'If you need to get back.'

Freeman put the sheets down and nodded. 'Okay, if you're sure.' She looked around as if she was trying to think of something else to say, as if the situation wasn't awkward. 'There's plenty of food in the fridge and cupboards so just help yourself. That is if Darren hasn't already finished it all off. Bathroom's just over there,' she said, pointing out the door, across the hall. 'If you need to go out, take Darren's key. I'll get another cut for you tonight.' She kept looking around as if she needed to explain it all.

'Thank you,' Lawton said, trying to help her out. 'You didn't have to do this. But I appreciate it.'

'No problem.'

Freeman led them back to the living room where Cotton had taken up a place on the settee beside Darren. He was feeding her Wotsits and she was greedily wolfing them down. 'I think she likes them,' Darren said, his face gleeful.

Freeman looked at Lawton apologetically. 'If he annoys you, you have my permission to punch him,' she said and then looked horrified.

Lawton just smiled gently. She knew she'd be doing this for the rest of her life now. Watching people realise what they've said, walking on eggshells around her.

'Okay. I'll leave you to it,' Freeman said. 'Darren? Don't be annoying.'

Lawton watched Freeman leave and turned back to Darren. 'She can be a bit of a fascist,' he said and fed another crisp to the dog.

She'd been at Freeman's barely an hour before Darren started asking questions. When Freeman had left, Darren had offered to make some lunch, and, even though it was only mid-morning, she accepted the offer. She wasn't quite sure what to do with the bacon and egg bun he served up, unable to fit it into her mouth. But eventually she managed and she had to admit it was delicious. Cotton stood in front of her, dribbling onto her socks.

'Thanks,' she said to Darren when she was done and he just nodded. He didn't need telling how tasty it was.

They sat there watching TV in companionable silence, Cotton sitting between them on the settee. Until finally Darren broke. 'You're a copper, right?' he asked and she nodded. 'So why don't you just, like, arrest him? Or just kick his arse?'

Lawton was going to ask who, but she knew who he was talking about, knew Freeman must've told her brother all about her. She felt anger stirring in her guts.

'Because they train you, right? So couldn't you just, like ...' He mimed some kind of kung fu and Lawton found herself staring at him, wondering if he was a bit simple. She stood up.

'I think I might go for a walk,' she said and Cotton jumped up at the word walk.

Darren stood up too. 'I'll come with you,' he said.

'No, it's okay.'

'No,' he said and pulled on a pair of shoes. 'I'm in charge of looking after you.'

Chapter 51

Freeman wanted to bring Andrew in again because of his visit to Lawton but Atherton had put his foot down. Lawton didn't want to press any charges, said there wasn't any reason to. He'd been persistent but hadn't hurt her and she just wanted to be left alone. Part of Freeman couldn't help wonder if there was more to it, if the neighbour had been right about seeing Andrew in the house with Lawton. But maybe it was nothing. Lawton didn't want to go ahead and see Lee punished for what he'd done, so why would she put a complaint in about Andrew when he'd done far less?

But now none of that mattered, she had something else. She could prove Andrew had lied again. She waited for Andrew to settle in before she spoke, letting Harrington make small talk before the official caution. Once Andrew looked suitably tense Freeman started.

'Why did you go there, Andrew? Why did you go and harass Dawn Lawton?' she said and watched Andrew bow his head, unable to make eye contact.

'I just wanted to talk to her,' he said.

'Why? How did you even know where she was?'

Andrew just sat there, silent, so Freeman slapped her palm down in front of him, making him jump.

'How did you know where Dawn Lawton was?' she asked again.

'I followed him.'

'Who?'

'Detective Gardner.'

'Jesus,' she said. 'Why? What was so important about talking to her?'

Finally he looked up. 'I need to find Katy. I thought she might know something. She's friends with her, isn't she? I thought she might be able to tell me something helpful.'

'And you don't think she would have already told us anything useful she had to say?'

'I don't know,' he said. 'I just need to know what happened.'

'Tell me again why you went home that day,' she asked.

Andrew closed his eyes and let out a frustrated breath. 'I already told you,' he said. 'That has nothing to do with this.'

'Tell me again why you went home that day,' Freeman said, more slowly this time.

'I'd forgotten my lunch. I went home to get it.'

'That's it?'

'Yes.'

'You didn't go out for any other reason?'

'No,' he said. 'Well, I suppose I was checking on Katy, to see if she was okay. But if I hadn't forgotten my lunch I probably wouldn't have gone.'

'And you didn't go anywhere else?'

Andrew paused, maybe trying to decide if it was a trick question, trying to work out what she knew. 'I went next door. I knocked to see if Katy was there. There was no answer so I left and went back to work.'

Freeman nodded. 'And you went straight back to work?'

'Yes.'

'What about on the way home? Did you go anywhere then?'

Andrew paused again, his eyes firmly on hers now. He knew she knew. It was just a question of whether he'd deny the reason he went there. 'I stopped at the shops on the way,' he said.

'Okay,' Freeman said. 'What for?'

'I needed some bits and pieces. I was passing and thought while I was out I might as well go.'

'What did you need?'

He shrugged. 'I don't know, just stuff. I don't really remember.'

'Well, it has been three days. You need me to refresh your memory?' She could see the anger behind his eyes now, knew she was getting to him. 'You went to B&Q on Tuesday just after twelve and you bought a wireless CCTV system. You bought it with cash you'd withdrawn the day before.' She held his gaze. 'Why?'

'Why what?'

'Why did you buy a CCTV system? What was it for?' Andrew was silent. 'Was it to keep an eye on her?'

'No.'

'No? It wasn't because she'd dared to leave the house without your permission? Because she didn't answer your call immediately like a good little girl?'

'No.'

'You didn't get so wound up about the fact she wasn't where she was supposed to be that you had to rush out and buy a security system for your home that you could monitor from work? Just to make sure she wasn't doing anything you didn't approve of.'

'This is stupid,' he said. 'It had nothing to do with that. It was for her safety.'

'Safety? What were you keeping her safe from in the house?' Andrew's face was red now, his jaw clamped together. 'Why would she be unsafe in your house? Who did she need protecting from?'

'I don't know. Him, maybe. Lee Johnston.'

Freeman shook her head. 'No. I think the only person who posed any danger to Katy was you.' She thought about what she'd been told earlier. 'Tell me again what happened when you got home on Tuesday after work.'

'I came in. I looked for Katy. She wasn't there. I went next door and knocked. There was no answer. I came back, waited. I was worried so I went round the back.'

'Why?'

'I don't know. I thought maybe they could be round there. I went to the door and knocked. It was ajar. I pushed it open and shouted. There was no answer. I noticed the mess and then the blood. I went in, shouted for Katy. There was no answer. Then I saw her phone.'

'And then?'

'I came outside and called the police.'

'You didn't look round the house for her?'

'No. I saw the mess and called the police.'

'And you didn't go back inside after you called?'

'No.'

'Why not? If you thought something had happened to Katy, why not check the house? What if she was upstairs, hurt?'

'I don't know. I panicked. I just knew I had to call the police.'

Freeman stared at him and he had to look away. 'I want you to think really hard,' she said. 'Because I know you've had trouble remembering things before. Did you go anywhere else in the house, other than the kitchen?'

'No.'

'Have you ever been in the house before?'

'No,' he said.

'Are you sure? Have a good think, Andrew.'

'I've never been in there. Why would I?'

'You tell me.'

'This is ridiculous.'

'So you'd never been in the house before that day. And you never left the kitchen. Is that what you're telling me?'

'Yes.'

'So why were your fingerprints found upstairs. In the bedroom, the bathroom, on the banister? How do you explain that?'

Andrew looked flustered. 'I don't know. It must be a mistake.'

'I don't think so,' Freeman said. 'So either you're lying about where you went that day. Or you're lying about visiting the house previously. So which is it?'

'Neither,' Andrew said. 'I've never been in there before. And that day I only went in the kitchen.' He stopped and looked down, his eyes flickering side to side. 'I'm sure I didn't go upstairs that day. I don't remember …' Freeman rolled her eyes. 'Maybe I did,' Andrew said. 'Maybe I forgot somehow.'

'You're good at that,' she said and watched as Andrew's brain whirred, trying to think his way out of his lie. 'Have you been in the house with Lee Johnston?'

'No.'

'Have you been in the house with Dawn Lawton?'

'No.'

'So how are your prints in the house? Upstairs?'

'I don't know,' he said, his voice shaking. 'I must've gone up that day. I must've forgotten. I'm sorry.'

*

Andrew left the station, not looking back, knowing Freeman would be watching him. He could practically feel her eyes burning into his back. Why wouldn't she leave him alone? She had nothing on him. He knew that. Why else would they have let him go? If they had something they'd have kept him there but instead he was free to go.

He knew he'd made mistakes and was angry with himself for that. He knew he should've said he'd gone upstairs that first day. How hadn't he realised they'd find out? It was such a stupid thing and didn't even help. It just made things worse for him. If he'd said he'd gone upstairs looking for her it would've been understandable. It would've been fine. But now they were thinking about

308

other possibilities. Like had he been in the house before. He didn't want them to know that. How would he explain that one?

As he walked to his car, his fists clenched and unclenched.

Stupid, stupid, stupid, he thought to himself, slamming the car door behind him. He'd probably ruined things now. He'd never be able to go back there. He'd never lie on that bed, never breathe in her smell. Never run his fingers across the wall, in and out of all the delves, the chunks of plaster that'd come off as she hit the wall.

Andrew slammed his palm into the steering wheel, ignoring the looks from passers-by. It was ruined now. Everything was ruined.

Chapter 52

Lawton threw the ball across the sand and Cotton launched herself after it, picking it up and running around in circles. At least she was enjoying herself.

Darren walked beside her, glancing at her every now and then, but not saying a word. She could be thankful for that at least. She knew he hadn't meant any harm with what he'd said and part of her could understand his questions. There'd been a time when she'd asked herself the same thing, sort of. Why *didn't* she just get him arrested?

The truth was it wasn't that easy. She'd seen plenty of women come in, their husbands or boyfriends charged and then let go and nothing changed. Mostly it just made it worse. They say the most dangerous day of an abused woman's life is often the day she leaves. It hadn't proved that way for her so far but maybe that was because she hadn't really left and Lee knew it.

But maybe it would've been different for her, being on the inside. She'd seen how her colleagues had reacted, how they'd rallied. But would they really have been able to do anything differently? They could've charged Lee for battery but it was unlikely he'd be held very long. And what would he do then?

She looked out to sea. The water was flat, shimmering in the sun. Cotton ran to her feet and dropped the ball, looking up expectantly. This time Darren chucked it for her and she ran off, tail wagging.

'I'm sorry I said that stuff,' Darren said.

'It's all right,' she said.

They stood silently again, waiting for Cotton to return but she'd found something to sniff and had forgotten all about them.

'Can I ask you something else?' he said. 'You don't have to answer.'

'Okay,' she said.

'Why don't you just leave him?'

Lawton sighed. The million dollar question again. If only she had the answer. 'I don't know,' she said. 'I love him.'

'Why?' Darren asked, his face distorted in confusion.

'I don't know,' she said. 'We've been together a long time. Sometimes we have fun.' She felt tired all of a sudden and sat down on the warm sand. Darren followed, his eyes never leaving her, waiting for an answer. She was silent until Cotton came racing back, standing in front of them, wanting to know why they'd stopped playing.

'Sometimes he hits her,' she said, her hand on Cotton's back. 'He uses her to make me stay sometimes. Says he'll hurt her or kill her.' She turned to Darren. 'That sounds stupid.'

'No, it doesn't. I wouldn't leave her there with him.'

311

Lawton tried to smile at him but the lump in her throat stopped it.

'To be honest, he sounds like a dick,' Darren said. 'If you want, I could beat him up for you.'

This time she did smile. And the smile broke into laughter. The idea of Darren Freeman, eight-stone weakling, beating up Lee made her laugh. And she couldn't stop. At first Darren looked hurt that she was mocking his offer but he softened and seemed pleased he'd made her laugh.

They sat there a little longer until a black cloud appeared over the sea, blowing in towards the beach. 'We should head back,' she said and stood up, brushing the sand from her jeans.

As they walked back, Darren tried more conversation. Asking how long she'd been a cop, if she liked it, why she did it. It felt good not to talk about Lee.

'Don't you want to be a detective, like Nicky? I mean, no offence, but that seems cooler than being, like, a normal copper.'

Lawton shrugged, the black cloud hovering overhead. 'I've thought about it,' she said. 'But Lee doesn't want me to do it. Thinks I spend too much time at work as it is.'

'So?' Darren said. 'Fuck him.'

'He wants us to have kids,' she said, immediately unsure why she'd told him.

'Do you want to have kids?'

She shrugged. 'I don't know,' she said. But she did know. She knew that no matter how long she stayed with him, no matter how much she loved him, she would never have kids with him. That was the only certainty in their relationship. Except he didn't know it.

He forbid her to use contraception, refused to use condoms. In the end, after an accident, she'd gone to the doctor. If he knew, he hadn't mentioned it yet.

As they walked back up the steps from the beach she tried not to think about the day she found out she was pregnant, the days leading up to it. How ashamed she felt. She knew he was seeing someone else, but wasn't sure if it was one person or several; it was never mentioned. But he kept digging at her, accusing *her* of cheating. By now he'd moved on from Dave. Now Gardner was on the scene. She denied it over and over but he insisted he knew, knew she was a slut. Sleeping around. And then he got his proof.

The symptoms were hard to ignore but he kept quiet, waited for her to break. In the end she'd gone to the doctor who confirmed she had an STD, needed treatment, and needed to inform her partner so he could be treated too. It was bad enough having to go there, feeling ashamed and judged. But knowing she had to go home and tell him was worse. She knew it was him, knew he'd done this, that he was waiting for her to come clean. To come forward and admit what a slut she was. She could see him revelling in it. She hated him, planned on leaving. But she didn't.

But she also didn't tell him the other news she'd got that day. Didn't tell him about the appointment to get rid of it. He didn't get to control everything. He had his secrets and she had her own.

Chapter 53

Lee stood by the window, trying not to be seen. He saw Andrew's car outside the house so he guessed he was home, guessed he didn't have anywhere to be so early on a Saturday morning. Technically Lee should've been at work, not that that usually bothered him, but the way things were at the moment, he doubted he still had a job.

He looked up and down the street and wondered if the police would be bothering him again, if he should just leave it. That other copper, the bird, had been around again the day before, asking him more questions. He'd wondered at first if she was there about the phones. He'd heard Scott had been arrested, had been stupid enough to lead her straight to them. He was pissed off that that gravy train had left the station, but at least Scott seemed to be keeping his mouth shut. He had to give him that. That'd be all he needed right now along with everything else.

But as it turned out she was just asking if he was mates with Andrew Blake. He had to laugh at that. Andrew was a tosser. He'd been telling tales to the police, telling them what he apparently heard on Sunday night, making it seem like something it wasn't. Maybe that's why he was doing this, maybe that's why he was getting involved. It might've hurt him a little bit, but it was going to hurt Andrew Blake more. Dawn too. He was looking forward to seeing what happened when the shit hit the fan. Besides, he was getting a bit sick of it all now. He just wanted things to get back to normal. And the sooner this was over, the sooner Dawn would come back.

Lee didn't even bother to put his shoes on, and the warm tarmac felt good against his feet. He looked over his shoulder before going next door. When Andrew answered the door he looked nervous and didn't invite him so Lee barged his way in.

'What're you doing?' Andrew said, following him into the living room. 'You need to leave.'

Lee sat himself down on the settee, his eyes settling on the bottle of beer on the table. It looked like it had just been put there. Andrew was starting early. Not much had been consumed yet, the heat of the air yet to cause the condensation to run.

'Get us a drink?' Lee said, making himself at home.

'Leave,' Andrew said again, his voice firmer this time. Lee almost believed he had some balls. Almost. 'What do you want?'

'I had that copper round yesterday,' Lee said. 'She wanted to know if we were mates.'

'I know,' Andrew said, his voice tight. 'I saw her.'

'I'm getting pretty sick of them hanging around,' Lee said and stood up, moving right in front of Andrew. He could see him sweating.

'It's not my fault,' Andrew said, but his voice was weak. Lee stepped back and shoved his hand in his pocket. He could see Andrew was curious and Lee

315

wondered if he should just go home. Let Andrew stew a bit.

'You should go. It won't do either of us any good if someone sees you here,' Andrew said.

Lee pulled his hand from his pocket. 'Fair enough,' he said. 'But I've got something you might want.'

Chapter 54

As they drove towards Lawton's house, Gardner asked, 'So how is it over there?' The night before, his place felt empty without her even though she'd only been there a couple of days. But at least he could get a seat on his own settee without the dog kicking him or grumbling about his presence. He'd wondered if he should call Molly and apologise but he knew he still wouldn't be good company, would risk only making things worse.

He'd wanted to call Lawton though, check she was all right, but he felt like he was intruding. And maybe he was being paranoid but it felt like she was drifting away from him.

'It's okay,' Lawton said, leaning against the window, her eyes on the passing world instead of him.

'Darren's not driving you mad?'

Lawton gave a little smile and finally turned, briefly looking at him before going back to the road. 'He's all right,' she said. 'Cotton seems to like him.'

Gardner had noticed that she'd left the dog behind. 'Well, dogs like children, don't they?' he said, feeling petty and childish himself as soon as the words came out. He pulled up outside the house and was relieved to see a space where Lee's car had been. Maybe he'd finally deigned to go to work. Or maybe he had better things to do. Gardner still wasn't convinced that Lee had had nothing to do with Katy's disappearance; he just couldn't prove it. Yet.

He wondered if it was too late, if Lee had killed Katy already, with intent or by accident, and had hidden the body. Despite the small amount of blood in the kitchen, he wasn't convinced that she was still out there. Why else would Lee hide her? What purpose would it serve to take her somewhere and hold her hostage? And of course, just because there was a lack of blood didn't mean she hadn't been killed in the house.

'I'll just be a minute,' Lawton said. She got out of the car, leaving him sitting there until he considered that Lee could be in there, waiting. Gardner climbed out of the car and caught up with her. She looked like she wanted to argue but kept quiet and unlocked the door.

The house was quiet, just the faint hum from the fridge coming from the kitchen. On the sideboard by the door was a small pile of letters. Lawton picked them up and flicked through, keeping hold of them while she started up the stairs.

'I'll just grab my stuff. Take a seat. I won't be long,' she said and disappeared upstairs.

Gardner watched her go and then walked through to the living room. He noticed a crack in the plaster, a few chips in the paintwork, and wondered if they were usual wear and tear or if they'd been caused by Lee throwing something. By Lawton hitting the wall.

He turned away and looked out the window. The street wasn't very wide, the houses opposite not too far away. Kelly Wood could easily see into the house opposite her, easily enough to see Andrew Blake in there. And yet ... no one helped. No one knew. He couldn't help but wonder how close someone would need to be to notice something was wrong. To feel that they had to help. He wondered if any of those people across the street had seen anything, heard anything. If they'd thought it was none of their business either.

Gardner listened to the sound of Lawton moving about upstairs, opening drawers and cupboards. He hadn't wanted her to come back, mostly in case Lee was here, but also in case the lure of home was too much. That she'd decide that her own bed was better than his or Freeman's, that she'd take her chances and come back. But, he supposed, the fact she'd decided to come and collect some clean clothes, toiletries, mail, meant that she was planning on staying away a while longer. That could only be a good thing.

He walked back to the bottom of the stairs and listened, moving only when he saw her legs between the banister. Not wanting her to think he was getting impatient or keeping tabs, he walked through to the kitchen and took a look around.

There was still traces of dust where they'd checked for fingerprints and the bloodstain on the floor was still visible. Obviously Lee wasn't big on cleaning. Gardner walked to the back door, thinking about Lee's claim that Katy could've used the spare key. He thought it was bollocks. Lawton claimed they'd gotten rid of the spare key ages ago. And how would Katy know where to find it anyway? He turned to go back to the living room to wait but something stopped him. He tried the back door but it was locked.

He went up the stairs to see how Lawton was getting on, walked along the hallway and found her sitting on the edge of the bed, reading a letter. He cleared his throat and she jumped, folding the letter and standing up.

'How's it going?' he asked and she gathered her things, sliding her mail into her bag.

'Fine,' she said. 'I'll just get some things from the bathroom.'

Lawton disappeared and Gardner walked to the window, which overlooked the garden. He leaned forward, looking across to Andrew's garden. He had a good view from there. And he wondered ... he looked at the pot that Lee had claimed the key was beneath and then looked for the same spot in Andrew's garden. He could see it just as well. So Katy must've been able to see into Lawton's garden too. What if she *did* know where the key was kept but only because she'd seen Lee hiding it before?

For a moment he wondered if Katy had let herself in that day. But the fact her phone was left, along with some blood, made it seem unlikely she was alone in the house. Even if she did let herself in, something had happened to her in there. Maybe that was the reason *why* something had happened, if Lee found her sneaking around maybe he lashed out.

'I might go away for a few days,' Lawton said, startling him.

'Where to?' he asked, surprised at the sudden announcement.

'My aunt lives in Scarborough. She's been asking me to go for a while. Maybe now's as good a time as any.' She scanned the room, picking up a few more items, stuffing them into a bag. 'It'll just be a couple of days.' She looked back at him. 'Darren's driving me mad. I could do with a bit of quiet.'

Gardner wasn't sure it was a good idea but he could understand wanting to get away from Darren Freeman. He looked past her to the bedside cabinet, a trace of blood still visible. Maybe leaving was for the best after all. The further she was away from Lee the better.

He nodded. 'Maybe the break will do you good,' he said, not adding that he thought the time alone might make her see sense. 'When do you want to go? I can take you if you like.'

'That's okay. I can get the train.'

He nodded again. 'All right. When?'

'This morning? I just need to check with Darren that Cotton can stay with him. My aunt doesn't like dogs,' she said.

Chapter 55

Freeman knocked on the door, wondering if she was wasting her time. She'd decided that seeing Rhiannon at home, away from Andrew, would be better. That she could speak to her in private, try and get the truth from the woman instead of what Andrew had fed her.

Rhiannon's house was a small terraced place. The houses on either side, in fact up and down most of the street, looked run down, unloved, as if the people who lived there couldn't be bothered to do anything to make the place more cheerful. That they hoped they wouldn't be there that long, that any cosmetic enhancement would be pointless. But Rhiannon's house was done up just like its occupant. Wind chimes hung from the porch, and each window was adorned with colourful-looking scarves rather than curtains.

She knocked and waited a while, wondering if Rhiannon had seen her coming and done a runner. Or maybe Andrew was in there, telling her to keep quiet until the police would go away. She tried again and this time saw the outline of someone through the frosted glass. When she finally opened the door, Rhiannon looked half asleep and not her best. She had no make-up on except for the leftovers of yesterday's mascara in flaky crumbs around her eyes. It took her a moment to process who was standing in front of her.

'Can I come in?' Freeman asked and Rhiannon stepped back, scratching her head. It was mid-morning but obviously Rhiannon had just got up. She was wearing her pyjamas – pink shorts and vest with pigs on – her feet swallowed by dirty-looking rabbits. Freeman tried to remember how old Rhiannon was. 'Is this a bad time?'

'No,' Rhiannon said. 'It's fine.'

'Did I wake you?'

Rhiannon nodded. 'I've got cold.' She led Freeman through to a room that stank of incense sticks, something that Freeman had dabbled with as a teenager but had quickly grown out of. She sat down and smell felt heavy on her chest. She wondered how Rhiannon could stand it all day.

'Has something happened? With Katy, I mean,' Rhiannon asked.

'No, not yet.'

Rhiannon nodded and waited for Freeman to say something.

'You and Andrew are friends, right?' Freeman started. 'Does he talk about his girlfriend much? Does he confide in you?'

'Sometimes,' Rhiannon said.

'What does he say?'

She shrugged. 'Just stuff.'

'What sort of stuff? About their problems?'

Rhiannon shrugged again and tucked her legs underneath her bum. 'Sometimes. Just venting, you know.'

'Can you think of anything specific?'

'Not really,' she said. 'But I don't think he was happy she quit her job. I think she was scrounging off him a bit and it bugged him.'

'He said that?'

'Yeah. And he's right. He shouldn't have to pay all the bills and stuff just because she didn't like her job. I mean, who likes their job?'

'So he told you he wasn't happy about that. What else?'

'I don't know. Nothing really. He's not a moaner. He puts up with a lot.'

'In what way?' Freeman asked.

'Just from Katy. Like her quitting her job. And she's a bit miserable, I think, like she won't go out when he asks her. And I think she calls all the time for no reason. Every time he checks his phone she's called like ten times. He always says, "I better go and see what the ball and chain wants",' Rhiannon said with a smile. 'And she always calls at lunchtime.'

'*She* calls him?'

'Yep. Every day, same time. And she yammers on about whatever. He usually goes outside but I can see him through the window. I can see he's getting annoyed but he won't say anything to her. I just think, if she wants someone to talk to, she should get another job.'

'And he tells you all this. That she keeps calling him. That she refuses to go out?'

Rhiannon nodded. 'I feel sorry for him. I know I shouldn't say it, because of, you know, what's happened, but I think he'd be better off without her.'

'You like him?'

Rhiannon's face flushed and she picked at the fur on her rabbit slippers. 'We're friends.'

'But you want to be more than friends?' Freeman asked and Rhiannon shrugged and twirled the necklace she was wearing.

'He's nice,' she said. 'And sometimes I think he likes me too. And I wouldn't treat him like she does.'

'So you'd do anything for him?'

Rhiannon looked up now, cautious. 'What do you mean?'

'Did Andrew ask you to lie for him the other day?'

'No.'

'Are you sure about that?'

'Yes.'

'Rhiannon, do you actually know that any of the things Andrew told you about Katy are true?'

'How'd you mean?'

'Well, you say he wasn't happy Katy quit her job, but he told me he was fine with it, that he made enough to keep them ticking over. And her ex boss told me that she liked her job, that she was surprised Katy left.'

'So?'

'After she left, she stopped seeing people, stopped calling them. Changed her number and didn't tell anyone.'

'So?' Rhiannon said again. 'That proves it, doesn't it? I don't know, maybe she has mental problems or something. Andrew tries to get her to go out but she won't. There's something wrong with her.'

'The only person Katy called, or who called her in the last few months was Andrew. Don't you think that's odd?'

'Yeah it is. But that's up to her, isn't it?'

'What about the fact that when Andrew left the office on Tuesday to go home and get his lunch, the day you and him both lied about, what do you think about the fact he stopped on the way home and bought a CCTV system that he could monitor on his phone. A system he was planning to install at home where Katy spends all day, alone.'

Rhiannon frowned. 'Maybe he's worried about her. Maybe she's depressed.'

'Did he tell you that?' Rhiannon shrugged but didn't answer so Freeman continued. 'And you think that spying on someone who's depressed is the best way to help them? You don't find it a bit odd. Creepy even?'

Rhiannon stood up now, looking more awake, seemingly forgetting about her cold. 'I don't know anything about that. All I know is that he's my friend. You don't know Katy. You can't say what she's like.'

'Do you know her?' Freeman asked. 'Have you met her?'

'No,' Rhiannon said. 'But he tells me things.'

'Exactly. He *tells* you. Doesn't make them true.'

'He hasn't done anything to her,' Rhiannon said. 'He wouldn't do something like that.'

'Like what?'

'Whatever it is you think has happened to her. Andrew told me you're harassing him. That you think he's hurt her. But it was the other man. His neighbour. Andrew said he beats women up. He said he's always accusing his girlfriend of cheating on him and stuff and then he hits her. Why aren't you picking on him instead of Andrew? He loves Katy. He just wants her back.' Rhiannon was crying now. 'He's not like that. I know him. I know he couldn't do anything like that.'

Freeman got up. She wasn't going to get anything from Rhiannon. She was brainwashed by Andrew. She got to the door and turned back to the other woman. 'Rhiannon, I think you need to be careful.'

'Why?'

'Because as much as you think you know Andrew, you don't. You know nothing about him. He's not the kind of man you think he is. And whatever he's done to Katy, he could do exactly the same to you.'

Chapter 56

Freeman met Gardner coming down the corridor. 'I'm going out for some lunch. You want anything?' she asked.

'I'll come with you,' he said and turned back the way he came. 'Anything useful from Rhiannon?' he asked.

'Nope. I think she's besotted with him. Can't see what a dick he is.'

'But you set her straight, I assume.'

'I tried. Not sure it worked.' Freeman shook her head. 'Did you drop Lawton off at the station?'

'Yeah. Watched her get on the train.'

'You think it's a good idea, her going away?'

'Can't hurt. And the further away she is from Lee the better.'

They walked down the stairs, through the corridor and out into the daylight. The sun was killing her already. She wished she'd remembered her sunglasses. Wished she'd remembered to put some factor 40 on even more. She could feel her skin crisping up already.

'Where'd she go?' Freeman asked as they got to the car. Fortunately she'd parked in the shade so the car was, relatively, cool.

'Scarborough,' Gardner said. 'Visiting her aunt.'

Freeman felt something pulling at her, a little nagging feeling, but couldn't say why. Maybe it was just the idea of Lawton going off alone.

'You don't mind her leaving the dog at your place?' Gardner asked.

Freeman tried to ignore the anxious feeling in her gut and replied to Gardner. 'No, it's fine. Gives Darren something to do other than watch TV all day.'

'Well, hopefully he won't annoy the dog as much as he annoyed Lawton.'

She started the car and weaved her way out of the car park. 'I didn't know he had been annoying her,' she said, and then tilted her head to the side. 'I suppose it's a given though.'

'That's why she went. To get away from his insistent jibber-jabber.' Freeman looked at him now. 'Actually, I'm not sure how true that is. I'm sure it's *partly* true, but I think she just wanted to get away from things in general.'

'Huh,' she said and pulled down the visor.

'What?' Gardner said.

'Nothing. It's just I got the impression they were getting on quite well.'

'Really? Why?'

Freeman shrugged. 'They seemed to be talking a lot. Darren said she'd opened up to him a bit.'

'Opened up how? About what happened with Lee?'

'He wouldn't tell me anything specific. But they went for a walk and he said she talked quite a lot.'

Gardner went quiet and stared out the window, and she knew she shouldn't have opened her mouth. Gardner was feeling like a spare wheel in all of this already. He was desperate to help Lawton, to make up for what he perceived was his mistake, and now she'd made him aware that Lawton was more interested in telling Darren her secrets than even speaking to him. She cautiously glanced at Gardner, wondering how to do some damage control.

'I don't think she told him anything really,' she said. 'I think Darren just bombarded her with questions and she finally answered him, probably to shut him up. I doubt it was anything personal. I'm sure Darren's the last person she'd talk to about anything serious.'

Gardner nodded and flipped his phone in his hand. She could tell he was itching to call Lawton but they both knew it was a bad idea. The last thing she needed was him crowding her. Maybe going to Scarborough was a good thing after all. Maybe having no one giving her their opinion on her life was what she needed most of all.

Chapter 57

Gardner knew it was ridiculous, that being jealous of Darren Freeman in any way, shape or form was absurd, but he couldn't help it. Why would Lawton choose to talk to him of all people? Darren was an idiot. He might've been capable of looking after the dog but he wasn't equipped to deal with Lawton and her life. God only knew what advice he was giving her.

He stared out the window as they sat in the car eating and watched a man walking a dog along the edge of the park. Apparently Lawton's dog had taken a liking to Darren too and, not that he'd ever admit it to anyone, ever, even that hurt a little bit.

'Penny for them,' Freeman said and he turned to her.

'I was just …' He didn't want to tell her that he was jealous of her brother, that he was bothered that the dog liked Darren more than him. He tried to think of something that didn't make him sound quite so pathetic. 'When I was at Lawton's I had a thought.'

'Go on then. Dazzle me,' Freeman said.

'Lee claimed there was a spare key.'

'Which has vanished. And that Lawton doesn't think exists.'

'True,' Gardner said. 'But I was upstairs in the bedroom that overlooks the gardens.'

'And?' Freeman said with a mouthful of sandwich.

'So what if there *was* a key and Katy saw where it was hidden?'

'So you're saying Katy let herself in? And then what? Hurt herself? What about your conviction that Lee did it?' Freeman said.

'I'm not saying he didn't do anything. I'm just saying there's a chance that someone could see the hiding place from next door so it's *possible* she could've got in with the key. After that? Then I doubt she was alone.'

Freeman sat back and chewed quietly. 'So she surprised him and he killed her?'

'Maybe.'

Freeman shook her head. 'I still think Andrew was involved. There's too much stacking up against him. He's lied about everything.'

Gardner sighed. She wasn't going to let go of the idea that Andrew hurt his girlfriend. 'So maybe Andrew found the key,' he said and she turned to him.

'But she'd already gone next door before he got the message,' Freeman said.

'But what if she didn't get in and just left,' he said. 'And maybe once Andrew got the message he thought, what a good idea.'

'And went home and took her next door to cover it up? So where's the body?'

'I don't know. But it's possible, isn't it? That if Katy could know where the key was, then Andrew could too?' Gardner said.

'Are you sure you can see into the garden well enough?'

'Pretty sure.'

Freeman screwed up her wrapper and threw it onto the backseat. 'Why don't we go and have a look? See if we can rattle Andrew a bit more.'

Chapter 58

Gardner followed Freeman up the path and she knocked on the door, hard enough that the glass rattled. He knew she was losing patience with the whole thing. That the lack of evidence one way or another was pissing her off. He didn't know why it was getting to her so much; investigations often went this way, but this one seemed to bug her more than usual. Maybe it was the fact that they still couldn't say definitively what sort of investigation this was: missing person or murder. The lack of body, the lack of everything, made it impossible to know. The fact it'd been four days since Katy vanished, along with the evidence from Lawton's house and the various creeps Katy had been in contact with recently, made it seem, in his head at least, that it was more than likely they should be looking for a body.

He stepped back to allow Freeman room to move and pulled out his phone, hoping Lawton might've texted him by now, letting him know she'd got there safely. He didn't even know how long the train took to get to Scarborough.

Freeman gazed up at the upstairs window before moving across and peering in through the living room window.

'Anything?' he asked.

'There's someone round the back,' she said and he started to walk down the side of the house to have a word with Andrew, see if he'd be willing to let them take a look out of his bedroom window.

'Shit,' Freeman said and pushed past him. He started to ask what was wrong but she was already gone and all he could do was try to catch up. Next thing he saw Freeman on the ground and someone rushing towards him.

Gardner grabbed hold, preventing Andrew from escaping. He obviously wasn't expecting them to both be there. But why was he so skittish all of a sudden? Gardner turned him around, ready to find out. Only it wasn't Andrew Blake he had hold of. It was Dominic Archer.

'What're you doing?' Freeman asked, brushing the dirt from her trousers. Dominic struggled against Gardner and looked like he was about to puke.

'I wasn't doing anything,' he said. 'I just wanted to see if she was back. I wanted to know if she was okay.'

'Really?' Freeman said. 'In the middle of a missing person investigation you thought you'd just turn up and see if she was here? In case we forgot to check?'

'I think it's time we had a little chat, don't you?' Gardner said and hauled Dominic back to the front of the house despite his protests.

The sound of a door opening made Gardner look up and he caught sight of Lee coming out of the house next door. Lee looked Dominic up and down. 'Is this your murderer then?'

Gardner ignored him and led Dominic towards the car but Freeman stopped and spoke. 'Have you seen Andrew Blake?' she asked.

Lee pulled a face and shook his head. 'Nope,' he said.

Gardner knew he wouldn't tell them if he had. And maybe it didn't matter anymore. Maybe they'd just found their man, maybe he'd been right about Dominic Archer. But why would he come back here now? What was he trying to do?

'I haven't seen him for a couple of hours,' Lee said, causing Gardner to turn back. 'Seemed like he was in a hurry though,' he said to Freeman. 'Mentioned something about a trip.'

Gardner glanced at Freeman. Had he fled? Had something she said rattled him, making him cut his losses and scarper?

'Do you know where?' Gardner asked, a bad feeling coming over him, something he couldn't explain, or didn't want to. An earlier conversation, something he'd dismissed right out, suddenly seemed to appear at the forefront of his mind.

Lee looked up as if he was trying to remember. 'I think he said something about the seaside,' he said.

Chapter 59

Lawton got off the train and looked around, trying to work out which way to go. She knew Scarborough a little – her aunt had lived there until a few years ago – but she'd never come by train before so she didn't know where the station was in relation to the rest of the town.

She moved out of the way when she realised she was blocking the exit and people were getting annoyed. She put down her holdall and pulled the note from her handbag. The address wasn't familiar to her but she'd looked it up on her phone and discovered it was somewhere close to the seafront so it couldn't be too hard to find.

Her eyes skimmed the words on the page. They were brief, made her feel unsettled, but still somehow persuaded her to come. She knew it was wrong, that there'd be consequences. But she couldn't stop herself. She knew she had to come.

She felt bad lying to Gardner. She knew he was doing his best to help her and all she'd done was push him away. But she couldn't face it, not with him. She didn't want him to know the details. That the person he thought he knew was actually a lie, a facade. She was trying to protect him as much as he was trying to protect her.

Lawton slid the piece of paper back into her bag and walked out of the station. She squinted in the bright sunlight, trying to get her bearings. She'd aim for the seafront and work from there. She thought the walk, the fresh air, might shake some sense into her … that by the time she'd reached the sea she'd have realised what she was doing. She'd call Gardner, come clean. Wait there for him and it'd be over. It was a lot to ask from the sea air.

She turned left and started walking, following the signs pointing to the South Bay. She welcomed the breeze coming in off the sea, listened to the seagulls squawking, drowning out her own screaming thoughts telling her not to go. To do the right thing for once.

As she walked through the streets, which became more familiar the closer she got to the sea, she thought about what she'd left behind at home. She'd go back, of course, but things would be different. Nothing was going to go back to the way it had been. Not after her secrets were out in the open. Not after they found out what she was doing there. And they would find out. She hadn't decided yet the best plan of action. She knew that would depend on what happened when she got there as much as the extent she let her conscience get to her. But even if nothing here was set in stone, she knew for certain that everything would change after this.

Part of her was relieved, that the burden of her secret was no longer on her shoulders alone. She could tell that no one else understood, not fully. They never could. But now it was all out there, maybe they could begin to try to understand.

She wondered if she would go back. To Lee. To work. If they'd take her. She wasn't sure which she wanted most. And though she knew neither were good for her, not really, she still felt drawn back. But maybe she should just make a decision for once. It might hurt, but perhaps she should walk away.

The cool wind hit her, rippling her shirt. It felt good and she considered just walking down onto the sand, sitting amongst the kids making sandcastles and poking jellyfish. She could just sit there for a while, enjoying the sound of the sea, letting it all go. Instead she turned onto the promenade and made her way along, dodging groups of people, families bickering whilst trying to keep hold of swiftly melting ice creams. She walked along, past the arcades, the lights and sounds giving her a headache within seconds. At each side road she paused, checking for a street sign, until she finally found it halfway along the front. She turned off, leaving the noise and the crowd behind.

She heard her phone ring and pulled it out, staring at the screen. She should answer, she knew she should, but instead she just put it back in her pocket. There were lots of things she should've done. Didn't mean she would.

It was only a hundred yards or so from the front. It didn't look like much but then most of the apartments and houses here didn't. She looked up at the window, wondering if she was being watched. She thought again about just turning and going. Maybe she could just get the next train home and forget it all.

But she was knocking before she even knew it, realising that it was too late to run now. That she'd made her decision even if it was a bad one.

There was no sound from inside the building and she wondered if she was too late. Knocking again, she stood back and looked up. Still no movement, no sound, no sign of life.

Lawton let out the breath she was holding and squeezed the handle of the holdall. Maybe the letter hadn't been an invitation. She thought about the words and wondered why she'd ever thought they were.

She turned and started to walk away but something stopped her. She'd come this far. Maybe it was her chance to make things right. She turned back to the house and tried the door, surprised to find it open. She went inside, suddenly aware she was holding her breath. She wanted to call out but was afraid of what might happen.

She stepped into the sparse living room and looked around. It was empty. And then she heard the door close behind her. She stopped but didn't want to turn around and see for herself. If she didn't turn, maybe she could deny any of it ever happened. But she did turn, did look, just as she heard the voice saying, 'I wondered if you'd come.'

*

Gardner tried Lawton's phone again but there was still no answer. He let it ring and ring. It wasn't even going to voicemail.

'Let's go,' Freeman said, already getting in the car, already decided that Dominic Archer, whatever game he was playing, could wait. Gardner followed her, phone still pressed to his ear.

As he was about to slam the door, Lee walked out of his front garden, standing in front of the car. He sort of smiled at Gardner.

'She didn't tell you, did she?' Lee said, looking happier than ever.

Chapter 60

Andrew stood in the doorway looking at Lawton. She looked like she wanted to leave but she just stood there, staring at him. He glanced out the window, down the road just in case. He didn't think she would have but it wasn't beyond the realms of possibility that she'd told Gardner and Freeman, that she would've let them in on her secret.

He watched her look around. She was nervous; he could see that. He could see she was desperate to say something, to ask questions, but she was holding back. She spun around, looking for something: a clue or a way out? Who knew? But he wasn't going to give her anything. Her eyes flickered from one place to the next. It was like watching a child try and work out a puzzle. He should've been angry really, and he was, but he wasn't going to let her see it.

'This won't go down very well, will it?' he said and she finally looked at him. 'You coming here. Not telling your colleagues. Doesn't look good.'

'I don't care,' she said and her eyes settled on the dining area. He knew what she'd seen and followed her as she walked through the archway, bending down beside the table, her fingers brushing the vase, smashed into dozens of pieces, the soil scattered, the flowers dying.

She looked up at him then, the question on her lips, and he smiled. She was desperate to know. He felt powerful, like how he'd imagined when he'd been in her house. It felt good. Maybe he should've been worried, but he wasn't. He knew he was in control.

Lawton stood up straight and her eyes flitted around, stopping on the closed door. She looked at him again before walking to the door. Her hand rested on the doorknob for a second before she opened it and went into the bedroom.

Her face was neutral, gave nothing away, but then that didn't surprise him. It was what she came for. He followed her. She'd come to a standstill just inside the door, her eyes on the bed.

Andrew moved behind her, blocking her exit, waiting to see what she'd do next. What this pathetic woman, this supposed police officer who couldn't even look after herself, would do next. Maybe she was wondering herself. He knew he was.

And so was *she*.

From her place on the bed, Katy looked up, first at him, then at Lawton, her eyes pleading for her friend to do something.

Chapter 61

Freeman put her foot down, heading towards Scarborough, hoping that anyone who was planning a day trip was already there and that the roads wouldn't be clogged with tourists. Gardner sat beside her, trying Lawton's number continuously, muttering to himself as he did it.

She watched his foot tapping as he listened to the endless ringing. It wouldn't surprise her if he keeled over long before they reached Scarborough. He'd told her it would take a little over an hour to get there, less if she put her foot down. But the fact was they had no idea where they were going so the time it took was irrelevant. Unless Lawton answered and told them where she was, it was doubtful they'd be able to do anything to help, or to stop whatever was going to happen.

'Why didn't she tell me?' he said. 'Or you? Or anyone? What was she thinking?'

'I don't know,' Freeman said. 'She must've had her reasons.'

Gardner put the phone down. 'Well, they were fucking stupid reasons,' he said.

'Don't blame her. It's been hard for her.'

'It still doesn't excuse the fact she knew and didn't tell us.'

Freeman knew she should keep her mouth shut and her thoughts to herself but maybe this time it needed saying. 'Are you pissed off because she withheld evidence or because she didn't tell *you*?

The look Gardner gave her was enough to stop her pushing it but she could see that there was guilt behind his anger.

'You're right,' he said. 'Why would she tell me this? She hasn't told me anything else.'

'Can you stop being a baby about this?' Freeman said, raising her voice to match his. 'Have you ever considered that she might've found it too hard to talk to you? That the reason she talked to Darren is *because* he doesn't know her? Stop making this about you. If you want to help her, let her deal with it in her own way.' She looked back at the road, hoping to see a sign telling her they were nearly there. She didn't want to be in the car with him any longer.

'You're right,' he said quietly. 'I'm sorry.'

She sighed. 'Don't be. Just don't blame Lawton for this. Whatever reason she had for not telling us, I'm sure she thought it was for the best.'

'I know,' he said. 'It's just …'

'What?'

'For a moment there, when Lee told us where Andrew had gone, I thought you were right.'

'About what?'

'About Lawton and Andrew. When you suggested they were seeing each other I thought it was ridiculous, that

Lawton would never do that. But when Lee said Andrew had gone to the seaside … I really thought she'd lied to us all. That she knew more than she'd told us.'

'Well, thankfully, she has nothing to do with Andrew,' Freeman said. 'But she did know more than she told us. She knew Katy was alive.'

Chapter 62

Lawton rushed over to Katy, bending down, checking her for injuries. She didn't seem hurt, not on the outside at least but she was crying.

'What did he do to you?' Lawton asked, brushing Katy's hair back from her face.

Katy just shook her head and whispered, 'I'm sorry.'

'It's all right,' Lawton said and took her hand. 'Come on. Let's go.' She tried to pull Katy up but she was dead weight, refusing to move. 'We need to go, Katy.' She stood upright and pulled her phone from her pocket. It was time to call Gardner. No matter what she thought would happen here, that she'd tell Katy everything was okay, that she could just leave, stay hidden, whatever she wanted, Lawton now knew she needed to tell Gardner the truth, if only because Andrew would never let Katy go.

'What're you doing?' Andrew said and moved quickly across the room, snatching the phone from her hand. 'You're not calling anyone,' he said and tried to get to Katy but Lawton moved in front of her. He might've gotten there first, but Lawton wasn't going to let him leave with Katy. Wasn't letting him near her again.

'Move,' he said to Lawton but she stood firm.

'How did you find her?' Lawton asked.

Andrew smiled and reached into his pocket, pulling out a piece of paper. She thought he was going to pass it to her but instead he read from it.

'Dear Dawn, I'm so sorry things have gotten out of control,' he said and Lawton felt her stomach clench.

'How did you get that?'

'Your boyfriend gave it to me,' he said. 'Turns out he's not as bad as I thought.'

Chapter 63

Freeman saw the sign telling them they were ten miles away but it meant little when they had no clue where Lawton was. She wasn't sure she believed Lee when he said he couldn't remember the address on the letter, as far as she could tell he was just stirring the pot. She wasn't quite sure who he was trying to get at the most by letting the police know where they all were, but at least his conniving was partially useful. He could've easily kept all the information to himself, just let Lawton, Andrew and Katy at each other, see what happened.

Gardner had been quiet for a while. He'd stopped trying to reach Lawton; she obviously had more on her mind than speaking to him, deciding to help Katy herself instead of involving anyone else. And maybe that would've worked if Andrew hadn't found out about it too.

She sighed, thinking about Katy Jackson, the fact that she was alive. Initially she'd been sure that the woman was fine but as the days went on that hope decreased bit by bit. She'd really expected to find a body. She couldn't get her head around it. Lee hadn't told them much, just that a letter had gone to their address, a letter to Lawton that he opened anyway. A letter he then passed on to

Andrew for reasons she didn't quite understand. He'd obviously read the letter in full, knew that Katy was alive, but claimed not to know anything else. He was probably lying, but then maybe Katy hadn't said much. Freeman doubted she was planning on coming back. So why send a letter to Lawton at all?

She was trying not to kick herself. She should've known as soon as Gardner told her Lawton was going to Scarborough. She'd seen the postcards on Katy's dresser. Why hadn't she made the connection immediately?

'You think Lawton knew all along?' Freeman asked and Gardner turned slowly, as if he'd been drifting off.

'I don't think so,' he said. 'She wouldn't let a full investigation go ahead if she knew Katy was fine.'

'Depends how much she wanted to help her.'

'I don't think she'd do that,' he said.

Freeman nodded. She didn't think so either, or at least wouldn't have thought so an hour ago, but now they knew she'd been aware at least a few hours and said nothing. And anything was possible with people. With people, you never knew a thing about them really.

She tried not to dwell on it too much. Maybe Lawton knew all along, maybe she didn't. They could deal with that later. For now they just needed to find them - Lawton and Katy - before it was too late. Before they could disappear somewhere else or before Andrew found them.

And that was what worried Freeman the most. Lee claimed Andrew had left a couple of hours ago. If that was true, he could've found Katy before Lawton got there. In which case, was it already too late? Would he and Katy be long gone, even before Lawton could get there?

She wondered what Andrew would do, if he was as dangerous as she'd thought or if he actually did just want to find his girlfriend. Freeman thought Andrew had hurt Katy and that wasn't the case at all. But if he was so innocent, why hadn't he called the police as soon as he found out? Why had he snuck off alone to find her?

Freeman shook her head. She was sure she'd been right about Andrew all along. He might not have killed Katy, might not have done anything that day, but there was a reason Katy left. And there was a reason Andrew hadn't told the police he'd found her. He'd missed his chance to hurt her once. She doubted he would let the opportunity go again.

Chapter 64

Andrew was moving around Lawton, trying to see Katy although Lawton couldn't tell which of them he was talking to. 'He was pretty pissed off, you know,' he said as he shook the letter towards them. 'That you'd been in his house, that you'd made it look like he'd done something to you. He is not happy about that.'

'It wasn't like that,' Katy said, her voice quiet, unsure.

'He thinks you tried to set him up. And it does look that way. Except I wasn't sure who you were trying to set up. Me or him. Obviously he's taking it personally.'

'It wasn't like that,' Katy said again.

'I guess he thought I had a right to know where you were. Didn't think he'd still give you the letter as well though,' he said to Lawton and moved closer to them. 'I suppose I should've known I couldn't trust him.'

Lawton felt her heart racing. How could Lee do this? That he'd read her mail was nothing new; she'd come to expect that. So why hadn't she thought he might know about Katy? He'd obviously covered it up. Usually he just left the opened letters out in the open to prove a point; sometimes he hid them for days or weeks, giving them to her when it was too late to do anything with them. But this time he'd covered his tracks. He'd made a copy of the letter and put it back, sealing the envelope. He didn't want her to know that he knew, instead telling Andrew, putting them both in danger.

But what if he was just trying to get himself off the hook? He knew Gardner would never stop suspecting him, so what if he just wanted an end to it all? What if he was, in his own way, trying to help? But why not just give the police the letter as soon as he found it? Because he'd never do anything that made things easy on Gardner. She wanted to shake him. But maybe he thought sending both her and Andrew to find Katy would force Andrew to show his true colours. Maybe, maybe, maybe... With Lee you could never know anything for sure.

'You need me, Katy,' Andrew said, leaning down to her, pushing Lawton aside.

Lawton stepped in front of him, saying, 'We're leaving.' Whatever Lee's motives, she could deal with that later. She knew they had to get out. Andrew might not have hit Katy before, but that was then. 'You need me,' he said again, ignoring Lawton, not looking at her any longer. 'You wouldn't have sent the letter if you didn't need someone.'

'She sent the letter to me,' Lawton said but he still didn't acknowledge her.

'You need looking after, taking care of. If you could survive alone you wouldn't have reached out. You wanted to be found. You want to come home.'

Lawton could hear Katy behind her, mumbling, maybe trying to disagree, but the words weren't coming.

'You said you were sorry,' Andrew said. 'And you should be. But it's over now. We can go home. You said you wanted to come home, right.' He reached for her and tried to pull her up.

Lawton couldn't let him take her. Even if he was planning taking her home, even if whatever he'd done to her before Lawton got there had, in his mind, made things right, she couldn't let Katy go with him. She could see in Katy's face that she knew she was beaten. She would go back home with him. She would apologise to everyone for running away. She would never let anyone in and would never let anyone help her again. They would probably move somewhere new, somewhere no one knew what had happened, what kind of man Andrew was. And Katy would shrink some more and he would win. But she wasn't going to let it happen. Lawton felt her eyes burn but wasn't going to let him see her cry. This wasn't about her.

Andrew had hold of Katy's arm, trying to pull her up, trying to leave.

'Leave her alone,' Lawton said, pushing him away.

'Keep out of it,' Andrew said and shoved her, hard. But she stood her ground, refused to move out of the way, keeping herself between him and Katy. She wasn't going to let him win. 'Get out of the way,' he said and when she still refused he pushed her harder. Lawton fell against the bed, stumbling. As she tried to find her feet, Andrew grabbed Katy, dragging her across the floor, out into the living room.

Lawton pushed herself towards them, taking Katy's other arm, holding on to her, trying to pull her back. Katy was crying now, Andrew screaming at her to let go.

She didn't see his fist until it was too late. She was on the floor when it registered. The familiar feeling, the pain echoing through her cheekbone. Lawton touched her face, hot where his hand had been.

The scream was unfamiliar though. And then she realised it wasn't her voice, it wasn't Lee standing above her. Katy looked ill, like she was going to puke. Andrew looked down at her, no longer gripping Katy's arm. He had another woman to deal with first.

'I'm sorry,' Andrew said. 'But it's your own fault. I told you to keep out of it. I *told* you.' He stood there, looking down at her, his fist clenching. She wondered if he'd hurt himself or if he was preparing for more. 'You never should've got involved.'

Andrew turned and took hold of Katy, this time pulling her upright, dragging her by the wrist to the door. Lawton could feel her face burning, her cheek pulsating, as if she could feel the bruise growing. She watched as Andrew dragged her friend away, Katy barely fighting at all.

I'm going to lose her, she thought.

And then she was on her feet. She could hear herself this time, her breath heavy. She launched herself across the room, pushing herself into Andrew, slamming him against the wall. He let go of Katy, the surprise on his face telling Lawton everything she needed to know. This man was a coward. He thought he'd stopped her but he hadn't. He didn't have control of her.

She felt her own hands curl into fists, felt the impact of them smashing into his face, sharp pain reverberating up her arm, but it felt good. The feel of his flesh under her knuckles, the trickle of blood, running across her fingers, warm, telling her she was doing it right.

Andrew put up his arms, blocking his face, but her fists still made impact, she didn't care where. She just needed to feel the pain. His, hers. It didn't matter.

He slid down onto the floor, curling up. She could hear him begging her to stop but she couldn't. Even though she could feel herself weakening, her arms tiring, she couldn't stop. She couldn't stop.

His face was distorting and she realised that she was crying and still she didn't stop. She knew she was just like him, like Lee, and still she didn't stop.

The hand on her arm shocked her, like a jolt of electricity. She spun around, ready to fight some more.

Katy's face stopped her. She looked afraid but didn't move away, not even when Lawton's fists were aimed at her. She just held on, saying nothing.

Lawton's tears caught in her throat, causing her to splutter. Her hands fell. Katy's did too. Katy just stood there and Lawton turned to Andrew, a crying, bloody mess on the floor. And all she could think was, *what have I done?*

Chapter 65

They arrived in Scarborough, were driving along the seafront, Freeman asking, 'Where now?' over and over, and all he could say was he didn't know. Freeman pulled in to the side of the road.

And then his phone rang.

He checked the screen. 'It's her,' he said and picked up. 'Lawton?' He listened as she told him where to find them, her voice croaky, worn out. 'Are you all right?' he asked but she didn't respond. Just said, 'We might need an ambulance.'

Gardner hung up and told Freeman where to go, they weren't far away. He called in for an ambulance and could see Freeman look his way but he didn't reciprocate. He didn't know the answer to her question. Didn't know who was hurt. Or how.

They were there in minutes and Gardner was out of the car before it'd come to a stop. He raced up to the door, pushing it open. Freeman was right behind him, almost running in to him in the hallway. The both looked at Katy. The woman back from the dead. She didn't meet their eyes, just looked down at her feet.

Gardner pushed through and saw Lawton sitting on the small sofa bed, her head down, her hands shaking. He could see blood on them. 'Lawton?' he said and took a step towards her and it was only then he saw the body on the floor. He turned to Freeman but she was already on it, kneeling down beside Andrew, feeling for a pulse.

Gardner stepped closer to the sofa, sitting down beside Lawton. He took her hand and she looked up, fear in her eyes. He could see a bruise starting to form on her face. A new bruise. He looked back to Andrew, at Freeman trying to check him over, wondering what had gone on.

'He attacked us.'

Gardner looked up at Katy. She was standing in the doorway, hands knotted. She didn't look at Andrew.

'He attacked us both,' Katy said again. 'She was just defending herself. Both of us.'

Gardner nodded and looked back at Lawton. She was glassy-eyed, staring somewhere into the middle of the room. She didn't agree with Katy. Didn't say anything at all.

Behind him, Gardner heard the siren and an ambulance pulled up outside. He watched as two paramedics got out and came to the door. They paused briefly, taking in the scene, before going to Andrew. Freeman stepped away and said, 'He's breathing.'

Gardner watched as the paramedics checked Andrew over and then got him onto the stretcher. As they started to leave, Gardner told them, 'We'll be right behind you.' He looked around the room, at the blood, the debris, and Freeman followed his gaze.

'I'll stay here,' she said. 'You take them to the hospital, make sure they're okay.' She glanced at Katy as she spoke, no doubt she had a million questions for her but knew it would have to wait. Until they knew what'd happened they had to assume they were standing in a crime scene. Going home would have to wait.

Chapter 66

Freeman escorted Katy to the interview room. She'd moved the chairs so the desk wasn't between them. For now she just wanted to talk and thought the less formal the better in order to get Katy to open up. As of yet they didn't know if Katy was guilty of any crime, whether she'd intentionally faked her own death, or at least her disappearance, and Freeman didn't want to push her too hard. She'd been through enough.

They'd taken her to the hospital the day before, along with Lawton and Andrew. Lawton had required a couple of stitches to her face and hand but was otherwise fine, physically at least. Katy appeared fine too but was shaken up. Shock, according to the doctor. They decided to hold off on questioning her until she'd had some rest. Andrew didn't fare quite so well and though he'd been kept in overnight, his injuries were mostly superficial. He'd live anyway. They'd bring him in later, as soon as he was discharged.

But for now, Freeman just wanted to hear Katy's story, to finally get the answers she just couldn't find before. At least now she knew why.

'Can I get you anything?' Freeman asked and Katy shook her head. They both sat and Freeman started, her notepad on her knee. She felt like a therapist. 'Do you want to tell me what happened?'

Katy nodded and then looked puzzled. 'Yesterday?' she asked.

'We'll get to that. But first tell me what happened on Tuesday. Andrew told us you went next door that day because you were worried about Dawn.'

Katy nodded again. 'Yes,' she said. 'We'd heard them fighting. Dawn and Lee, I mean. We heard them a lot but that night it was worse. I wanted to go the next morning but Andrew kept telling me to leave it be. Not to stick my nose in. But it kept bothering me. I couldn't stop thinking about it and I hadn't seen Dawn. Usually I see her leave for work but I didn't. So that day I just decided to go, I needed to know she was okay.'

'So you decided to go next door and you called Andrew first. Is that right?' Katy nodded. 'Why did you call him?'

Katy looked down at her hands. After a moment she spoke quietly, almost too quiet for Freeman to hear. 'I always tell him where I'm going,' she said. 'In case he worries.'

Freeman tilted her head, trying to get Katy to look at her. 'Why do you think he'd worry if you went out?' Katy was silent and Freeman saw a tear fall onto Katy's jeans. 'Katy? You can tell me.'

She finally looked up. 'He doesn't like me going out. He wants me to stay inside all the time, he wants to know where I am.'

'He forces you to stay in? Doesn't let you see people?'

Katy shook her head. 'It wasn't always like that,' she said. 'I don't know when it changed. I didn't notice. I …' She looked Freeman in the eye. 'I'm so stupid.'

'No, you're not,' Freeman said. 'He manipulated you. He wanted to control you.'

Katy's tears came faster and she wiped her face with her sleeve. Freeman handed her a tissue. 'It's not your fault, Katy,' she said and waited for her to meet her eye again. 'And you're stronger than you think. You went out that day because you thought it was the right thing to do. Even though you knew Andrew wouldn't like it, you still did it. And you didn't always tell him if you were going out, did you?'

Katy looked up sharply. 'I did,' she said, as if Freeman was accusing her of doing bad things.

'You'd been going to see Dawn, hadn't you? For a while. Andrew didn't know about that, did he?'

Katy started crying again, shaking her head, saying sorry, over and over.

'It's okay,' Freeman said. 'It's a good thing.'

Katy stopped, looking at Freeman like she didn't understand. Like being told she'd done something good was an alien concept. 'It meant you were still in there,' Freeman said, tapping her head. 'He doesn't control you. You knew you had to leave.'

'But I didn't. I just let him do those things,' Katy said.

'But you were finding a way out. And that day, when you went next door, you found a way out, right?' Freeman said. 'Tell me what happened.'

Katy took a deep breath. 'I called Andrew. He was in a meeting that morning so I knew he wouldn't pick up. I left him a message. I don't know why I did it. I'd been there before without telling him. I just … I'd seen his lunch in the fridge and I thought he might come back early. I thought if I told him I was going it would be okay.' She wiped her face again, took another breath. 'So I went and knocked but there was no answer. I knew Lee had gone out, I'd watched him drive away. But I hadn't seen Dawn so I went around the back to check. Usually when I went round we'd sit in the kitchen so I tried the back.'

'How did you get in? Dawn wasn't there, was she?'

'No. I knocked but there was no answer. I was going to just leave but I thought I could see something on the floor.' She looked away again. 'I knew where the spare key was.' Freeman sighed. So Gardner was right. 'I'd seen Andrew taking it before.'

'Andrew? When?'

Katy shrugged. 'I don't know. A few times. Sometimes he'd say he was going out for a while and I'd see him go into next-door's garden. I watched him take the key from under a pot. He'd go inside. He'd be there a little while. Twenty minutes, half an hour or something, and then he'd come home.'

'What was he doing?'

'I don't know.'

'Was he going to see someone? Lee?'

'No, I don't think so. The first time I went to see Dawn I was going to ask her about it but I just couldn't. But every time he went I'd have a look out and ….' She paused, looked embarrassed. 'He only went when they weren't in. I never asked but …'

'But what?'

'I think he was curious about them.'

'About Lee and Dawn?'

Katy nodded. 'He'd sit and listen to them when they were fighting. He'd tell me to stop talking so he could hear them. I think he enjoyed it.'

Freeman tried to control her revulsion. She knew Andrew was sick, but this? He was some sort of misery tourist. Not like he didn't get enough of it at home. He was probably going around to see the aftermath of Lawton's abuse. No wonder he lied about going upstairs.

'Keep going,' Freeman encouraged. 'What happened after you opened the door?'

'I saw a photo frame on the floor, smashed. I shouted for Dawn but there was no answer. I had a look around, shouted upstairs. I was going to go up but it felt wrong. Like I was intruding. So I went back in the kitchen. I wondered if I should call the police but it was just a broken frame and I knew she was in the police anyway.'

'How did your blood get in their kitchen?' Freeman asked.

'From the frame. I picked it up. I was curious about what it was, why he'd break it. I guessed it was him. Anyway, I picked it up and cut myself. It was deep, dripping all over the floor,' she said, holding up her hand, which was still bandaged. 'I dropped the frame again and went to the sink to wash it. I wrapped my hand in a towel and then I realised what a mess I'd made so I tried to clean it up but it was hard. I looked in the cupboard under the sink for something to use and I found money.' She looked surprised at herself as she said it out loud.

'I picked it up. It was quite a lot. It crossed my mind it was her escape money but it wasn't very well hidden. It was just there, right when I opened the door.' Katy looked down at her feet again, her face flushing, ashamed of her actions.

'My phone started ringing. It was Andrew calling me back and I knew he'd be angry at me,' she said, her voice breaking. 'I was going to answer but I looked at the money and I just … I don't know, I knew I had to take it. I ignored his call, which I knew would make him even madder. I didn't really think. I knew he'd definitely come home now, to check up on me, that he'd probably lock me in. So I just took the money. I left the mess. I didn't really think about it. I just locked the door, put the key back and left. I walked for a while, not knowing what I was going to do. I ended up at the station and then I got on a train to Scarborough. I just … I don't know why. I always liked it there. My dad took me there. I just wanted to leave. That was it. I just wanted to escape. I never thought all this would happen.'

'What about your phone?'

'I just forgot it. I realised after I left but I knew I didn't have time to go back for it. I wouldn't have kept it anyway, but I didn't leave it on purpose. It didn't occur to me that the police would get involved. I thought Andrew would look for me, that he'd know I'd left him.' She shook her head as if she couldn't believe it.

Freeman sighed. They'd checked the trains and no one had recognised Katy. She guessed a woman on a busy train to Scarborough didn't stand out in anyone's memory.

'I didn't want to get anyone in trouble,' Katy said. 'I just wanted to leave. He made me leave my job, I don't have anything. I just saw the money there and knew it was my only chance. I'm sorry.'

'It's okay,' Freeman said.

'It was my only chance,' she said again. 'You have no idea what it was like.'

Chapter 67

Gardner stood in the corridor, listening to Molly's voicemail kick in for the third time. He wasn't sure if she was ignoring him or just unavailable but he had a sneaking suspicion it was the former. And who could blame her? He'd just hung up every other time, unsure of what to say, but now decided he needed to say something, at least try to make things right. But as he listened to the beep his mind was a blank and he finally hung up without saying a word as he watched Andrew make his way along the corridor, his hand clutching his ribs, his face black and blue, almost unrecognisable.

He let him in to the interview room first, almost feeling sorry for him as he winced trying to sit down. That Lawton had done this to him – he couldn't reconcile it in his mind. Nor could he decide how he felt about it. He was glad she'd stood up for herself. But there was standing up and there was this. He wondered how she was feeling about it. She hadn't said much at all.

'Why am I here? I'm the victim,' Andrew said.

'That remains to be seen,' Gardner said. 'Why don't you tell me what happened yesterday? Why you chose not to inform the police that Katy was alive as soon as you found out?'

'I wanted to know she was all right,' he said, looking like he was in pain with every word spoken.

'Fair enough. But why didn't you inform the police?'

'Like that bitch from next door, you mean? She knew too. Have you asked her why?'

'I will. But right now I'm asking you.'

'Katy didn't want me to. She was scared that she'd get in trouble for wasting police time,' Andrew said.

'And you knew that before you saw her? You didn't think the police should know she was alive and well? After all, you were suspected of hurting her. Why didn't you want us to know she was okay? You could've got yourself off the hook. Or did you think that seeing as you were already a suspect, what the hell?'

'No,' Andrew said. 'I love her. I was going to bring her home. We would've come here together.'

'I don't believe you,' Gardner said. 'Why did you attack Dawn Lawton?'

'I didn't,' he said.

'Katy claims you did.'

'I'm the victim,' Andrew said, pointing at his face. 'She did this to me for no reason. I barely touched her.'

'So you're admitting you did assault her first?'

'It was an accident. She wouldn't leave us alone.'

'So you hit her.'

'It was an accident. I didn't want to hurt her. I apologised to her and she did this. Maybe you shouldn't feel so sorry for her after all. She's as bad as he is.' He leaned forward and then appeared to regret it, gasping in pain. 'I want to press charges,' he said.

Gardner left Andrew and found Lawton. She looked like she was almost asleep as he went into the office. He couldn't ignore what'd happened, the fact she'd withheld knowledge about Katy's whereabouts, the fact she'd pulverised Andrew's face. But he'd try his hardest not to let anything stick, to not let anything happen to her. It was the least he could do. Maybe the only thing he could do.

'How is he?' she asked as he sat down beside her and Gardner wondered if she was genuinely concerned about Andrew's wellbeing or if she was just working out how much trouble she could be in. If he knew Lawton, it was probably genuine.

'He's all right,' Gardner said. 'A few cuts and bruises. Maybe the odd broken rib.' Lawton winced at this and he thought maybe he should've kept the details to himself. He sighed and sat back. 'He wants to press charges,' he said and Lawton just nodded.

'Fair enough,' she said.

'No, it's not.' He sat up straight again and looked her in the eye.

'I lost it,' she said. 'Yes, he hit me first but not like that. I could've stopped him without going that far but I just lost it. I really thought I was doing it for her. But I wasn't. I was letting my own frustration out on him and it wasn't fair. It wasn't right.'

369

Gardner sighed. 'Maybe you should keep that to yourself,' he said but she shook her head. 'You have every reason to be angry,' he said.

'Maybe. But not with him. Not like that. If he wants to press charges, let him. I don't care. I deserve it.'

Chapter 68

Freeman waited for Katy to say more but she was quiet, still. The only sound was the buzzing of the strip light above their heads. 'I know what he did to you. At least some of it,' Freeman said. 'I get why you thought you had no other options. He forced you to leave work. He stopped you seeing your friends, your family. Wouldn't let you talk to them. I saw your phone records. I know he withheld money from you. I understand why you did it.'

Katy nodded. 'But I could've just told someone. If I wasn't so pathetic, so stupid, I would've told someone. Instead I just ran away. Made a huge mess of things.'

'Who would you have told?' Freeman asked. 'When would you have told them?'

Katy shrugged. 'My mum?'

'When was the last time you talked to her?'

'A few weeks ago, I think.'

'And were you alone?'

'No. Andrew was there.'

'Right. Because he was always there. Because he was always watching you.'

'But I went to Dawn's. I could've told her. I did tell her some things, just not … I couldn't.'

'And why not?'

'I don't know,' Katy said. 'Because I'm stupid.'

'You're not stupid,' Freeman said, taking Katy's hand. 'He wore you down. He made you feel like you were stupid, like you didn't deserve anything better. But you knew, deep down, it was wrong, that's why you talked to Dawn, that's why you reached out. But it's hard. You knew she was in the same situation, that she was a police officer, and she couldn't do it either. It's not your fault, Katy. It's him.'

'But Lee was beating her up. She has reason to be scared. Andrew doesn't hurt me.'

'He doesn't hit you, you mean?'

Katy nodded. 'I felt bad for moaning to her about my problems when I knew what was going on there. It was so stupid.'

'No it's not. It's the same thing and you know that. Deep down you know that. That what he was doing is just as bad as what Lee's doing. Don't ever feel guilty about that.'

Katy stood up now and went to the window, staring out at the view, such as it was. 'Am I going to get arrested?'

'No,' Freeman said.

'But Andrew said—'

'Andrew doesn't know shit,' Freeman said. 'What happened yesterday? When he showed up?'

'I heard the door. I didn't even check first, I just assumed it was Dawn because I'd sent her the letter. I didn't ask her to come, I was just trying to explain because I felt bad about what'd happened, about the police getting involved, about the money. Even about Lee being

372

questioned. I don't even know if I wanted her to come,' she said and sat back down. 'Maybe I did subconsciously, that's why I put the address on the letter. Maybe I thought she'd sort everything out for me, with the police. Or maybe Andrew was right and I wanted to be found.' She sighed. 'Maybe when I heard the door I just thought everything would be all right. I thought it would be her and she'd know how to fix things. But then I opened it and it was him.

'And I didn't even say anything, didn't try to stop him coming in. I just stood there and watched him walk by me into the living room. And I just closed the front door like it was totally normal.'

'And what happened?' Freeman asked.

'He just sat down, stared at me. I couldn't look at him, I was scared. And I thought that Dawn had told him where I was and I felt angry about that. He didn't say anything for ages so I just apologised. And he still didn't say anything for so long until finally he asked me if I had anything to drink. I actually thought nothing would happen, that maybe he just was happy he'd found me, that we'd go back home and nothing would change. And then he got up and walked around the room. He picked up a vase and threw it at me.' Freeman watched Katy's lips tremble but she let her go on. 'He's not usually like that. He doesn't get angry like that. I was so shocked, I screamed,' she said. 'He asked me why I'd written to Dawn and not him, why I'd been sneaking around behind his back, how I could do it to him. I just kept telling him I was sorry but he wasn't listening. He was so angry, I thought maybe he would really hurt me this time.

'I kept saying I was sorry. I said I'd get my things and we could go home but he said maybe we should go somewhere else instead.' Katy stopped and took a breath. 'He said that if we went home we'd have to get our stories straight. And then there was a knock at the door. He told me to stay in the bedroom, to be quiet.'

'And then what? Dawn showed up?'

'She wanted me to go with her. Andrew didn't want me to.' She took a breath and looked Freeman in the eye. 'He hit her. That's why she hit him back. She was only trying to defend herself. And me. Please don't let her get in trouble.'

Freeman walked back down to the interview room, trying to keep up with the other woman. 'In here,' she said and opened the door.

Katy stood up and ran towards her mum, who hugged her tightly, telling her she was sorry, that everything would be all right.

'It's okay,' Katy said and her mum shook her head.

'No. I should've brought you home sooner,' she said. 'I can't believe I let this happen to my baby.'

They both started to cry and Freeman backed away. 'I'll give you some privacy,' she said.

Chapter 69

Freeman had told Darren to make himself scarce so he'd taken the dog for a walk, leaving the three of them in Freeman's flat. She said she'd make some drinks and disappeared herself, leaving Gardner and Lawton alone.

Andrew had decided to drop the charges against Lawton, possibly knowing that no one in the police station would be on his side, that it would be pointless. Gardner couldn't help but think Lawton was disappointed by this, that she'd wanted to be punished for what she'd done to him.

'So,' he said, trying to decide on the best way to say it.

'I know what you're going to say,' she said.

'And?'

She shook her head. He'd been pushing the idea of pressing charges against Lee but she wasn't going for it. It drove him mad, that she wouldn't do it, that she didn't feel it was necessary, but also that he couldn't let it go, that he was going to push her away even more. And yet he couldn't give it up. He wanted Lee to pay for what he'd done.

'I don't want to do it,' she said, reaching out to the warm spot the dog had recently vacated. 'I don't want to go through that.'

'You'd rather continue to go through this instead,' he said, indicating her bruised face, even though he knew this latest injury wasn't Lee's doing.

Lawton let out a long breath and Freeman came back through with two cups of tea. She looked at Gardner and nodded towards the kitchen. He followed her through and knew as well as Lawton had pre-empted his words, what Freeman was going to say. Didn't stop her saying it though.

'Leave her alone,' she said.

'I can't. How can she not want to send that piece of shit down?'

'I don't know. But she doesn't. So drop it.' Freeman handed him his cup of tea. 'She might change her mind eventually, but she'll do that in her own time. You nagging at her isn't helping anyone. So just shut it.'

She left him standing in the kitchen and went back through to Lawton, asking her if she wanted anything to eat. Gardner wondered how she found it so easy to act like nothing was going on, to act so naturally, so relaxed with Lawton. But he was glad she could. Someone had to.

'Did Gardner tell you they caught the guy breaking into houses?' she asked and Lawton shook her head. 'Well, it wasn't Dominic. Turns out he was just your bog-standard stalker. This other guy made another attempt. He managed to pick a woman who was alone this time but he also picked the wrong one to mess with. She broke his nose and knocked him out. He regained consciousness just in time to get arrested.'

Chapter 70

The sun was already working overtime when Lawton got up the next morning, its rays sneaking in through the gap in the curtain, waking her before she was ready. She lay there in the unfamiliar room for a while, looking at the cracks in the ceiling, the cobweb on the light fitting. She could hear the TV in the living room, surprised Darren was up already. She wondered if Cotton had woken him, having decided to sleep on the settee with him the night before.

She felt as if a weight had lifted somehow but couldn't put her finger on what it was. She didn't feel happy, just freer than she had for a while, as if things were right. Maybe it was the fact Andrew wasn't pressing charges. She felt bad about what she'd done to him and would've understood if he'd gone ahead, but it was a problem she didn't need, an incident she didn't want officially recording, not if she was going to continue in her career.

Perhaps it was that Katy had been found alive and, if not well, as least, well, alive. She was pleased that Katy's mum had come and got her. That she wouldn't be going back to Andrew. She hoped she would stay in touch but understood that it might be too hard. That Lawton would always remind her of Andrew, of the prison he'd made of her life, killing her in slow motion.

Lawton closed her eyes, thought about her bed at home. How the morning light would hit the other side of her face, how alien this felt. She felt a tug, an emptiness, in the space beside her. She ran her hand across the sheet, cool and unused by another body. She took a breath, knowing what it was that made her feel different this morning. She knew it was time. She just wasn't sure how to tell him.

Lawton got up and dressed and found Darren stretched out on the settee, Cotton curled up on the chair, the one she wasn't supposed to get on. Freeman had wanted at least one dog hair-free zone to remain.

'Morning,' she said and Darren looked up, turning the volume down.

'Hey,' he said. 'You want breakfast?'

'No, that's okay,' she said and sat on the arm of the chair, stroking Cotton's head. She cleared her throat, unsure why she felt so nervous. 'I'm going home,' she said.

'What?' Darren said, turning the TV off completely. 'Home, like, to him?' She nodded. 'You can't.' Lawton tilted her head at him and he shook his head. 'You know what I mean. I mean, shouldn't you tell Nicky or Gardner first? I don't think you should just go.'

'It's not their decision.'

'I know. But still,' Darren said. 'Why do you want to go back there?'

Lawton wondered herself. She'd had a lot of time to think over the past week and those thoughts had varied wildly. She would leave for good, she would go back to stay. She hated him, she loved him. She wasn't sure the exact moment she'd made the decision but she knew that morning, lying alone in bed, that she missed him. Missed him being beside her.

She felt different, changed somehow. She wasn't sure how that would translate, if she would be different when she was with him. But she knew she had to go home.

She'd listened to Gardner, even agreed with a lot of what he'd said. But she knew she wouldn't do it, wouldn't press charges. Maybe she always knew she would end up back home.

But something was different. She couldn't explain it, couldn't explain any of it.

'Maybe now things are out in the open, it'll change,' she said but Darren just frowned at her. 'Will you keep Cotton though?' she asked and Darren looked at her like she was mad. She looked down at the dog and felt longing for her already, even though she hadn't gone anywhere. 'If your sister says it's okay, of course.'

'Sure,' he said. 'But why?'

'She likes you. It'll be better for her here.'

'Okay,' Darren said but still looked worried and Lawton wasn't sure if he was concerned for her or that Freeman and Gardner would be furious with him for letting her go. Probably a little of both.

Lawton bent down and kissed Cotton's head. 'I'll come and visit her,' she said and stood up. She hugged Darren too and walked to the door. 'Thanks,' she said.

As she walked away she knew she was doing the right thing, at least the right thing for now. Leaving Cotton with

Darren would make it easier, one less thing to keep her tied, that next time she decided to leave it would be that bit easier. That she would chip away at it until one day she could just walk out and not look back.

She knew that day would come. Just not today.

Note

Help and information about domestic abuse can be found here:

https://www.womensaid.org.uk/

https://www.refuge.org.uk/

http://www.lwa.org.uk/index.htm

Like Lawton, many victims are reluctant to leave an abusive home because of concerns for leaving a family pet. The Dogs Trust has a scheme called The Freedom Project which finds foster care until the owners can find a new home. More information can be found here:

https://www.dogstrust.org.uk/help-advice/hope-project-freedom-project/freedom-project

Acknowledgements

Many thanks to Donna Hillyer for her editing skills. To Stan for his early input. To family and friends for their support, especially Mam and Dad, Donna and Chris, Jonathan, Maria, Paula, and Diane. To Stephen for the technical support, listening to my endless jibber-jabber, and everything else. And to Cotton and Tina for occasionally behaving themselves.

24222630R00230

Printed in Poland
by Amazon Fulfillment
Poland Sp. z o.o., Wrocław